MARRIED TO A SPY

Alec Waugh has set his new novel in Tangier where he has been an intermittent resident for twenty years. *Married to a Spy* is not, however, 'another Tangier novel'. It is a dramatic story of fast-moving action and suspense based on the assumption that the Basque liberationists decide to launch a series of guerrilla attacks against southern Spain, using Morocco as their base.

The British secret service sends to Tangier, to keep an eye on things, an Englishman in his middle thirties who is married to an American ten years younger than himself. He is bringing into danger not only himself but her, and one of his main problems is that, without jeopardising security, he cannot take her fully into his confidence. Thereby he is endangering his marriage.

This situation provides the framework for a story, at once romantic and exciting.

This is ALEC WAUGH'S 50th book
he has also written:

NOVELS

The Loom of Youth (1917)
Kept (1925)
Nor Many Waters (1928)
So Lovers Dream (1931)
Wheels within Wheels (1933)
The Balliols (1934)
Jill Somerset (1936)
No Truce with Time (1941)
Unclouded Summer (1948)
Guy Renton (1953)
Island in the Sun (1956)
Fuel for the Flame (1960)
The Mule on the Minaret (1965)
A Spy in the Family (1970)
The Fatal Gift (1973)

SHORT STORIES

My Place in the Bazaar (1961)

TRAVEL

Hot Countries (1930)
The Sugar Islands (1958)

AUTOBIOGRAPHIES

The Early Years of Alec Waugh (1962)
My Brother Evelyn and Other Portraits (1967)
A Year to Remember: A Reminiscence of 1931 (1975)

MISCELLANEOUS

In Praise of Wine (1959)
A Family of Islands (1964)
Wines and Spirits (1968)
Bangkok: The Story of a City (1970)

ALEC WAUGH

MARRIED TO A SPY

W. H. ALLEN · LONDON
A Howard & Wyndham Company
1976

PRINTED AND BOUND IN GREAT BRITAIN BY
RICHARD CLAY (THE CHAUCER PRESS) LTD,
BUNGAY, SUFFOLK
FOR THE PUBLISHERS, W. H. ALLEN & CO. LTD.,
44 HILL STREET, LONDON WIX 8LB

ISBN 0 491 01837 1

Acknowledgement is made for the use of quotations from
A Streetcar Named Desire by Tennessee Williams which
appear in *Four Plays* published by Secker & Warburg.
© Copyright, 1947 Tennessee Williams.

FOREWORD

This is a piece of fiction. Its plot presupposes that the Basque Liberation Committee, which at present operates from south-west France, decides to open a base for guerrilla activities in Morocco. The British Government, in view of its awkward status in Gibraltar, instructs its Secret Service to send a representative to Tangier to 'keep an eye on things.' Its own attitude is ambivalent.

No such situation exists, and for many years M.I.6 has not had a representative in Tangier. But if the Basques were to change their tactics, incidents such as this story recounts might well take place.

I have been visiting Tangier regularly since 1955; since 1969 I have run a flat there. I am a member of the Tangier Theatre Group, the Yacht Club, and I have served on the Church Library Committees. I know nearly all the members of the Anglo-American set and have been the personal friend of six successive American and five successive British Consul Generals, but this book does not contain a single portrait of any living resident or visitor. It is a piece of fiction.

The second half of this book was written at the Macdowell Colony, Peterborough, New Hampshire. I should like to express my warm gratitude to the management for its hospitality.

ALEC WAUGH

PART ONE

PART ONE

1

Adrian Simms was woken by the muezzin, calling from a
minaret. There was no need to look at his bedside clock. It
was early June. Tangier was on Greenwich mean time.
About quarter past three. He could do with another two
hours sleep. But he had been roused from a vivid dream. His
mind was racing. He would need a few minutes' reading to
control and compose his thoughts. But he did not want to
switch the light on and wake Beryl. An Englishman thirty-
five years old, he had been married for four years to an
American, an Oklahoman, ten years younger than himself.

In his bachelor days, he had maintained that one of the
pleasantest things about a love affair was the waking first
in the early morning; the gentle rousing of one's companion,
the few minutes of cosy cuddling, the drowsy love-making,
the falling asleep in each other's arms, then three hours later
the waking together, refreshed to a world refreshed. But that
was one of the things that died out in marriage. One of the
many things . . . He checked. That wasn't fair. Some things
went. Others came to take their place; many others.

Beryl was breathing quietly beside him as he slid away;
he tucked the bed-clothes round her. Having no resident
maid, they left their bedroom door ajar, so that the air could
circulate freely through the flat. Soundlessly he crossed the
passage into his dressing room. He had left a book open by
his bed, a Simenon. The bed was soothingly cool. The drama
of the narrative steadied his nerves. In a few minutes the
lines began to blur. He switched off the light.

The room was in dusk when he awoke. Half past six. He
pulled back the shutters and the brightness of the early sunlight made him blink. The sky was cloudless. Another radiant
day. His flat was on the second floor of a new two-storied
maisonette, three-quarters of a mile from the centre of the
town. It stood on a broad avenue—the Boulevard de Paris.
Already the town had come to life. Veiled Moslem women

3

were carrying their bread baskets from the baker's. A couple of Moroccans in long hooded *djellabahs* were pushing a hand-cart laden with furniture. Sheep were grazing on an empty stretch of grass across the road. A fully loaded bus grunted up the hill, discharging thick black fumes. Below the flat a group of untidy men were gossiping. One of them, his guardian, waved at him. 'Good morning, Monsieur Adrian.' Everyone called him 'Monsieur Adrian'. He liked being known by his Christian name.

'No chance of a bath yet,' he thought. There was a water shortage and the water which was turned off around nine o'clock at night did not usually go on till seven. He went into the bathroom and turned the tap. As he had expected, there was a gurgle and then silence. 'Best open up,' he thought.

It was a largish flat that he had thought himself lucky to find when he had been posted to the British Consulate eight months earlier. It was furnished with a low Danish sofa, two Danish chairs, a long low Danish table that he had bought when he was stationed in Copenhagen. On the walls were framed travel posters. There were thick locally-made floor rugs. A central passage divided the two main rooms. The other side faced a garden. It was a flat that looked its best during the day. As he drew back the curtains and opened the shutters, letting in the sunlight, Adrian felt that he had no reason to resent his lot. He had only one complaint to make of the flat, its lack of books. He wished he had had the chance to build up a library.

At its far end was the small room that he used as his own study. As always when he entered it, he thought, How would it strike the police if they broke in? Was it or was it not what they would expect of a thirty-five-year-old vice-consul? It was a short narrow room. The shelves lining one of the walls were filled with photographs, reference books, stationery, a small cardboard letter file. The break-in would be made, presumably, at night. The intruders would not switch on the light, which would show through the shutters and attract the attention of the guardian. They would flash a torch round the room. Would anything strike them as unusual?

4

There was a small steel desk; its surface littered with ink bottles, paper-weights, pens, pencils, a calendar, sealing wax, stationery, blotting paper, a paper knife. One side of the desk contained a filing cabinet. It was almost empty. Adrian kept his working files in the consulate. Above the well of the desk was a drawer that locked. It contained the kind of thing that a prudent man would keep locked away: cheque books, passport, passbook. There was also a diary, in which every morning he wrote his entry for the day before.

'A quiet day,' he wrote, 'the *levante* was blowing in the morning which made the beach uncomfortable; lunched alone; nothing unusual at the office; the Garlands gave a cocktail party, about thirty guests, had an interesting talk with the Spanish Vice Consul who told me that twenty-five per cent of the Spanish colony were leaving because of the Moroccanisation of small businesses. He foresaw that there would soon be a lack of minor technicians, shoe repairers, barbers, that kind of thing. Returned to the flat for supper, discussed with Beryl our project of giving a supper party for the theatre club after the next performance.'

It seemed a reasonable entry. Before he closed the book he arranged a piece of thread diagonally across the page. If the thread were disturbed, he would know that he had been broken in upon.

The days when he had made love he marked with a Greek A. It was five days since he had made such a mark. Some days were marked with a B. It was quite a while since a night had been so commemorated.

Five minutes to seven. Time for the news. He went into the kitchen, filled a small bowl with a handful of cornflakes, poured milk over it, and went into the room where he kept the radio. It was narrow, furnished in the Moroccan style: low cushion-strewn settees covered in white and blue, a deep red fabric three feet high stretched above them: the curtains were of the same white and blue; with the valance above them in the same deep red. The white walls above were bright with local landscapes. When the Simms' had dinner guests, they would serve cocktails in the drawing room, then come in here for coffee and liqueurs. It was a good place for talk. Sitting up straight kept your mind alert. Aldous Huxley had once argued that the art of conversation had decayed since the company started to loll back in armchairs after meals.

Adrian turned on the radio, low so as not to disturb Beryl. The news came from Gibraltar, relayed from London by the forces' wireless. The reception was usually excellent, and the headlines this morning came through clearly. Kidnappers in the Argentine had been appeased with a large ransom. A hi-jacked aircraft had landed in Kuwait. It was raining in England. Nothing about Spain.

Then the full news came through. 'The hi-jackers have been taken into custody,' he learnt. For three days their exploit had been top news. And that, he told himself, will be the last that anyone would hear about them. The trial would be delayed, postponed; there would be appeals; a sentence would be delivered. In a year or so the prisoners would be released surreptitiously when everyone had forgotten all about them. It was tantalising never to know how a story ended.

The news from Britain was equally tantalising. How little this bulletin of facts and personalities told one about the realities of English life, of how the average family was surviving under a cascade of rising prices. Most people, he presumed, lived on a shoe string as he did himself. That shoe string was not elastic. Would London seem the same place when he got back to it? Seven-fifteen, the water should be on by now, he thought. It was.

Slowly his face emerged from its lathering of soap. He had never learnt to use an electric razor. He enjoyed the cleanliness of a morning shave. He would stand grubby and soiled before a mirror, in no condition to face the world. Then stroke by stroke, he would become himself again, ready for anything. Here I am, the old me, he'd think . . . Six months ago when Beryl was on holiday in America, he had grown a beard. He looked, he had come to feel, too, like too many other people. There were advantages in an intelligence agent being unobtrusive, but you could carry anony-

6

mity too far. He had been in this game now eleven years. He did not seem to be headed anywhere. Better to make himself someone who was easily recognised, easily remembered. 'Oh yes, Simms, of course, that fellow in Tangier with the beard.' He had thought too that it might make an impression upon Beryl. After four years there was a danger of her taking him for granted. With a beard one could ring changes on oneself.

He had changed his style already several times. At the moment his upper lip was bare, so was the upper part of his lower lip. His beard was a thick but narrow band of hair, starting half an inch below his ears and running along his jaw; the neck was closely shaved. His whiskers were bushy, tapering to a point below his cheek. He was debating the question of cutting off that point. The hair on his head had not yet begun to thin. He kept it clipped fairly short. He did not want to look a hairy man. He aimed at a continental neatness. He was due to go on leave in September, perhaps he would return with those whiskers trimmed. In the meantime it was well enough. He felt he was making the best use of his possibilities. He had never been vain about his looks.

He stepped on to the scales. 167 lb. A reasonable weight for a five foot eleven man. No sign of a paunch. Reasonable: that, he supposed, was the appropriate adjective. For his appearance, and for himself.

Adrian always went out to breakfast. Their Fatima did not arrive till nine. Beryl set her own alarm clock for a quarter to, in case she overslept. It was an arrangement that suited Adrian very well. He enjoyed his quarter of an hour's walk into town; and he enjoyed reading his paper *Le Matin* without interruption. His office opened at nine, but he liked arriving there a little early, to get his desk in order before the telephone began to ring. It was going to be hot. Yesterday the temperature had touched 70°; most men wore short-sleeved open shirts at this time of year, but he was wary of the climate. Lyautey had called Morocco 'a cold country with a hot sun'. He preferred to wear a collar and tie under a linen coat. He liked to look formal in his office. He could leave his jacket behind him on a hook when he went out to lunch.

He pushed open the door to Beryl's bedroom. As far as he could judge, she had not moved since he had slipped away four and a half hours back. She was still on her right side breathing quietly. She probably would not stir until the alarm clock went. The world was divided into two groups, the early risers and the late risers. It was a question of metabolism. He and Beryl were in that respect two different creatures. Tonight at eleven, just when he was feeling drowsy, she would be bright-eyed, anxious 'to go places'. It was one of the matrimonial hurdles that no couple took into account in their days of courtship, yet maybe it was one of the more frequent causes of disharmony. 'I have piped to you and you have not danced.' He shrugged. If one was aware that it was a hurdle, one could cope with it.

With the Spanish school next door to him, the road that led to the central Place de France where he breakfasted was at this hour crowded with boys and girls, carrying books and satchels. Half of them were Moroccans. Quite a few were of mixed parentage. They were laughing and chattering together. Against the wall, forty or so yards from one another, a couple of beggars were sitting on their haunches, with outstretched hands. He gave each ten centimes, as he did every morning. They showed no gratitude. A little further on, the road turned and ran steeply down towards the shops. There was a series of stone seats along the kerb. On one of them sat, quite often, his favourite beggar. He was very old. He wore a clean white *djellabah*. His beard was neatly trimmed. He had an amused smile and appeared to find life entertaining. Adrian gave him a twenty-centime piece and was rewarded by a blessing.

The Café de Paris was across the street. It faced south and after ten o'clock was in the sunshine. From eleven onwards its row of green chairs was crowded, but now only a couple were occupied. He bought a copy of *Le Matin* and took his place at one of them. He always had the same breakfast, a large glass of orange juice, a small black coffee, and a soft boiled egg. It cost him the equivalent of forty pence. As Moroccans do not use egg cups, he brought his own. He opened *Le Matin* at the second page. He took it in preference to *L'Opinion*, the opposition paper, because he was absorbed by its cartoon—an American product called 'Juliette de mon Cœur'. Each instalment ran for about six weeks. The current drama was working to its climax. Juliette, the heroine, was in a desperate plight; at odds with her boyfriend, her father threatened by the police. He could not imagine what God out of the machine would rescue her. But he knew that within a week one would.

He turned back to the first page which set out the news he had already heard over the radio on the day before. As he did so he looked over his shoulder into the interior of the café. By the clock was sitting a neatly dressed young Moroccan, bearded, tall, and handsome. 'Ho, Ho', he thought, 'here we go again.' He turned back *Le Matin* to the second page. From his inside pocket he took a sheet of paper on which a series of numbers had been written. He put a circle round several letters in the 'Juliette de mon Cœur' dialogue, and folded the paper back to the first page. As he sipped his orange juice, he studied the Moroccan interpretation of Colonel Gadaffi's attitude to the Fuel crisis, then laid the folded paper on the table.

'If you will excuse me, sir.' The handsome young Moroccan was standing at his side. He held out his copy of *L'Opinion*. 'If you have finished with your paper I wonder if you would exchange yours for mine.' He spoke French as though he were a Frenchman. 'But of course.' The Moroccan took *Le Matin*, put *L'Opinion* in its place, bowed, and turned away. Nothing in his behaviour would have suggested to any onlooker that the two knew each other.

Adrian picked up *L'Opinion* and turned to the second page; there were no pencil marks at the foot of the third column. 'Odd,' he thought. But even so a nil report was a report at that, just as a drawn cricket match is a match with a result. He ran his eye down the first page headlines. There really was not anything there to read. Back to the treadmill.

The British Consulate General was a dignified formal building as befitted the important mission that it once had

9

housed, and which Harold Nicolson's father, later to be Lord Charnock, had administered at the turn of the century. The gateway with its royal coat of arms emblazoned over the entrance suggested solemn deliberations. There was a large stone block by which visitors had mounted and dismounted. It belonged to another day. The residence was square, solid, and two-storied. Adrian's own ground-floor office was small but light and airy, a cheerful room. He wished he had more work to do in it. The hours that he had to spend here were slow in passing. This looked like being an average day. He could afford to spend half an hour on the London newspaper that had arrived the previous evening, two days late. He turned first to the cricket page.

The telephone rang. A familiar female voice was at the other end. The Consul General's secretary. 'Can you come and see the CG right away?'

The Consul General—Mark Littlejohn—a bulky, burly man was bald, red-cheeked, clean-shaven. From a photograph you would have expected him to be genial. But he was not genial. In his middle fifties, he was a man, Adrian suspected, who had missed the boat. Something had gone wrong somewhere along the line. He ought at his age to have a better appointment. His wife, a divorcée when he married her, was not with him at the moment. She was in London, cherishing her twenty-year-old daughter. The fact that she was in England suggested that she had lost interest in her husband's career. The daughter was more important.

'Ah come in, Adrian, come in, sit down. Another of your mysterious missives.' He said it genially enough. But his words had a sarcastic undertone. 'Mysterious missive indeed', as though he resented having messages sent in cypher to his own office. Well and perhaps he did, at that. If he did, Adrian did not blame him. He put the envelope in his pocket. 'Thank you very much, sir.'

'Not at all, not at all. Delighted to be of service.' The 'to be of service' was delivered as though it was in quotes. That, too, had a satiric undertone. 'Is everything under control?' he asked.

'Yes, thank you, sir.'

'We're not giving you too much to do, I hope?'

'Oh no, sir.'

'We have to give you something, just for the look of things. The Italian Consul General was talking to me about you the other day.'

'About me, sir?'

'Not about you, personally. About what you are doing here. "I hear," he said, "that you've got a new Vice Consul." "That's so," I said. "What on earth do you find for him to do?" he asked. I told him that you looked after passports. "Surely that can't keep him very busy?" "You'd be surprised," I said. "I am," he answered, and his eyes twinkled. He's an amusing chap, as I guess you know.'

'I scarcely know him, sir.'

'Is that so? Yes, I suppose it is, moving on different levels as it were. Still he's worth knowing, a real sense of humour. Not surprised that he was supercilious about your being here. We've become a backwater. The last American Consul General wanted it downgraded. I told them that in Gibraltar, when they insisted on your coming here. "What on earth am I to find for him to do?" I asked. "Don't worry about that," they said, "we'll keep him busy." I hope they do.'

'Oh yes, sir, thank you.'

'I'm glad of that. Very glad of that. Never been one of your cloak and dagger merchants. Just a straightforward Whitehall employee. Here to give you an alibi. But I can't do that, can I, unless I keep you fairly busy.'

'Of course not, sir.'

'Otherwise my staff would get suspicious. Can't have that. The less I know about what you're doing, the better I'll be pleased. Want no responsibility if anything goes wrong. Remember that Vice Consul in Montevideo. They warned you of that, didn't they?'

'Yes, sir, they warned me of that.'

'Good luck to you, then, that's all that I can say. Good luck to you, my boy.'

Littlejohn watched the door close behind Adrian, then

lifted the telephone. 'Could you ask Miss Fitzgerald to come in,' he said.

His secretary, Frieda Fitzgerald, had been on his staff for seven months. She was, so he had learned from the dossier when she had been posted to him from London, twenty-seven years old. Her father, a regular army officer, had commanded a Brigade on Alexander's staff where he had won a DSO: he was now passing what were presumably his last months of service before retirement in the MS branch at the War Office. He had a house in Hampshire, was the father of three sons, the eldest of whom was a lieutenant commander in the Royal Navy. Frieda had taken a BA degree at Cambridge in modern languages. Before her posting to Tangier she had served as a secretary at the Ankara and Vienna embassies. She was rather tall and thin, with dark hair and a fresh complexion. Littlejohn felt curious about her. She was a good mixer. Tangier was a social place. He saw her about at cocktail parties. Everyone seemed to like her. But he knew very little about her. She was friendly, but she was not forthcoming. Her name had not been linked with anyone's.

He wished he knew her better, and most days tried to find an excuse for an informal conversation. This morning the Tangier Theatre Club provided an occasion. The Club, which was mainly run by American and British residents, had had a committee meeting on the previous evening. Frieda was one of the members.

'How did your committee meeting go?' he asked.

'All right.'

'Did you chose a play for the next performance?'

'*A Streetcar Named Desire*.'

'I'd hoped that you were going to have *An Inspector Calls*.'

'The committee thought it was too English.'

'Mayn't some of your audience find *A Streetcar* too American?'

'Only a few, and our last play was English. We like to take it in turns.'

'And the Americans do a lot for the club, don't they?'

'They lend us the old legation for our Poetry Reading.'

12

'Of course, of course,' he hesitated. He wanted to prolong the interview. 'Have they given you a good part?'

'I don't know yet. The casting's tomorrow night.'

'Who do you expect?'

'The usual ones. Beryl and Sarita as the leads'.

'Sarita?'

'Sarita Jerez. The Spanish CG's daughter-in-law.'

'Of course, of course. Stupid of me to forget her. What about the Moroccans? Have you any of them? I wish we could get more Moroccans to join in that kind of thing. The trouble is, isn't it, that they won't bring their womenfolk.'

'That's one of the troubles.'

'When they come to cocktail parties they sit in a group together.'

'Exactly.'

'But it would be nice if you could get one or two of the young Moroccans.'

'We are getting one this time. Pablo Monterey.'

'Do I know him?'

'Perhaps you don't. He's not really a Tangerine, though he has a flat here. He runs a family estate near Tetouan.'

'I see.' He hesitated. He was reluctant to end the conversation.

'Where's the casting?' he asked,

'At my flat, at six.'

'I might come around.'

'You'd be very welcome.'

She had a rich contralto voice . . . Did a half-smile flicker over her lips? There were times when he wished that he had not to maintain the dignity of his position.

Back in his room Adrian locked his door, then unlocked his desk, and took out his cypher book. It was a short message. 'Check new apointee American School' it ran. He struck a match and set it to the sheet of paper. Pensively he watched it burn. The American School was a well-run flourishing concern supported by Washington, that provided education for the children of American residents and for promising Moroccan students. I can deal with that, he thought.

13

He put through a call to the American Consulate. Could he speak to James Murray. Murray was the one of the three vice-consuls with whom he had built up a personal relationship. They played golf together sometimes. 'Good morning James. There's something you can do for me.'

'Yours to command.'

'Am I right in thinking that you've got a new compatriot on the staff of the American School?'

'You are'.

'He'll be at the party for the ship this evening, won't he?'

'He's been invited.'

'Then he'll be there. I'd like him to be introduced to Beryl.'

'Of course.'

'She gets rather homesick for compatriots of her own age.'

'I'll bet she does. We all do.'

'Thank you, that's settled. By the way, what's his name?'

'Sven Jurgensen.'

Most days Adrian lunched at the Yacht Club. A mile and a half away, it was a walk to which he invariably subjected visitors. 'In three minutes,' he would say, 'you can get the whole essence of Tangier.' The same trees that shaded the church yard of the Anglican church protected the gravestones of a Moroccan cemetery. Above the roofs of a row of one-storied shops you could see the yellow ochre walls and rounded bastions of the original medina. 'The Portuguese built it,' he would tell his visitors, 'then gave it to Charles II as part of Catherine of Braganza's dowry. But Charles looked a gift horse in the mouth. He suspected that it would be a heavy drain on his exchequer. He needed his money for other things. Pretty witty Nell and all that went with that. He sent out Samuel Pepys to case the joint. Pepys agreed with him. If England wanted a foothold on the Mediterranean why not cross the straits and take the Gibraltan. So the English blew up most of the fortifications and went away. That was typical of Tangier,' he would tell his visitors.

The roadway below the wall was jammed with carts and

14

cars. Tangier had acquired a reputation for crime and violence, but nothing could have seemed more orderly and peaceful than this crowded area. Adrian himself always felt completely safe in the narrow winding streets that ran down from the Kasbah. For generations the same families had been living here, in the same shops, selling the same kind of merchandise, to honest, self-respecting families. It was not here that visitors got 'mugged' but in the new parts of the town, and not by members of the old families, but by newly arrived thugs from Casablanca. When anything happened in the Kasbah it was the visitor's own fault; men who were half drunk and behaved stupidly.

'The Vice Consul in Montevideo.' But that was another matter altogether. It was a classic incident. More than one reference had been made to it at that course at Hendon. 'Don't be like that fellow in Montevideo,' he had been warned: a man who went outside his brief: who tried to make discoveries for himself. 'Leave the risky work to your agents.' Was there any risk for him here? He did not think there was. But how could he be sure? He did not really understand the half of what he did. He had only been told as much as he needed to know to carry out his immediate job of work. Watch Spain, he had been told. Ignore Morocco except as far as Spain's concerned. Leave the Moroccans to manage their own affairs.

Most days Beryl joined him for lunch. But not invariably. She had a good many activities. She was on the committee of the theatre club. She played bridge. She took her turn at flower decoration in the church. It was unusual for him to see her before he left for breakfast. Her plans might very often change during the morning. She never rang him up unless she had to. 'You sound so businesslike in the office,' she would complain.

'I'm very likely not alone.'

'I know and I don't like it when you can't concentrate on me.'

He had an idea that sometimes she would not come down

15

to the beach even though she would have preferred to, so as not to be taken for granted.

'Is my wife here?' he asked the doorman.

'Yes, Monsieur Adrian, she come an hour back.'

She was already seated at a table, a jug of sangria beside her. She was wearing a pale blue bikini. She was light haired and her skin was acquiring a becoming tan.

'You look a dish,' he said.

'Hurry, I am ravenous'.

He was back within ten minutes.

'I've got a surprise for you,' he said.

'A nice surprise?'

'I think you'll think so. A young American's joined the teaching staff. I've arranged to have you meet him.'

'What kind of an American?'

'I've no idea. I'm relying on you to tell me.'

'So it's one of those things, is it?'

It was not by any means the first time that he had enlisted her support. In Copenhagen she had twice been very useful.

'And I suppose that once again, you are going to keep me in the dark, you're going to give me no idea as to what you want to know.'

'I want to know everything you can find out.'

'And you're not going to tell me why. You're not going . . . yes, yes, I know, you explained it all to me before. If you gave me any clue as to why you're curious about this guy, it would put ideas into my head; I couldn't be trusted not to let him guess what I knew; I'm not a trained interrogator . . . Why aren't I, by the way? Why don't you send me on the same kind of course that they sent you?' She spoke lightly, teasingly. 'I might be very useful.'

'You're far more useful to me the way you are.'

'That's what you say. But you don't know how much more useful I might be. Why not try it my way, this once.'

Her eyes were twinkling.

'I find it very hard not to do anything you want,' he said.

'How pleased with myself I'd be, if I could break down your reserve.'

'Wouldn't you rather despise me if you could?'

'Give me a chance and see.'

Her teasing excited him in a funny way. It was a kind of aphrodisiac, a form of mental flagellation. 'Do you know what I'd really like?' he said.

'You tell me what you'd really like.'

'I'd like this to be one of those hotels in the country where I could say to the manager, "I'd like to have a bedroom for the afternoon."'

'Like that day at Fontainebleau.'

'Exactly, like that day at Fontainebleau.' But that had been on their honeymoon. Things were different now.

As a bachelor, he had envied the spontaneity of married couples, who did not have to plan their love-making in advance, who would suddenly find themselves 'in the mood', who would never know when they woke to a new day whether they would make love during it. In an affair you always knew in advance; weekends planned ahead, lunches when you kept the afternoon free; everything foreseen. Free love was not free at all. That was how he had thought before he married. But now in marriage, a whole week might pass without his making love. Five days without a single A. He looked at her across the table, enviously. When he walked down to the beach he had no idea that he would be feeling in this mood now. But now that he was, what was the use? They had their respective afternoons planned out. She was going to linger on the beach, read a novel, have a second swim, play bridge between four and six, then get dolled up for the party; while he would doze in a deck chair, then take a taxi to his office.

'What's the name of this American?' she asked.

'Sven Jurgensen.'

'Sounds Scandinavian.'

'That's what you'll be telling me tonight.'

After the party, they'd go to the Parade for supper. Perhaps they'd recapture the mood they were in now. High time there was another A in that diary.

2

US naval officers unlike the British turned up in mufti to
Consular cocktail parties. Beryl wished they wouldn't. They
looked so unromantic, so impersonal in their conventional
dark suits. 'I'll probably recognise Sven Jurgensen because
he'll be the one young man there with a little style.'

He wasn't though. In his dark suit, white shirt, black tie
he seemed as much turned out to pattern as the rest. But
whereas they in mufti looked ill at ease he seemed to be
wearing a familiar uniform. He was tall but not over tall. He
looked strong. He was clean shaven. He was quite handsome
in a healthy way.

'Tell me about yourself,' she said. 'Where are you
from?'

'Utah.'

'Not a Mormon?'

'Yes.'

She looked at the glass in his hand. It was yellow coloured.
Is that apple-juice?'

'It's not.'

'How come?'

'I'm not in Utah now.'

'Have you abandoned the Word of Wisdom?'

'So you know a bit about us?'

'A little, not a lot.'

'Have you had any Mormon friends?'

'A few.'

'I'm not a good example. I break all the rules.'

'A Jack Mormon?'

'So you know what we're called?'

'Doesn't everyone know that?'

'Not everyone.'

'Have you always felt like that?'

'By no means.'

'When did you start having doubts?'

18

'Quite recently. Four months ago. It was rather awkward. I was on a mission.'

'So that explains it.'

'Explains what?'

'Your suit, why it seemed familiar; like a uniform. It's what you wore on your mission, isn't it?'

'Correct.'

'I've seen Mormon missionaries sometimes. They are unmistakable. They look so clean, so healthy'.

'That's the idea, the girls compare us with their own young men who smell of booze and cigarettes.'

'How do you feel now about cigarettes and wine?'

'I never smoke. I never took to it. Perhaps because I never inhaled.'

'What about wine?'

'It doubles the fun.'

'Of everything?'

'Of everything.' There was a twinkle in his eye.

'Tell me about those doubts?' she asked.

He shook his head. 'Some day.'

'Too long a story to tell me now?'

'It isn't that, it's . . .' He hesitated. 'I'll need to know you a lot better.'

'Don't take too long.'

'I won't.'

She felt cosy with him. It was amusing to be with someone her own age. She wasn't, all that often; Adrian was ten years older, and most of the men in the British Colony were even older. She liked to meet men on equal terms. Adrian had had a ten year start, he was running around with girls when she was going to children's parties. She must see more of this young Jurgensen. 'Why don't you join the theatre group?' she asked.

'Nobody's suggested it.'

'Well, I am now. Our next show is *A Streetcar Named Desire*, I'm on the committee. The casting's tomorrow night. I could take you round.'

'I'll be very grateful.'

19

Of the two or three bars to which Tangerines went after cocktail parties, the Parade was the most popular, and in most ways the best. Started directly after the war by an American GI who was reluctant to return to the USA, it was small and intimate, decorated with large romantic oil paintings by a local artist. It had banquette tables round the walls; its bar was covered like a tent. Its founder had been extremely popular with females, and it was the one place to which it was safe for them to go unchaperoned. They would sit on stools along the bar, ordering hamburgers or bacon and eggs when they felt hungry. He acted as their chaperone. If anyone undesirable tried to approach them, he would ward the intruder off. He did not discourage anyone whose friendship he adjudged appropriate. They were for the most part attractive well-dressed ladies in their middle forties. The bar had the appearance of an herbaceous border.

With a pleasant garden which was widely patronised during the summer, it opened at seven-thirty but was rarely crowded before ten. It was a place to which people 'went on afterwards'; usually for a one-course meal.

Adrian and Beryl went there after the cocktail party at the American consulate.

'I know what I'm going to have,' said Adrian, 'scrambled eggs and bacon. Are you going to have your usual vol-au-vent?'

'And with a Flag-Pils,' That was the local Moroccan beer —a rather bitter but a wholesome beverage. 'And you'll be surprised,' she said, 'at how much I have to tell you. Do you know much about the Mormons?'

'Only what I've read.'

'*A Study in Scarlet*, I suppose?'

'That's the best known, isn't it?'

'And the least accurate. You've a lot to learn. Are you ready to listen to a lecture?'

He listened thoughtfully as she delivered it, 'What do you make of that?' she said.

'A young man who's lost his faith is very vulnerable.'

'That's what I thought you'd say.'

20

'I'd like to learn how he lost it.'

'So I'm still on my assignment?'

'Most certainly.'

'Did you have a close look at him?'

'Not very.'

'Enough to realise that he was quite good-looking?'

'Can't say I did.'

'Men never know when another man's good-looking.'

'Oh, come now.'

'No, that's true. Unless a man's queer he can't tell whether another man's got "it".'

'And that's what this fellow has?'

'If I were a spy, I'd welcome the assignment.'

'You would?'

'You can guess, can't you, what I'd say to you if I really were?'

'I guess so.'

'That the best way to find a man's secret is to go to bed with him.'

'Then it's lucky that you haven't got a real assignment.'

'But what would you say if I were to make you a practical proposition. If I were to say, "You want to know all about this fellow. You go off to Marrakesh for three days and see what I have to tell you when you come back."'

'I don't think I should welcome that proposition.'

'Not if I brought you the exact information that you needed?'

'Not even if you did that.'

'Then I'd say you aren't a first-class agent: that you don't put your profession first. Can you expect me to respect a man who doesn't put his profession first?'

She was teasing him again, just as she had teased him that afternoon at the Yacht Club, and once again he found his excitement rising. Tomorrow morning he might well be marking a letter B in his diary.

'Suppose I were to make a bargain with you?' she said.

'What kind of a bargain?'

'Suppose that I were to promise not to enjoy myself, to hold back?'

'Do you think you'd be able to keep that promise?'

'It would be fun seeing if I could.' He burst out laughing. She was an enchanting creature. Maybe there would be a B in his diary tomorrow morning.

Back in the flat, he found that already the water had been turned off. Damn, he thought. He would have liked to have shaved. He passed his hand over his chin. A little rough. Perhaps he ought to get an electric razor. Still there was a basin of water beside his bath. It wouldn't be the first time that he had shaved in cold water. Five minutes later his skin was tingling and fresh. He squirted some Brut lotion into the palm of his left hand, rubbed his palms together, and smoothed his face. He had the sense of a new day starting, just as he had had that morning at half past seven.

Beryl was seated at her dressing table. She raised her head. He could see her reflection in the glass. His liveliness subsided. Her face was as white as a clown's.

Every ten days or so she would coat her face with a cream that as it dried hardened into a solid mask. Unless she left it there untouched until the morning it would not achieve its rejuvenating purpose. Damn, he thought, damn, damn, damn. There would be no Greek letter in his diary tomorrow.

Beryl was still asleep when he left next morning. She had turned towards him in the night. Her cheeks were still flaked with the white mask. He did not know whether she would really look any prettier because of her modern treatment but she would think she did. 'One wakes feeling so terrible, so parched and dry. One can't stand the sight of oneself. Then one puts on the cleansing cream. One feels so wonderful; reborn. One feels like that all day.' Surely there would be a Greek letter in the diary tomorrow morning.

To his surprise, he saw in the inner room of the Café de Paris the elegant young Moroccan who had laid *L'Opinion* on his table the previous morning. He was surprised, he was also annoyed. Twice running. That was the kind of thing that people noticed. Had he a special message, or was he going to make a practice of breakfasting there regularly, so as not to attract notice. Perhaps he wanted to make the exchange of papers a daily occurrence. At any rate he himself had no message to send.

He read through *Le Matin*, responded to the drama of the heroine's problem, refolded the paper, and laid it on his table. Five minutes later the Moroccan came across. 'I wonder if we could exchange newspapers,' he asked.

Adrian watched him cross the roundabout. He wondered where he was going now: Adrian knew nothing about him except the name; and he could not be sure of that. He was the 'cut-out', the man who made the contacts, who went to the places where he himself could not go. He did not even pay him his money. That was paid into a Gibraltar bank. He did not know how much. He had been told that his information was reliable. He himself set questions to which he quite often did not receive an answer. He had other sources of information. Where would the man be in an hour's time? Did the Moroccan authorities know about him? For all he knew he might be in their pay; he might be a double or a treble agent. Was he himself suspected by the Moroccans? He had to go to the police station fairly often. English tourists were constantly getting into trouble. He had his own special contacts. But he wondered if the British Consul General had any idea of how completely he was in the dark himself.

His 'cut out' paused in the midway island of the Place de France, and looked about him. There was no policeman on duty there, and it was an awkward crossing. The Rue de Fez was a two-way street, and the traffic going south came from two different directions. There was no traffic light.

The 'cut out' looked round him a second time, then began to cross, looking in two directions. He was halfway across, when . . . But it happened so quickly that Adrian could not tell what had happened. At one moment Tangier was following its own affairs in its usual inconsequential manner, everyone occupied with his and her own affairs, then suddenly there was a blowing of whistles, a sounding of horns, a shouting; a traffic jam was forming, a body was lying in the roadway, the body of a young and elegant Moroccan. One of the waiters from the Café ran across.

Adrian did not move. He did not want to figure as a witness; besides what had he to report? He had seen nothing. The waiter returned.

'Is he badly hurt?' Adrian asked.

'Dead.'

'Who was he?'

'Someone who comes here sometimes. I don't know his name.'

A couple of policemen joined the scene. An ambulance drew up. The body was hoisted on to it and the crowd dispersed. Adrian rose. There was no point in his staying any longer. He took *L'Opinion* with him. He wondered what had happened to the copy of *Le Matin* which the victim had had under his arm. No letters were encircled in the 'Juliette de mon Cœur' caption.

Back in his office he opened *L'Opinion* to its second page. A number of letters in the third column were ringed. He locked the door and took out his cypher. 'Tuesday June 15' he read. 'Now what on earth does that mean?' he asked himself.

3

Mark Littlejohn stood on the ninth tee. He had the honour. He was playing his Spanish colleague. It was their second time round the nine-hole course, and he was one down. But he had won the last two holes. His opponent, several years older than himself, was, he suspected, tiring. 'I'll win this hole,' he thought. 'Then for the hell of it, we'll play the first hole again, and the drinks will be on him.'

Littlejohn addressed his ball with confidence. The ninth was a straightforward hole. It was a long par four, and his opponent would not be able to get on in two, whereas he himself had, on the first time round.

The green was guarded by two shallow bunkers. It was a question of placing your drive so that the approach lay open. There were no intervening hazards. The fairway sloped gently to the left, then lifted towards the green. It was lined with pines and gumtrees. Littlejohn shifted his feet. 'Steady, don't press,' he told himself.

His club went back. But as it did, he remembered suddenly that he had forgotten to put a call through to the Spanish hospital where one of his staff had had a minor operation two days before. 'Damn,' he thought, 'damn, damn, *damn*'. His head went up. His club head met the ball cleanly, but at an angle. The curving ball glistened in the sunlight, white against the pale blue of the evening sky. If it reached the rough, he would never be able to get on in two. He watched it anxiously, as it neared its apex.

It was sinking, sinking. Sometimes when he was watching a ball, more often when he was watching an opponent's ball, it seemed that just as it was about to sink, it acquired a new impetus, an extra access of power, presumably because a breeze had caught it: it went on, on, on. Would that happen now? He strained his eyes. They were not as good as they had been. He played in glasses, which at a distance blurred the landscape. The ball was dropping slowly, slowly, with diminishing pace, with diminishing length too. Would it reach the rough? With any luck it wouldn't. But it did. It landed in a ditch.

'Damn,' he thought, but didn't say it. A Spaniard would be shocked by a display of feeling. He stood away from the tee, and waited.

The Spaniard knelt down to put in his peg. Senor Jerez was a tall, thin man on the edge of sixty. He was clean-shaven and thin-featured, punctiliously well-dressed. He was one of those irritating opponents who do not hit the ball very far, but hit it very straight. He took a short flat swing. The ball went low but straight. It pitched a hundred yards away and ran on for another thirty. He would make certain of his five.

'I'll play a second ball,' said Littlejohn.

This time his shot was clean and true. It landed well beyond his opponent's and ran on for another forty yards. Why couldn't he have done that the first time? Then he could have got his four, won the hole and halved the match.

'Are you going to have a look for that first shot?' the Spaniard asked.

He nodded, but he might have spared himself the trouble. The ball lay under and behind a root. 'How like me' he thought. 'The game in my pocket. I had only to concentrate, but that's the one thing I can't do. My attention wanders at the important moment. I miss my opportunities; that's why at my age, I'm in a dead-end job like this. I've had my chances, but I've let them slide. That's why I'm alone here, with a wife who doesn't consider my career sufficiently important to deprive her daughter of her company. A failure in my career, a failure in my marriage. The man who lifts his head on the eighteenth tee.' The incident was typical. On the hill, beyond the course, the sun was shining on the cemetery, pinking the stones. That's where I ought to be, he thought for all the good I'm doing here.

He looked at the Spaniard enviously. In one way Jerez was in the same position as himself. He too, was in a dead-end post. This was his last assignment. His career in retrospect would seem as moderate as his own. But their positions were dissimilar. Jerez came of an old family, a rich family. He had not needed to be a success. His role had been to perform a public duty: dutifully. His final years would be spent in an atmosphere of prosperity and respect.

In another respect too, there was between them a similarity of position. Jerez' wife was in Madrid. Her health was frail. She had not wanted to take on the duties of a consul general's wife. She had persuaded, had had no difficulty in persuading her daughter-in-law, a twenty-nine year-old widow, to take on her responsibilities. It had seemed reasonable for a Spaniard and a Catholic to make a decision of that kind. To Spaniards marriage was an inexorable, willingly accepted obligation. Did Jerez have a *petite amie* here? He might well do. But Littlejohn had heard no gossip. A man like Jerez would know how to organise a thing like that.

Jerez got his five. Littlejohn just missed the long putt that would have halved the hole for him. He should have won that hole. 'What will the victor take?' he asked.

'Sweet sherry. In public, I must support my country's industry.'

They sat on the terrace in the evening sunlight, cosily in tune with one another. Littlejohn did not speak Spanish. He had rarely been in Spain. The Spaniards were more foreign to him than the Moroccans. Yet he felt more in tune with Jerez than he did with anyone in Tangier. On the whole, he did not really like it here. Tangier was a curious place and had had a curious history.

It was not surprising that it should have acquired a series of special characteristics, attracting a variety of international expatriates. Life here was inexpensive. The climate was good. The old town was beautiful. Some of the new residents converted old Moorish houses in the Kasbah into picturesque wandering homes on different levels with fanciful tiles and windows. Others built themselves modern villas on the mountain. They had charming gardens. The English colony was the largest and the most influential: it was also the most fashionable. It was this fact that made Littlejohn feel ill at ease.

27

He had previously served in Bordeaux and Oporto: that was the kind of place he liked—where the British community had long-based family connections through the handling of wine—solid, substantial, respectable, and respected. In places like that he could be, as the representative of the Crown, the centre of the community. It was different here. He would be glad when he had finished his tour of duty.

He finished his scotch and soda; he would have liked a second, but he remembered that the Tangier theatre were having their casting evening.

'Isn't your daughter-in-law on the committee of the theatre club?' He asked.

'She is.'

'They're casting their new play tonight. Why don't we go down?'

'That's an idea.'

Their cars were parked side-by-side. Littlejohn's was a large roomy Simca, a family car. Jerez' was a low slim Hispano Suiza. Their cars underlined the difference between them. 'You lead;' said Littlejohn, 'your car will weave its way through traffic blocks.'

Frieda's flat consisted of two main rooms off which two small bedrooms opened. The dining-room had been cleared and a bar arranged against the wall. Most of the group had glasses in their hands. James Murray, the director stood in the centre.

'Now I'd like to try that scene between the sisters. On page seventy-eight. That's you, Beryl and Sarita. It's one of the big scenes. It's where Stella realises the kind of woman her sister has become.'

Beryl and Sarita stood together. Sarita was dark slim, tall with her hair knotted low upon her neck. She had long-fingered hands which she moved expressively as she talked. Beryl was shorter by five inches; her slight plumpness and her pale bronze hair made her an effective foil.

'Don't they look good together' Jerez whispered, 'Such luck for Sarita. I don't know what she would have done

28

without Beryl here. I felt a little doubtful at first about her coming. This is a curious place. You don't need telling that. But when Beryl arrived I knew it would be all right. They are so in tune, so much a team. Look at them now'.

Sarita had started her key speech.

'I never was hard or self-sufficient enough. When people are soft, soft people have to shimmer and glow. They've got to put on soft colours, the colours of butterfly wings, and put a paper lantern over the light. It isn't enough to be soft. You've got to be soft and attractive, and I'm—I'm fading now. I don't know how much longer I can turn the trick.'

Murray interrupted them. 'That's fine. That's enough. You'll be just right, the two of you. Now let's hear one or two others. Pablo, I thought you should be right as Michael. Will you read the scene with Sarita, the one that begins on page seventy-eight.'

A tall, wiry young man came forward. He was dark-skinned, his hair was black and straight. He was obviously half Moroccan.

Littlejohn leaned across to Jerez.

'Who's that?' he asked.

'Pablo Monterey.'

'Of course, yes.' The man about whom Frieda had talked to him the other morning. 'The man with an estate near Tetouan?'

'Exactly.'

'I haven't seen him before.'

'He isn't about here much. He goes to Madrid quite often. His grandfather was one of the Moors who fought for Franco. He was killed at Teruel.'

Littlejohn looked at Pablo with curiosity. He was very handsome. He moved with a feline grace. He had been cast for the role of a rough, uncouth ex-soldier. He did not seem to fit the role particularly, but he had an appropriate accent.

'He's the kind of man I ought to know about and don't,'' thought Littlejohn. Once again he was afflicted with self-doubt. He was not doing his job efficiently.

Littlejohn looked about him. He had been in this flat

29

several times before. It was one of half a dozen in the town that were being constantly sublet to English and Americans posted on short assignments. But he had not been here since Frieda had taken it over.

He noticed some photographs on the desk in the living-room. One of them showed a small family group, with a large house in the background. Frieda was at his side.

'Is that your home?' he asked.

'It was: or at least I thought of it as my home. It was my grandfather's. I spent most of my holidays there when my father was on duty somewhere. I've never really had a home.'

'Do you still go there on your leaves?'

She shook her head.

'My grandfather died three years ago, My uncle sold it.'

'You must miss it.'

She nodded.

'I went there for the funeral. My parents were in Australia. They couldn't come back for it. I had to act as hostess. My uncle's wife wasn't well. So I stayed on after the rest had gone. It was very strange, having breakfast alone with him on that last morning. He was closer to me than my father was. He was there in the holidays. He used to visit me at school. He had no daughter. A succession of four sons. I was special for him. I could tell him things. He could tell me things. That last morning at breakfast I knew what he was feeling. "This must be a wrench for you," I said. I could go straight to the point with him. He could go straight to the point with me. He nodded. "I've always dreamed that this would be my home," he said, and even after I had realised that I couldn't keep it up after paying death duties, I used to indulge in fantasies, thinking I might win the football pools. As it is, I shall go back to London this afternoon, and never spend another night here in my life. When I came back as a school boy for the holidays, my father would put up a notice "welcome home to the heir of Brockleigh". That's how I thought of myself. *The heir of Brockleigh*. I shall have enjoyed my inheritance for just three days.'

Littlejohn picked up the photo and looked at it closely. It was the kind of house that typified a whole way of life. There had been such a house, a couple of miles outside the Somerset village where he had been brought up. He had been to it, often enough for cricket matches and for Christmas parties. He had known the sons of the house by their Christian names, but they had belonged to a different world. He had recognised that and so had they. It was the English caste system to which nobody referred. All that was over now. The "big house" in his own neighbourhood had not been big enough to be taken over as a show piece by the National Trust. It had been sold to meet death duties and the head of the family had moved into a more modest house. The kind of house in which his own father had lived, as the local doctor. Exactly as had happened to Frieda's uncle. There was no difference now between girls like Frieda and girls like his own step-daughter, except for the basic difference that Frieda had been brought up in a big house and his own Julia had not. Was this one of the reasons why he was conscious of a difference in Frieda?

Jerez was again beside him. 'I suppose you know everybody here,' he said.

There were some twenty in the room. Littlejohn knew most of them by sight, but there were one or two whose names eluded him. It was a tendency of which he was becoming increasingly aware. Others of his own age were noticing the same thing, at least they said they were. It was a weakness against which he had to be on his guard. At the end of the day he would run over the names of the people whom he had met during the last fifteen hours. It got him off to sleep more quickly than counting sheep. He took a second glance round the room. There was one face that he did not recognise. 'Who's that young man talking to Sarita?'

'Sven Jurgensen?'

'Who's he'?

'The latest staff addition at the American School.'

'He's quite good-looking.'

'So Sarita thinks.'

31

They laughed together. 'Does that mean she'll cast him as her leading man?'

'Not in this play. He joined too late.'

'But next time.'

'We shall see.'

'What about Frieda?'

'Your secretary?'

'Yes.'

'She's the extra woman—the one that everyone confides in.'

'I'm glad she's in this. I suggested that she should. She needs friends.'

'Who doesn't?'

'Perhaps she does more than most. She's on her own. What does Sarita think of her?'

'She likes her, quite.'

'Not more than "quite!"?'

'She doesn't know her very well.'

'That's what her trouble is, I'd say. No one knows Frieda very well.'

'Don't you?'

'There's a barrier between secretary and employer.'

How he wished there weren't. She made him feel inquisitive. She made him feel aggressive. He wanted to break down barriers, discover what she was really like. If only he could take her out to dinner, work her into a mellow mood, lead her on, provoke her, question her . . . He checked, no, no . . . not again, not that. He had been warned. He knew the geography of that road. He had learned his lesson . . . Better talk to Beryl.

He looked about him. Beryl was standing by herself. He walked across to her. 'Time I was on my way. Have you got your car?' he asked.

She shook her head. 'Adrian has the car. I walked'.

'Can I give you a lift?'

'I'd be very grateful. I'll say goodbye to Sarita and I'll be ready.'

He noticed that the two women kissed each other, in the

32

French fashion on both cheeks. 'And that's a date for Tuesday,' Sarita said.

'Most certainly.' She turned to the young ex-Mormon. 'And we've got a date for tomorrow.'

'I won't forget it.'

What fun they all seemed to be having, all except himself thought Littlejohn. He felt wistful as he watched Beryl climb the stairway of her flat. Lights were showing through the shutters in the sitting room. Simms would be waiting for her. They would have a cosy evening. What a long time since he had had that kind of evening.

It was shortly after eight. Adrian had been listening to the news. He switched it off when he heard the click of Beryl's key. 'No, no keep it on,' she said. 'You need to hear it.'

'Not when you're here with a day's gossip.'

They had not lunched that morning at the Yacht Club. 'I haven't heard your voice all day,' he said. 'Will you have a whisky? That's what I've been having.'

They sat facing each other in the Moroccan room, barely seven feet apart, with a small table in front of each; sitting straight upright; How right Huxley was. 'Tell me about the Mormon. Is he fitting in?'

'He's coming round tomorrow with Sarita to try out his part. If you come back early, but not too early, you'll have a chance of seeing him.'

'I'll be there.'

'And there's another thing. Have you anything planned for us on Tuesday, at lunchtime or the late afternoon?'

'Not that I know of. Why?'

'Sarita asked if I would go with her to Ceuta. There's a "do" on there.'

'Tuesday. Isn't that the fifteenth?'

'Is it? I don't know. The fifteenth, yes it must be.'

Tuesday the fifteenth, that last message he had received from his Moroccan cut-out.

'Did she say what kind of a do it was?'

'No.'

33

'Do you think you could find out?'

'Well . . .'

'I don't mean make an issue of it. Couldn't you ring up and say that of course, the Tuesday is perfectly all right, if that is essential, but that in point of fact, I had got something tentatively planned, so that it would be more convenient—if it wasn't absolutely essential for her—to go on the Monday or the Wednesday.'

Beryl looked at him, intently. 'Is this one of your top secret orders?'

'Yes.'

She went into the narrow passageway where the telephone table was. Adrian could hear her across the passage. 'Sarita, this is Beryl. I'm wondering how important Tuesday is, that actual date I mean . . . Yes, yes I see. No, no there isn't any problem. It's just that Adrian had something he'd like to have me do . . . No, no it's not important . . . another day will do as well for him . . . and yes, of course if for you Tuesday is the only day . . . That's fine I'm looking forward to it. I've always wanted to see Ceuta and tomorrow you'll come round to go over Sven's part with him. Wonderful, wonderful.'

'And that, as you gathered, is that,' she said as she returned. 'Disappointed?'

'Nothing could matter less.'

'You seem to have a great many alternatives in your devious profession.'

'It's all a game of make-believe,'

Next morning he codified for Gibraltar a message that ran 'Suspect something subversive happen Ceuta Tuesday.'

I wonder, he thought, I wonder.

He rang through to fix an appointment with the Consul General. He was given an unusually warm welcome.

'I had an agreeable talk with your wife, last night,' he said.

'So she told me.'

'I hadn't realised what an attractive girl she is. You're a lucky fellow.'

'I think so, sir.'

34

'There's a lot to be said for Anglo-American marriages. A mixture of what's familiar and what's foreign. You must always be getting small surprises, which is something one doesn't often get in marriage. Well, what have you got for me this morning. Another of your secret messages?'

'I'm afraid so, sir.'

'Don't be afraid. That's what you're here for. If you weren't bringing me these messages, I should start worrying. Come along now, hand it over, and one day quite soon, I'll be asking Frieda to fix an evening when you and your wife can come round for a quiet dinner. We ought to know each other better.'

Adrian hesitated. He wished that he and Littlejohn were, he would not say on better but on closer terms. He wished he were really on Littlejohn's staff. Could he risk it? Perhaps he could. Perhaps he should.

'There's something, that I'd like to ask you, sir.'

'Fire away.'

'Have you heard of anything special that might be happening on Tuesday?'

'Happening where. Here?'

'In Ceuta.'

The expression on Littlejohn's face changed, became aggressive and aggrieved. 'Do you think you should ask me that kind of question? You have your work to do and I have mine. You have your sources of information and I have mine. My sources tell me what I need to know, your sources tell you what you need to know. Our interests may overlap, at times. If they do, our respective sources will inform us. Isn't that the correct answer to your question?'

'Yes, sir. I'm sorry, sir.'

'That's all right. I can guess how you must feel at times: lonely and on your own.'

'Thank you, sir, thank you very much indeed.'

Back in his own room, he shrugged. Had he blotted his copybook? In a way, perhaps, but nonetheless, he felt closer to Littlejohn than he had before.

4

Tangier time was an hour behind Spanish time. The two young women started off on the Tuesday shortly after ten. It was a clean bright morning; the sky was cloudless, but a wind was blowing. It would not be a scorching day. 'Let's take it quietly and drive in turns,' said Sarita.

It was the first time they had made an expedition of this kind. It was the first time they had really been alone together. They had liked each other, instinctively from the start. They had been meeting constantly, at parties; at charity committees. They had made a point, as often as possible, of sitting next to each other. But their conversations, their 'you and me' conversations, had always been interrupted. They had never had any equivalent of a double date. Yet they had come to feel that each was the other's closest friend. This was a genuine occasion.

They took the new mountain road. The colours were soft and varied, springlike in their freshness. The streams were bright with oleanders. The hill sides were dotted with small white houses.

'And now perhaps you can tell me what all this is about?' said Beryl.

'Once we've crossed the frontier.'

'You're being very mysterious.'

'Diplomats have to be; haven't you learnt that from Adrian?'

'That's all I have learnt from him.'

'Really?'

'Yes, really.'

'I thought you had been his secretary.'

'What gave you that idea?'

'It's the idea that everybody has.'

'How little one knows of what people say about one.'

'It isn't true then?'

'Not by any means.'

'Funny, it's the only explanation we could find of how you came to marry him.'

'Is that so complimentary—to either of us?'

'I don't see why it shouldn't be. You're ten years younger. You're American. He's English. You're extremely pretty.'

'Thank you.'

'He isn't rich.'

'Who is, these days?'

'Some young men look as though they might be some day.'

'And you don't think he does.'

'Do you?'

'Quite frankly, no.'

'He's not a glamorous Adonis.'

'He's reasonably good looking.'

'But even so.'

'You think I've thrown myself away.'

'You're saying that, not I.'

'I think I'll have to tell you how it came about.'

'You will?'

'It would save trouble, wouldn't it?'

'Perhaps.'

And it would be a relief to let herself go, with Sarita; to lay her cards upon the table. 'Look back four years' she said. 'That makes me twenty-one. Just graduated, majored in Eng. Lit. If I'm to get a master's I must do a thesis. I've never travelled. I've been a good daughter, reasonably. Now is the time to touch my parents. Why not a thesis on the Medicis. That means Florence, and that's the kind of thing an American girl can put across. There was no battle, no discussion. A recommendation from the Dean, and there I was. One who had never been outside the US, in Italy, in Florence, in mid-June. Can you see me? Over four years ago, remember.

'So that's how it began?'

'On a guided tour; I was late only just made it, and there I was breathless and a little fussed plumped down beside a reasonably good-looking man—you will admit he's that, reasonably I said, not more than reasonably. And he may not have been particularly young; ten years older than myself, at least, but he wasn't middle-aged. And he was well dressed, in a casual English way, a sports coat with flannel trousers, but his shirt collar wasn't open and he had on a tie. One of those stripey ones that in England mean you're the member of some club. And he had a pleasant leathery smell: no, not tobacco, I'm glad to say. I didn't take it all in at once, that was later, when I was thinking it over, adding up. As I said, I got in late: he was on the window seat, I leant across him to look out—it was then that I got that leathery smell: later I realised it was Brut, his toilet water, but that was later, yes a good deal later. I leant across him to look out. "Is this your first time here?" he said. It was, I told him. "In that case you'd better have my seat." That was a nice thing for him to do now wasn't it? And I liked his voice. Very English, but it wasn't fluted in the way English voices can be. We began to talk, and I found myself liking his voice, more and more. He told me that he had a job at the British consulate. I asked if it was with the British Council. No, he said. He was a kind of diplomat. He had been here a year and expected to stay another. He told me a lot about the things we passed: very knowledgeable. I asked him why, if he knew Florence so well, he bothered to come on a trip like this. "To refresh my memory, and also it's part of my job to see what kinds of tourist come here and how they behave." '

'Did he talk to you about his job?'

'No, he left that till later, till a good deal later. By the time the tour was finished, we had become quite cosy. It was just on noon. "Why don't we have a drink?" he said. "Why not?" I answered. "I've got a flat here: rented from an Englishman who has had to go to Davos for his health. It's got a fine view of the Arno."

'It had a very fine view of the Arno and it was a delightful flat: with old furniture and bookcases and hangings, and modern pictures that were not too modern: thick rugs and lots of cushions. That flat was the key to the whole thing. The setting is so important. I don't know how it is in Spain . . .'

38

'I can tell you how it is in Spain. It almost isn't. We're strictly chaperoned.'

'We aren't, thank heavens. But this flat was something different. I'd never seen anything like that in Oklahoma. There was a huge double bed with side curtains and a canopy. It seemed to say "Hullo" to me. It was the flat not Adrian that said, "This was meant for you." In a month I had to go to Venice, to round off my thesis. A month would be the perfect time. Long enough for us to get to know each other; not too long for it to go too deep. We'd each have perfect memories of each other: the kind of thing that everyone should have once, at least.'

'That's what we all think, at the start.'

'And then it doesn't turn out that way.'

'Is that what you discovered?'

'Yes and no. The month was perfect. There were so many things to do in Florence, and in the towns near Florence: in Pisa, Sienna, Lucca. He didn't seem to have any work to do. There was something new to do every day, with the feeling that everything had to be crowded into those four weeks. It was good too to think that the gilt wouldn't wear off the gingerbread. Another thing too, the immediate future was exciting; the month in Venice. Then back in Oklahoma:—a career opening out for me. When I caught my train out of Florence and craned my neck to catch my last glimpse of the Duomo, I could have cried, I was so happy. The perfect month; a treasure for all my life.'

'Then I suppose you spoilt it all by going back, trying to recapture it.'

'No, it wasn't that.'

'Then he did. It had gone deeper with him than it had with you. He was the older after all.'

'No, no, it wasn't that.'

'What was it then?'

'You'll be surprised. I found that I was pregnant.'

'What, weren't you on the pill?'

'Of course, but I'd been careless, nothing had been happening in that way for quite a while. I could have cursed myself. I did curse myself, but there it was. And there I was stuck in Venice, with no alternative to going back to Florence.'

'Why not go home? You could have fixed it there.'

'I thought of that, but I didn't want to cut short my time in Europe. How would I explain it? It would be a black mark against me. Much better to go back to Florence. He'd be able to find me a doctor.'

'Wasn't that the best way of ruining a perfect memory?'

'I didn't think it was. I wasn't going to be a nuisance. We were good friends. He'd take it the right way.'

'And did he? It looks as though he had, though not in the way that you'd expected.'

'That's what I'm coming to. I couldn't have been more matter-of-fact about it all. "I'm ashamed of myself", I said. I've been an ass. I'm humble and I'm contrite, I hate being a nuisance, but this is how it is. The Pill has let me down. I don't know anyone that I can ask."

'He smiled. It was a very friendly smile. The kind of smile that makes it easy to be confidential. "No problem," he said. "I know just the right man for you, the only thing is," he paused, "I wonder if that is really the best thing. It sounds rather an old-fashioned thing to say, but . . . I lost my father in the war; I've got a feeling about taking life. Listen now. There's an alternative. We are at the moment for quick decisions: What I suggest is this, that we go round this afternoon to the British Consul, that I say to him 'sir, I am trying to persuade this young American lady to become my wife. She knows nothing about me. She needs some solid facts. Will you read to her the appropriate extracts from my dossier. She can then decide whether her father would consider me capable of maintaining her in the social and financial status to which he had accustomed her.' If what the consul tells you is not adequate, then we can go to the doctor who will solve your problems on another level. May I add that I hope you will accept his estimate." What would you, my enchanting Sarita, have said to that?'

'I would have said what I'm certain you did say, "Let us

dispense with the Consul General, except in as far as we shall need his services to get us married." '

There was a pause. 'Is there anything that strikes you as curious about that?' asked Beryl.

'I don't know. Let me think . . . No, I can't see anything particularly curious, except that I think it's an unusual and romantic story.'

'Then I'll tell you what is curious about it: that I found myself taking those rather solemn vows to a man who had never said to me "I love you, will you marry me?" '

Again there was a pause.

'And what about that pregnancy?' Sarita asked.

'Nothing. Still born, prematurely.'

'So you need never have been married at all.'

'Exactly, and shall I tell you what endeared me to Adrian more than anything, that he never did say that, not even jokingly. There's this about Adrian, and it's quite a lot, he's never said a thing that's made me feel less well about myself: he's always built me up. I don't know what he thinks about half the things that we discuss; the English leave so much unsaid; they guess at what's in each other's minds. But this you do know, when you're right with them, you're right.'

'I call that a very romantic story. Ah, here's the frontier.'

It was Beryl's first visit to Ceuta. She had often wanted to go but Adrian had made difficulties. It wasn't worth it, he had said: they might have to wait in a queue for hours. The Moroccan customs were very tricky about currency. She had wondered whether Adrian had not a professional reason for not wanting her on Spanish soil. At any rate with Sarita's diplomatic visa there was no delay. 'And now,' said Beryl, 'you can tell me what's the purpose of this excursion.'

'A high ranking Spanish Admiral is paying us a visit.'

'And that's top secret?'

'It's supposed to be.'

'Why is he coming here?'

'I've not been told; but it is important. There is going to be a conference. You know that Ceuta is a point at issue between

41

the Spaniards and Moroccans—a kind of African Gibraltar. So it's not being publicised as a conference. Just a social visit. We're going to have lunch in a restaurant, quite informal, no protocol: my father-in-law has taken one of the Moroccan ministers, I don't know which. Because it's informal they asked me to bring you, to disarm suspicion and we'll get an exceptionally good lunch. So it's luck for us.

'But my, what a business these security men have with their little secrets.'

'I don't need telling that.'

'Does Adrian take you into his confidence?'

'Scarcely at all.'

'That's strange. For a husband not to be able to discuss his business problems with his wife.'

'Most of my friends think I'm lucky not to be bored with anecdotes about stocks and shares.'

'What did Adrian tell you about his work before you married?'

'He gave me one of Graham Greene's novels, *The Heart of the Matter*. He said that was the kind of racket he was in.'

'How did he get into it?'

'That's what I asked him once. He laughed. "The way my kind of Englishman gets into everything. The old school tie connection." '

'The English are unbeatable. They are all caricatures of themselves.'

It was one o'clock. 'We'll be ravenous by lunchtime,' Beryl said.

'Don't worry; there's a café restaurant on the hill with a view to beat all views. Let's have some wine there and some tapas.'

The view was breathtakingly dramatic. They could see the whole isthmus with its clustering houses, its port with its two approaches, and the Moroccan mountains in the background.

'You've been everywhere. I've been nowhere. Have you seen much that's as good as this?' said Beryl.

'Only Rio.'

'Thank heavens we've given ourselves time to see it.'

'We mustn't give ourselves too much time. We mustn't neglect the town itself. It's charming, so Spanish, iron-wrought balconies with little squares and palm trees. We mustn't linger over our wine too long.'

'We won't, we won't.'

They didn't. 'Time for the big event,' said Sarita.

5

Adrian walked on to his balcony. Quarter past six, quarter past seven in Ceuta. He could not expect them yet. Spaniards keeping Spanish hours. They would not lunch till three. They would not hurry over lunch. They would need a siesta afterwards. And then why not a swim. They wouldn't start the drive back till the air had cooled. 'Expect me when you see me,' she had said.

Don't be impatient, he adjured himself. They wouldn't hurry. They might be held up by customs, in spite of Sarita's diplomatic number plates. Two hours at least, at the very least.

It was ridiculous of him to worry. Why at this of all times should he find himself remembering that this was a dangerous game. That car crash in the Place de France. One moment a man had picked up a paper from your table. Two minutes later he was lying dead. Why was he worrying about that now?

Impatiently he paced the room, paced and repaced it. He could not settle down to read. If he mixed himself a drink, he'd soon need another. A second would become a third. They mustn't come back and find him weaving.

The minutes passed: became half an hour, became an hour. Again he opened the long window, walked out upon the balcony. It was silly of him, ridiculous. They couldn't be here yet. Quarter to eight. Too early; much too early. He looked to the left, then to the right, then straight in front. Nothing but taxis, bicyclists: a bus on the main road; a lorry, then another bus: yes, get yourself a drink, he said, a strong one, but only one. Just to steady your nerves; one look to the right, a final one. Then shut the window. One more look, but . . . yes, surely coming from the south that was an Hispano Suiza. The long lean line; a spasm of relief; then following it, came one of fear. They ought not to be back so early.

44

They must have left Ceuta soon after four. Something must have happened; nothing disastrous though, or they'd not be coming here, they'd be going to the consulate, unless, but no, it couldn't be . . . The car drew up beside the kerb. His heart was pounding. The door swung open. A short, plump leg with a brown open sandal, Beryl's leg, so Beryl had been driving. Beryl must be all right. And so must Sarita: otherwise they'd have driven to the consulate. Beryl was standing on the pavement. She looked cool and fresh: not grimy after an exhausting journey. And there was Sarita, trim and elegant; nothing had happened.

He stood in the doorway, opening his arms. His anxiety was over. 'Welcome,' he called. 'Welcome.'

One glance at Beryl was enough to warn him, though. There was on her face an expression that he could not explain; that he could not define. Something had happened.

'We want a drink,' she announced. 'Both of us. A scotch; a strong one, ice but scarcely any soda. You'd better get yourself a pretty strong one too. Then we'll start telling you.'

They went into the main not the Moroccan room. 'I want to loll back on cushions,' Beryl said. 'Oh yes, and we'll need food; food, that's what we need isn't it? Sarita.'

'I'll say we do.'

'I should have thought that you'd have had enough at lunch to last you for a week,' said Adrian.

'You would, wouldn't you? We'll explain. Best bring in a loaf of bread and a hunk of cheese. Then we can help ourselves. The whisky first, though: fast and strong.'

The two young women looked at one another. 'Who's going to tell him?' Beryl said.

'You start and then I'll interrupt.'

'But where shall I begin?'

'Does he know why we went there?'

'He might, you never know with these cloak and dagger men.'

'He knows we went to Ceuta?'

'He doesn't know why.'

45

'Unless he has some very dubious sources of information that I know nothing of.'

'Which he may well have.'

'Which he very well may have.'

Adrian interrupted them. 'Now please, stop teasing. I know you went to Ceuta—but that's all I know.'

'Ah, but are you sure it is?' This was from Beryl. 'You were very curious to know why we were going there. You felt there was a special reason. You wanted to know what it was. Why were you suspicious?'

'Someone like myself always is. That's what my job's about.'

'Is it? I suppose it is. I suppose we had better tell him. We went there, my dear husband, because a high grade Spanish Admiral was on a visit, nothing official, no protocol, no agendas, but a cosy little conference with a Moroccan minister. The Admiral had come over in the ferry; he was going back in it that night: there would be exploratory talks; that's the word isn't it Sarita?'

'That's the word.'

'And they organised a cosy little lunch party in a beach side restaurant—only ten of us in all. Everything very elegant; sherry to start off—not too dry a one; an Amontillado, we had "tapas" with it—anchovies, olives, cheese on toothpicks. Then there was a paella—it was very rich, but it wasn't sweet, and it wasn't stodgy—the way it is so often at the Yacht Club.'

'And there was a dry white wine with it. Spanish wasn't it?'

'It must have been, being in Spain, mustn't it?'

'I've not had much white Spanish wine I've liked.'

'Have you had much white Spanish wine?'

'Well, now you come to mention it, I haven't. There's that very sweet one.'

'The diamanté?'

'Yes, but usually when a Spanish white wine is dry, it's almost tasteless.' Wasn't this called "Monopole"?'

Would they never get to the point, Adrian thought. They

46

were playing a game with him. They were playing a game with themselves. They were deliberately avoiding a conclusion, tantalising him, making the preliminaries last as long as possible. They were excited: almost hysterical. They must have been under strain. This was their way of exorcising it. They must play it their own way.

'And the paella was so good,' Beryl was continuing, 'that I was afraid of eating too much of it.'

'That we wouldn't have any appetite left?'

'I wondered how many courses there would be.'

'You counted the knives and forks.'

'I asked you how many courses Spaniards had.'

'Did they have a cheese course before the dessert?'

'Would there be two entrées?'

'I wouldn't forgive myself if I had had no appetite for a special course.'

'Why couldn't they have a menu printed?'

Oh, hurry, he thought, hurry. I can't stand more of this.

'Then they came round with a red wine; a full one, wasn't it?'

'Was it, no, surely not, a rather light one, a kind of Beaujolais.'

'Of course yes, I remember. That made us wonder whether there wouldn't be a heavier one to follow.'

'If there were, there would be two entrées.'

'But I said, "no, they might have the heavy red wine with the cheese." '

'How hard it is to remember exactly what happened next.'

'I remember once I was in a motor smash, oh quite a minor one, but it happened so quickly that if I'd had to give evidence in a court of law, I'd have contradicted myself. A good lawyer would have tied me into knots.'

'That's how it was today. That entrée, now. I can't remember what it was.'

'Oh, but of course you can. It was that chicken, done in the Russian way with the butter in it.'

'Yes, so it was, I remember now: how good it was and the butter oozing out, sometimes it's dried up, over-cooked. I

47

thought whatever there may be to follow, I'm going to finish this.'

'I wonder what there would have been to follow?'

'We'll never know.'

'You're right, that was something that we'll never know.'

'When people talk about the best meal that they've ever had, I shall say "the best meal I ever had was a meal I never finished. That lunch at Ceuta." '

'I said at the time, no matter what the second entrée is or isn't, or even if there isn't one, this is the best lunch that I have ever had.'

'I had actually put a morsel in my mouth. I was thinking "thank heaven there are at least four mouthfuls left. And then just as I was thinking that, there was that motor cycle shrieking by and then the crash.'

'Didn't the flash come first?'

'Did it?'

'Light travels faster than sound.'

'But they were so close they'd have been instantaneous.'

'Were they? I suppose they must. There was the flash and crash. Then the noise of crockery.'

'Then there were the bullets. That cyclist in the roadway.'

'And half a dozen people shouting.'

'Most of it in Spanish. I couldn't get what was being said.'

'Then there was the screaming: there must have been at least five people screaming.'

'At least two of them were women.'

'And all that blood.'

'How many people would you say were killed?'

'There was the man who threw the bomb.'

'Was there only one?'

'That's hard to say. There was so much shouting.'

'And then there were those two policemen herding us across the street, clearing the terrace, and the photographs.'

'What happened to all that food?'

'I bet it wasn't wasted.'

'Within half-an-hour we were out of the place.'

'Longer than that. I'd say three-quarters.'

48

'Then the staff settled down to a banquet.'

'What else?'

They were thoroughly enjoying themselves, they were still in an electric mood, but they had sufficiently calmed down for him to ask them questions.

'Let's get this clear,' he said. 'You were sitting out there on the terrace, when a motor cycle went by and the rider tossed a bomb among you; the sentries fired on the cyclist as he rode on; they hit him and they killed him. Was he the only one?'

'As far as we could see.'

'Was he a Moroccan or a Spaniard?'

'I'd say he was a Spaniard; but he was dark.'

'Were many of your party hurt?'

'A couple were quite badly hurt. The Spanish Admiral was slightly wounded.'

'What did your father-in-law do? Did he stay on?'

'Only for a while. He told us to go, that he'd be back almost as soon as I was; he has a faster car. In fact I'd better go round there now. Thanks for these whiskies, Adrian, I needed them. I'll see you tomorrow, Beryl.'

'So you still feel equal to that rehearsal?'

'Why not? We've got to have our showdown with that Mormon.'

They parted in the liveliest good humour. It was clear to Adrian that their adventure had brought them very close. He might turn that to good account, he thought. 'And now what about our dinner. You don't want to exhaust yourself with cooking. What about the Parade?'

'Not till we've had a talk. I've got a lot to say. Fix me another whisky and I'll start.'

Her manner had changed completely. The exuberance had vanished. She had become serious, in a way that he had not seen her often. She took a long slow sip. 'Now tell me,' she said, 'and I have to know: how surprised were you to learn about this afternoon?'

'That's not an easy question.'

'You knew that something might happen?'

49

'I suspected that something might happen.'

'What made you suspect?'

'I had learnt from one of my sources that something was due to happen on the fifteenth of June.'

'Did you know that it was going to happen in Ceuta?'

'When you told me that you were going there with Sarita, and that she was being secretive about it, I put two and two together.'

'Did you know it might be dangerous?'

He hesitated. The man who had given him that information, who had dropped on his table the newspaper that contained that information, had been a dead man two minutes later. 'There's always danger in this game,' he said.

'Yet you let me go off on this trip knowing that I might be in danger?'

'To some extent I am myself in danger all the time. In a sense you, as my wife, are in danger all the time.'

'Yet you didn't feel that you should warn me? Yes, yes, I know. I have to be kept in the dark. As long as I'm in the dark, I can be of use to you. You've told me that a dozen times. And my going there today was useful to you.'

'As it happens, yes.'

'And you like to have me around, in that way?'

'I've told you that a dozen times.'

'I know you have, and I've believed you, but if I am going to be around, it has to be on different terms. I've got to know what you're about. Yes, I know what you'll say. That you have signed the Official Secrets Act, that it is part of your duty as an agent not to tell me things. If you insist, I shall understand. I shall say "Well, that's fine. You go your way, and I'll go mine. I'll catch the first plane back to the USA, find me a lawyer and go straight to Reno." '

'But Beryl . . .'

'No, no, please; let me go on. I'm not blaming you, I remember the way we married. I was in a mess. You got me out of it. You had no thought of marriage when you met me. I had told you I was on the Pill. If you had thought of me from the first in terms of marriage, if you had thought of me

50

as a wife, as a life's partner, it would have been another matter; you would have told me about yourself, you would have explained yourself, told me the kind of life that you were asking me to share. You would not so much have been offering me yourself as a way of life. I might have said, "Yes, I should like to share that life," or I might have said, "No, I'm sorry, but I couldn't stand it," but that's not how it was. There was an immediate problem. Should I have an abortion or shouldn't I, that's how it was, wasn't it?'

'That's how it was.'

'So that it's only now, four years later, that the question comes up of the kind of life I have to share. And I'm asking myself if I can share it and all the way back in that car, I've been telling myself I can't. The uncertainty's too great, I know too much, and at the same time too little. If you had said to me last week "There's a danger of something happening if you go to Ceuta," it would have been up to me to decide whether I wanted to go or not. I could have said, "Yes, fine, I'll risk that. Or I could have said, "No, that's too much, I'm sorry." You can see that, can't you?'

'I can see that, yes.'

'You don't think I'm asking too much?'

'No.'

'I'm not holding a pistol at your head. You may say to me, I'm sorry, I've signed the Official Secrets Act; there are some things I can't tell you. If you say that, I shall understand. "I quite see your point of view," I'll say. "It's too bad, but there it is. I'm not the kind of wife you need." I'll go back to America and we'll get divorced: there'll be no question of alimony. We'll put back the clock four years. We'll each go our own way, without recriminations. That's fair, isn't it?'

'That's fair.'

'Well, what do you say?'

He smiled. 'I accept your ultimatum.'

She stared. She had expected him to argue, to play for time, to insist on qualifications. But not at all. 'I completely see your point,' he said. 'I should have thought of it before. It wasn't fair to you. I'll put you in the picture right away.

I have been sent here on a specific assignment. You know that the Basques are trying to get liberation from the Spanish government. They are resorting to guerilla tactics. As you know they blew up the Spanish Prime Minister some while ago. They have been operating from a base in France. We have reasons for believing that they are opening or have opened a new base in Morocco. My job here is to find out all I can about that base. It's as simple as that.'

He made it sound so simple that she did not recognise for the moment what he was offering her. He was so very undemonstrative. He told her so little of what was on his mind. As she had said to Sarita, she did not know what he was thinking half the time. She had wondered sometimes whether he was contented with their marriage? Did he feel that he had been trapped? He had not particularly wanted to be married. He had been perfectly contented with the way things were. Professionally he had been better off, probably, as a bachelor. Marriage had limited his opportunities of meeting devious persons. She had often wondered whether he did not sometimes regret his marriage. Well, if he had wanted a way out he had had his chance now and he had not taken it. Warmth filled her heart. A new tenderness enveloped her. But she must not be too demonstrative: that would embarrass him: that would be unEnglish. She clapped her hands. 'What fun we are going to have,' she said.

Next morning Adrian entered a B in his diary.

Shortly before noon Littlejohn sent for Adrian. He looked ill at ease. 'I expect that you know what's on my mind,' he said.

'No, not exactly, sir.'

'You don't; then I'm surprised, or at least perhaps I'm not. I've got so much upon my mind, that I can't expect you to know what's worrying me the most. It's your wife being there.'

'But Beryl . . .' He checked. He was surprised. He hadn't expected this. He hesitated. Better leave Littlejohn to explain. There was a pause. Then Littlejohn went on.

'You gave me a warning and I put you in your place.

Perhaps I was wrong. I don't know. Anyhow, that's passed now. But your wife being there. How did that come about?

'Sarita asked her. They are very good friends. It seemed an amusing excursion for them both.'

'You had nothing to do with her going?'

'Nothing.'

'It would be quite impossible for me if you had. You see that, don't you?'

'I see that, sir.'

'London has instructed me to give you certain facilities of communication. And I'm aware that you have connections in this area that are unknown to me; that's common and accepted practice, but I couldn't have the wife of someone who is technically on my staff, someone who is a member of our community indulging in subversive activities unknown to me.'

'I quite see. Yes, sir.'

'You can give me your assurance, your word that you had nothing to do with arranging your wife's visit to Ceuta yesterday.'

'I give you my word, sir.'

Back in his office, Adrian asked himself, 'Did I lie?'

No, he hadn't lied, but he might well have to be extremely cautious on another occasion to ensure that he did not.

The morning's copy of the previous day's *Times* lay on Littlejohn's desk. He turned to the sports page. Middlesex were doing well. They had a good side this year. He glanced at the other matches, then pulled his writing pad across the desk.

'My dearest Vera,' he wrote. 'I don't want to fuss you. I know that you have a great deal on your plate right now, that this summer is an important one for Julia. She may have to make decisions on which her whole happiness will depend, she needs you at her side. At the same time she surely will not want to stay on in London the whole summer. You are planning, I know, one or two visits in the country. They may well prove important for her. She may meet people who are useful, but at the same time there's no reason why she

53

shouldn't meet people who could be equally useful here. You know how social Tangier can be in the summer . . . The mountain people are filling up with guests—so that other things being equal, I don't see why you should not come out here. It really is important for me that you should. This isn't an important post, and I'm not at a point of crisis in my career, but I do feel incomplete without you. You have been such a help to me in all my postings. You are so efficient, such a good hostess, everybody likes you. I should be able to do my job so much better. And there are one or two rather difficult points at issue at the moment. Couldn't you manage to come out here at the end of June? The P.D.S.A. meeting is on the first Saturday in July. As usual they are having it on our grounds. It would make all the difference if you were here for it. Please, please, please.'

He read the letter over, folded it, and put it in an envelope, but he did not close down the flap. He would read it again after lunch. He must get this letter right.

The mail left at half past four. The office re-opened at four o'clock. Littlejohn went to his room at half past three. He re-read his letter. He did not see how he could improve it. At the same time he did not feel confident that it would achieve its purpose. Vera's mind was set on having this summer with Julia in England. And perhaps she was right—from Julia's point of view. A mother's instinct. There was more for Julia in London than in Tangier. From Julia's point of view and from her own . . . for Julia's point of view was hers. Julia came first, but from his point of view. That was another matter.

He shrugged. He replaced the sheet of note-paper in the envelope and stuck down the flap. It was the best that he could do. But was it good enough? He drew his writing pad across the desk.

'Dear Frank,' he wrote. 'I've been thinking over the talk we had last month. I think you're right. I've had as much here as I can take. I'm headed nowhere. If you still want me I'm your man.'

There was no need to say more than that. Frank and he understood each other. He had to have a second string to his bow.

Beryl had not gone down to the Yacht Club at midday. She was tired and she had that rehearsal. Better to fix herself an omelette, then take a long siesta. She was more than curious about her Mormon. She had not yet had a real talk with him, but she was no luckier that afternoon. 'Listen,' she said to Sarita afterwards, 'we've got to have a real talk with this man. Next time we have a rehearsal, let's arrange it so that the three of us are left together afterwards.'

'Does that mean you are planning a campaign?'

'It doesn't. No.'

'Maybe that's just as well. I am.'

'What would you have done if I'd said Yes. Tossed for him?'

'We might have agreed to share him.'

'What an idea.'

'It might have been rather fun.'

'And then compared notes afterwards?'

'Oh no, really shared, not separately, together.'

There was a twinkle in her eye.

'I believe you mean that.'

'Of course I do.'

'You speak as though you had experienced that.'

'There's not much I haven't experienced.'

'I thought Spanish women were heavily chaperoned.'

'That's how we learn to be discreet. We take every opportunity we can get.'

'You make me seem very innocent.'

'I've read a lot in American novels about swinging couples in Suburbia.'

'But that isn't what you meant when you talked about sharing our young American.'

'I was thinking of trios. Spaniards are too afflicted with pride, with *machismo*, to be swingers; sharing two girls though is another matter.'

55

'You certainly put ideas into my head.'

'You stay around, I might have some more ideas before too long.'

Later Adrian said:

'You're very quiet.'

'Yesterday was quite a day.'

'I saw Littlejohn this morning. He's feeling restive. I believe it would be a good idea if I went over to Gibraltar for a day.'

'When do you aim to go?'

'Friday.'

'By air?'

'No, I'll take the ferry.'

'Shall I come too?'

'No need unless you want to.'

'I don't think I'll bother.'

Friday would be a good day for a rehearsal.

6

It was hot on Friday. The *levante* had been blowing for three days, but it dropped on the Thursday night. The sea was calm. The customs shed was crowded. A couple of group tours were crossing. There were four separate queues; tickets and passports had to be examined by both the Tangier and the Gibraltar authorities. It was hard to tell if one was in the right queue. Everyone was shouting. The ship was due to sail in forty minutes. Half the Moroccans did not know how to fill out their emigration forms. There was delay after delay. Adrian found a hotel guide who took his passport and forms and ticket. 'One moment,' he said, 'one moment.' With half a dozen passports in his hand he pushed to the head of the queue, then opened a side door. He was back in quarter of an hour. He was delighted with a two dirham tip. Adrian had brought no luggage. The customs officer did not frisk him. Then there was a shambles at the gangplank. No proper queue was formed; everyone was pushing in from every angle. Adrian relaxed. He let himself be pushed from behind and from both sides. In five minutes he was on the gangplank. It had taken him three quarters of an hour to get on board. Every time he made the crossing, he vowed that next time he would catch the plane. But as soon as he was on board, he knew that it was worth it. The plane journey was too quick. On the ferry you really felt that you were going somewhere; leaving one world, entering another.

Twenty years back there had been an Alec Guinness film called *The Captain's Paradise*, based on the Gibraltar ferry, in which the Captain had a different wife on each side of the straits. Halfway across he changed round the photograph in his cabin. In the film it had been a thirty hour crossing. In fact it was a two and a half hour crossing. But even so there was a sense of changing from one world to another.

As always he went straight into the dining-room. The waiters were half Moroccan, half Spanish-speaking

57

Gibraltarians. But the atmosphere was completely English. Emmet had designed the decoration above the serving counter. Adrian ordered the kind of breakfast he would never think of having except on a ship or train. Fried eggs and bacon, toast and marmalade, and because it was a British ship, tea not coffee. He had had cornflakes and coffee before he left the flat. Gibraltar time was an hour ahead of Tangier time. He would be eating a heavy lunch within four hours: but he was confident that he would settle down to it with a hearty appetite.

The ship started to draw out as the eggs and bacon were set in front of him. The customs and the gangplank had been a shambles, but the ship seemed half empty. The seats undercover were full of Moroccans, but there were less than twenty people on the top deck. Half of them had a hippy look; men and women alike were wearing Levi's. The men were bearded and long-haired, most of them were stripped to the waist. Adrian began to pace the deck. They were less than halfway across. But the Rock because of its height, seemed nearer than Tangier. How Gib had changed since he had seen it first twelve years ago when he had come here on a package tour. Gibraltar had scarcely existed then as a tourist centre. The Spanish frontier was still open and Spanish workers came across every morning, returning every evening. There was no need then for all these hotels and blocks of flats.

On that first visit, the first thing he had seen was the square tower of the old red Moorish castle and the brick wall that had run down from it. Now the hillside was so cluttered with white barrack-type buildings, that the Moorish tower did not stand out at all. You had to search for it. The new buildings overtopped it.

The ship was half an hour late. Midday by Gibraltar time. He had suggested to his boss, Lewis Marshall, that they should meet at the Lotus, the Chinese restaurant, at a quarter to one. If he got there early, as probably he would, there would be time for an extra gin and tonic. They usually went 'dutch' when they went together and Marshall was a moderate man. One aperitif and his share of a bottle of wine was enough for him. Adrian had a suspicion that today he himself could use more than that nominal ration of one aperitif. To his surprise however, he found his chief waiting at the docks.

Marshall was twelve years older than himself. He was due for a promotion. He was tall, heavily built, dark haired, slightly bald. He was always tidily dressed. He was a good athlete and a good mixer. In spite of the difference of age Adrian felt at ease with him. He was touched at his having come down to meet him. 'On a hot day like this, I couldn't have you toiling up and down Main Street on your trotters,' Marshall said, 'And that's the last thing I'm wanting for myself. Bathing trunks right away, that's me. Let's go up to the Rock and have a Bloody Mary at the pool. Lunch, by the way's on me. Once in a while, I can charge you on the house.'

Marshall had come to meet him in a chauffeur-driven car. 'I've given up driving,' he explained. 'It isn't safe. I start thinking about other things, and there's such a hell of a lot of things to think about; things I can't afford not to think about. You've got to concentrate here; look at this street now.'

It was indeed as crowded a thoroughfare as you could find, with its flocks of tourists, young service wives pushing prams, and the pavement on one side or the other always too narrow for two to walk abreast. Adrian looked to right and left. They were as regards their contents shoddy enough shops for the most part, half of them Indian. Though Gibraltar was advertised as a free port, tourists were short of money; and watches were the only expensive articles they cared to buy, while the Moroccans for the most part, and the Tangier residents over for the day, stocked up on groceries; they could also buy duty-free bottles of gin and whisky, if they were delivered to the ship in threes. But you would find no quality goods in the clothes shops. It no longer paid Burlington Arcade to run a branch for service officers. Even so it looked a real place, and after you passed the shops you were in an atmosphere of solid Georgian architecture, the best period of English building. There was the convent, the chapel and the law courts and behind and higher up the hill there was the garrison library.

'I can't bear to think of England not owning this,' said Adrian.

Opposite a spattering of shops was a dignified row of what once had been service living quarters, and at the end of the street a large gate with emblazoned shields and beyond it were the crosses of the Trafalgar cemetery. It was more English than most of England.

'What do you think of our new Policewomen?' Marshall asked. They were trim and smart, with short tight blue skirts, and short tight-fitting jackets, with high heeled black shoes, white gloves, and military style caps.

'They won't harm the tourist trade.'

'And now for that first Bloody Mary,' Marshall said.

They sat in the sun; they were both deeply tanned. No fear of sunburn. 'Now tell me all the Tangier gossip,' Marshall said. 'What's this about anonymous letters attacking one of the church wardens being put in the collection box?'

'There are some very eccentric people in Tangier.'

'You're telling me. What about Bill and Eric?'

'They're still together.'

'Charles and Freddie?'

'They are not.'

'Change your partners, all. I sometimes wish I lived there. Never a dull moment. But people there must get a rather inbred feeling?'

'Most of them do. I'm lucky in having an American wife. I see more of the American colony than the British. And the Americans are always changing. They aren't residents. They are posted and then move on. That makes for variety.'

'What about our CG?'

'Complaining that he hasn't got enough to do.'

'He's got something there. That's something I want to mention to you later. Now what about the second half of this

Bloody Mary. Shall we have it now, or shall we swim first then have it while we wait for lunch?'

'Swim first, I'd say.'

'So would I. Let's to it.'

The water was cool, but not so much cooler than the air outside that they wanted to linger in it. Swimming was an effort. They were soon seated at their table. 'These Bloody Marys are the best thing they make here,' Marshall said. 'In this heat, I'd like a white wine for lunch. Which do you prefer? French or German?'

'French, I think.'

'So do I. Let's look. Let's have a good one. Good wine is something you can't get in Tangier. That's one of the things that went with Independence. There used to be such a variety of wines, particularly Spanish, that it was almost worth going over for them. Still what you get is cheap and wholesome. The wine list here isn't as long as it used to be, but there's a Chablis that isn't bad.'

He's certainly doing me well, thought Adrian.

Almost too well, he was to think ninety minutes later when at the end of an excellent lunch—with one of the best bottles of wine that he had tasted for many moons—Marshall said, 'And now, let me recommend with that cheese—they do manage to get a really good sharp cheddar here—a glass of tawny port. They've got a Harvey's hunting port. And why not make it doubles while we're about it.'

And very excellent port it was. Good port was one of the things he missed in Tangier where you could get only inferior ruby. Yes, he was being done well: ominously well. There was the air of an occasion, too much the air of an occasion about it all. Soon he'll be coming to the point. He did.

'I'm so very glad that you've come across,' he said. 'You've been on my mind. What you were saying about the C.G. is pertinent. His feeling that he hasn't got enough to do. He hasn't. Tangier hasn't the importance that it had. It ought to be downgraded. It will be soon, and when it's downgraded, so'll be the other, what I call, ancillary activities, that go with it.'

Ah, here it comes, thought Adrian. I'll anticipate. I'll

61

make it easy for him. 'You mean that there won't be any need any longer for what Graham Greene would have called "Our Man in Tangier". '

'Precisely. You get my point. I knew you would.'

'I should have thought that the recent case in Ceuta would have made you feel there was a need for me.'

'You would have thought so, wouldn't you? And that's something else I wanted to talk about. How did you get on to that?'

Adrian explained.

'I see. That's very interesting; you were quick to cotton on; you earned yourself a good mark there. You're the right man in the right place all right: which so often in our game isn't so. You've done very well, but there is going to be a downgrading everywhere, and Tangier is one of the posts that are likely to be downgraded.'

'Although the Basques are still quite active?'

'I know. That's what I've been telling them. But they don't seem to attach the same importance to Gibraltar that they did—at least not so much to Gibraltar, as to Spain generally. You know the way it is. Sometimes there's one issue that seems all important. They concentrate on it, get it out of focus, then suddenly overnight they decide that it isn't important any longer, that that particular problem can be solved another way. That's what's happening now with Spain. It's being moved into another category. In a year's time they may have changed their minds; have come to feel that they were right the first time, and that Spain does matter in that way. But in the meantime . . .'

'In the meantime I may get posted somewhere else?'

'Precisely.'

'And when is that likely to happen?'

Marshall shrugged. 'Nobody can tell. I don't suppose you ever read Ian Hay's book about the first war, *The First Hundred Thousand*. No, I thought as much; too long before your time. It had a very amusing chapter about the War Office; it talked about the practical joke department. That department is still functioning.'

'So I've got to be ready to move at a moment's notice?'

'Precisely.'

'And where do you think I'm likely to be sent?'

'That's just the point.'

'Back into the pool?'

'Where else?'

There was a pause. I was right, Adrian thought. I was being done too well. He could read the small print all right. When he had joined up with this special branch he had been warned that you were offered no guarantee. There were certain pension and health benefits, but your engagement could be terminated overnight. Your salary was tax free. No account of expenses was kept. 'The firm' as it was called was very generous when things were going well. But it was ruthless when things were not. Maugham had described his own enrolment in the Secret Service: 'There's just one thing I think you ought to know before you take on this job, and don't forget it. If you do well you'll get no thanks and if you get into trouble you'll get no help.' That advice had been given in 1914. In essence, things were no different now. Fifteen years ago Adrian had been prepared to run the risk; the work had promised to be exciting. He had nothing else in mind. He was young. He was full of confidence. He had no responsibilities; why not give the thing a chance? He had never regretted his decision. There had seemed no reason why he should. Everything seemed to be going well. He hadn't put up a black. Whatever happened England would need a secret service. But suddenly the policy line had changed. Retrenchment was in the air. He was one of the junior members in the firm.

'What would you advise me to do?' he asked.

A look of relief crossed Marshall's face. He had been spared the awkward job of having to explain what the situation was. He did not need to prevaricate. 'I've been thinking about this,' he said. 'My suggestion is that you should go to London, sooner than you planned. When is your next leave due?'

'At the end of August.'

'And we're in June now. There is no reason, is there, why you shouldn't go right away?'

'None at all.'

'Who did you see there last?'

'Templeton.'

'He's in Berlin now. The man to see is Sonning. Have you ever met him?'

'Not that I recall.'

'Not a bad chap. Rather formal. Stuffed shirt. Punctilious. Don't quite know how we got into our racket. I'd have thought he was a 5 man rather than a 6. Perhaps he was kicked upstairs, but he's not a bad chap. I'll drop him a note, telling him to expect you. It makes all the difference meeting the right man. If your name comes up, you're a real person to him, not a number. I may be quite wrong of course. I hope I am. My hunches miss the target far too often. But meeting Sonning won't do you any harm. I'm glad we've had this talk. You've been on my mind. And I've enjoyed our lunch. Now for a little shut-eye before the office opens.'

He moved away from the table, found a long chair with a rest, and put his feet up. Within a minute he was breathing steadily. Adrian followed his example, but though his eyes were closed his mind was racing. What if this hunch was right. What did he do next?

7

In Tangier three hours later, the rehearsal had just ended. It had been held in the Simms's flat. It had been an early meeting. Two of the cast had to get away. At six there were only the three left, Sarita, Beryl, and Sven Jurgensen.

'Now let's relax,' said Beryl. 'We deserve a drinkie, we've never had a genuine gossip, just the three of us, and Sven, we've got a lot to ask you. We need the full story of your change of conscience and we mean to have it.'

She put Sven in one corner of the sofa. Beryl sat beside him, Sarita on the other side in a chair drawn at right angles to the sofa. 'So you're under fire from both sides,' said Beryl. 'The truth, the whole truth, and nothing but the truth, that's what we're after.'

'Why should you be so inquisitive?'

'It's something new in our experience. Sarita's a Roman Catholic. She believes in all of it, but she's not fanatical. She takes it for granted. She does not let it worry her. I'm an Episcopalian; it's been much the same with me. I've taken it for granted. I'm supposed to take communion three times a year, of which one must be Easter. I take it rather more often as a matter of fact, because I like the service; I like going early, so that I've got my decks cleared. I've done my church for the day, and anyhow Matins is a dreary service and I don't like being preached at. I go here, because Adrian does; he sees it as a duty to back up the chaplain. But as for believing it literally, when I make my general confession at early service and say that the memory of my sins is grievous unto me, the burden of them intolerable, it simply isn't true; they aren't. I accept the fact that one should make a confession of some kind and that that's our particular church's way of doing it. Isn't that how it is with you, Sarita?'

'I suppose so, yes. I don't know that I've let myself think about it much.'

'You see, Sven, that's the way it is with us and I imagine

that's the way it is with most churchgoers, but it must have been different with you.'

'Mormons are different.'

'In what way different?'

'We believe different things.'

'But so do Sarita and I believe different things. So do the Methodists and the Baptists believe different things. We all believe different things. But you must have believed your different things differently; and to lose faith suddenly like that, there must have been something very special. Some particular moment of . . . what's the word, Sarita?'

'Illumination? Revelation?'

'Yes, that's the word, revelation, like St Paul going to Damascus.'

'It can't have been gradual?'

'Or was it? Were you losing faith gradually, underneath the surface, without realising it?'

'Like the way one falls in love sometimes. One's seeing a person, day after day, enjoying being with him, without realising that it's more than liking, and then there it is suddenly, wham, bang.'

'Was this how it was, Sven? Tell us.'

They shot the questions at him, one after another, not giving him a chance to answer. It was a teasing, affectionate interrogation. It was a game; they were on the brink of laughing. They were very close to one another, at the same time they were very close to him. It was exciting in a subtle way. Beryl remembered Sarita's remark about their sharing him, how Sarita had said 'It might be rather fun, you know.' It had seemed to her ridiculous at the time, but now she thought, yes, it could be rather fun. Sven was enjoying himself too.

'There was, there must have been, a moment of revelation. There was, now wasn't there?' she said.

'I suppose so, yes.'

'That's what we said. And that's what we want to know.'

'You've got to tell us, Sven.'

'He's hesitating, Sarita, isn't he? We're on the track.'

66

'Come on now, don't hold out on us.'

With every question it became more exciting. It *was* like a seduction. He was on the verge of yielding. They leant forward across him, their faces close to his, and to one another's. 'Come now, tell us, Sven, tell us. There was now, wasn't there?'

They pressed their questions on him, relentlessly, laughingly. 'Come on, Sven, tell us.'

'There was one particular moment. There must have been, what was it?'

'You've got to tell us.'

They grew more persistent; more and more persistent. Suddenly, utterly, he yielded. 'OK, you're quite right, yes there was.'

'Ah.' The word broke from Sarita's lips in a long sigh of triumph. She stretched out her hand to Beryl's, her fingers twining between hers. Their eyes met, smiled; it was an instant of union.

'Come on,' Sarita said, 'we won't bully you any more. Tell us in your time, in your way.' She leant back in her chair, releasing Beryl's hand.

'It's going to surprise you, this.' he said.

'That's what we've been waiting for.'

'It may shock you.'

'That's what we hoped.'

'Well . . . you know, don't you, that we go on our missions as a pair, a couple.'

'Of course.'

'My companion made a pass at me.'

'*What?*'

It was such a surprise that it left even Sarita speechless, for a moment. 'Come now, you must tell us all about it.'

'There isn't much to tell.'

'Oh yes, there must be. You must tell us everything. What was he like?'

'That's just the point. He wasn't like that at all.'

'Like what?'

'Like the kind of young man who would do that kind of

thing. He wasn't effeminate. Far from it. He was a good athlete, fine at basketball. He was healthy, handsome, strong, and came from a very important family. He was a hero to me. I'd always looked up to him and his folks; I was proud when they assigned me as his companion. I felt honoured. I enjoyed working with him. He being what he was made everything more exciting. I wanted to get converts, for his sake: so that our mission would be remembered. Then for this to happen.'

'Was it quite unexpected?'

Completely. That's what made it such a shock. I've never associated him with that kind of thing. Girls seemed to like him. He liked girls. There was one particular girl in B.Y.U. . . . well, I'm pretty certain that something was going on between them. He talked about girls a lot. He would light up when he saw a pretty one. And then for him . . .'

'You had no suspicion of any kind?'

'Not in the least. That's what shocked me most . . . if it had been worked up to, if I had foreseen a crisis, but it wasn't like that at all. One evening, it was in our fourth month there, he walked into my room and said, "This nonsense has gone on long enough. I'm going to sleep with you tonight." So cold bloodedly, so matter-of-fact, no preliminary speech, no saying how this thing had grown on him, how he'd fought against it, how it had proved too strong for him. I'd have had some sympathy, some respect for that, but . . . for him to stand there, leaning against the chest of drawers, looking so handsome, "We've got to be practical," he said. "We have to behave when we're on a mission, we can't go to a night-club and pick up girls, yet we can't starve ourselves. We're human beings, we've got to make do with one another."

'I've only got to shut my eyes to see him, that scene, it's unforgettable . . . nothing can wipe it out; and I had such respect for him before . . . I didn't know what to say . . . nothing except "no, no, no." He began to argue. Chastity was bad for one, he said. It set up inhibitions. One's mind could not work properly if one's body was restless. One had

68

to throw sops to one's appetites. You know the kind of thing. As I listened, I made up my mind. I couldn't go on with him for a companion. Another twenty months with him . . . the strain! We could never be natural with each other again. We'd be useless as a team.

'I interrupted him. I said I'd go and ask the Mission President to transfer one of us. He asked me what explanation I'd give, and I said "What else but the truth, that we don't get along, we don't see things the same way?"

'But he said that I couldn't possibly say a thing like that. The President would suspect something—he'd be watched. It would get back to his parents and his whole future would be ruined. He got terribly upset and excited. "I can't let a thing like this happen to me!" He kept saying that.

'I told him that I at least took my mission very seriously and I felt God wanted missionaries to tell the truth. And then he went absolutely cold. That's what shocked me the most. He told me that if I asked for a transfer he'd tell them it was my fault, that *I* had approached *him*. Did I think they'd believe me or him, with his family and background? He suggested that I write home and say I'd lost my faith and wanted to come home. "After all," he said, "your whole life isn't bound up in Utah and the Church the way mine is. Some of the questions you've asked in our discussions—you know you don't believe everything we're supposed to preach."

'Imagine! I was so shaken I could hardly get the words out. Had he told me *he* didn't believe everything? And he shrugged and said, "Remember that French King who said Paris was worth a mass? Utah—my whole life—that's worth pretending to believe, isn't it?"

'I was absolutely shattered. It made him and his whole life a sham. And he'd been such a hero to me, that's what was the worst. He stood there telling me what I could do, how he would be glad to help me every way he could. He actually said he'd write and say how unfortunate my loss of faith was and that he felt sure it was only temporary—that I'd find my way back to the church in a year or two.

69

'So—well, you know I had nothing to say to an offer like *that*! I simply walked out. I wrote and told my folks what had happened and they understood. But I was really at a loose end. I decided to travel around awhile and in Athens I ran into this American who had been at the American School here and told me they had an opening. So I applied right away.'

He paused. How miserable he looked. Both their hearts went out to him.

'So that's the way it was,' Beryl told Adrian later. 'I'm a pretty good spy, aren't I? Worth my weight in gold?'

'Which is exactly what I'm going to need.' He told her what Marshall had said. 'Is it all right for you to go back to America at once?'

They had adopted the custom of taking separate holidays. It was good for them both, and for their marriage. She would go for three weeks to America while he went to London. Then they would have a wonderful refreshed week together. They called it their Honeymoon Holiday.

8

Adrian's mother lived in Highgate, in a second storey maisonette in Hampstead Lane. She had lived there ever since her marriage in 1937. She had seen no reason to leave. It was convenient: two sitting rooms, two bedrooms. Her first child, her daughter Marian, had been born just before the war broke out. When she became pregnant for the second time, eighteen months later, her husband had said "this flat is soon going to be too small, but it'll serve us till the war is over'.' Then he had been posted to the Middle East and killed at Alamein. And his widow had gone on living there. The flat had been the right size during Adrian's and Marian's schooldays. Then Marian had married and though the flat had become too small again, it had been useful to Marian to have a base in London, useful to have somewhere to leave her children when she went on a holiday.

Adrian arrived there twelve days later in the early evening. His mother leant out of the window. 'I'll throw the keys down to you. Catch.'

The telephone was ringing as he came up the stairs. 'That's very kind of you,' he heard her say. 'I'm almost sure I'd love to, but I'm not quite certain of my plans. Adrian has just come back from Tangier. I don't know what his plans are. May I ring you back tomorrow morning?'

Usually Adrian planned his visits to London carefully in advance. 'You have to,' he would say, 'if you want to see the people that you want to. Londoners plan so far ahead.' But this time he had made no plans. Mails to and from Tangier were difficult. He would not have had time to get answers to his letters. He would make his plans by the telephone, when he arrived.

'There's a letter for you in the hall,' his mother said. The address on it was typewritten. It was a plain envelope. Probably, almost certainly from Sonning. He put it in his pocket.

'I won't be a second, mother dear. I'll be right down.'

He opened the letter at once. 'I have received Marshall's letter. I shall be, of course, very glad to see you. I shall be away next week. Will you call here on Monday, the nineteenth, at eleven.'

Eleven. No question of lunch. No chance of getting to know the man. And the whole of next week a blank. Well, he should be able to fix up something for himself.

He was down in the drawing room within five minutes.

'It's good to see you, my dear boy,' his mother said. She was as always undemonstrative. In his twenties he had wondered why she was so undemonstrative. Was she on her guard, he had later asked himself. Without a husband, had she been resolved not to become absorbed in an only son? It would have been bad for him; bad too for herself. Had there been any other men in her life? He had not been aware of anyone. But he had been away at school so much. It was hard to believe that nothing had happened to a young and attractive woman in all that time. He had brought two parcels with him. One held a bottle of whisky.

'That's kind of you, that's very kind,' she said. When she opened the sideboard, he noticed that there were four other bottles there already, two gins, a whisky, and a vodka. She was always very punctilious that way. She was never out of anything.

'I expect you'd like a glass of whisky right away.'

'I would, yes, thank you very much. And I've brought this Spanish toilet water, Maya. Beryl swears by it.'

'Now that really is most kind.'

She had expected him to bring her whisky. It would be he who drank it, after all. But the Maya was something new for her. She took the bottle out of its case, unscrewed the top: poured a drop into the palm of her hand, rubbed her palms together, held them to her face. 'Oh, that's most pleasant, refreshing with a little sting and a clean smell. Is this what Beryl uses?'

'When she can get it. We mostly get French products in Tangier.'

I shall enjoy using the same toilet water. She's the same colouring as me, isn't she? What suits her should suit me. It's absurd, isn't it, that we've never met?'

'That's what she always says, but Tangier is a long way off.'

'Does this interview that you've come back for, mean that you've to be posted somewhere else?'

'It may do. I can't tell till I've had the interview.'

'Is that tomorrow?'

'No. Not till Monday week.'

The telephone rang again. It was the same kind of conversation as the other one. 'That's very sweet of you, Hilda, but may I ring you back tomorrow. Adrian's just come over and we haven't sorted out our diaries yet.'

'What a busy life you lead,' he said.

'Oh no dear, heavens, no, but I have to fill my time. I can't spend the whole day watching the telly.'

'You must do more than that while I'm here. We must see what shows are on.' He was careful always to take her to a couple of theatres and some cinemas. He must not appear to be using her house as a hotel.

'You'll be going down to see Marian, I suppose,' she said.

'Of course. I was thinking of the weekend after this.'

'Have you written to her?'

'I've dropped her a note telling her I was coming over. I'll telephone tomorrow.'

'Why not telephone tonight? Her diary is very crowded.'

Everyone's diary seemed to be very crowded. 'I'll ring her after dinner.'

'Why not now? She's going out this evening.'

'That's a good idea.'

He had an idea that mother and daughter had been in conference. Had he upset their plans? As a schoolboy, at Oxford, and recently as an official with a post abroad, he had been made to think that everyone at home planned their lives round him, because he was the absent one. They had always known in advance what his plans were. This was the first time he had diverged from the usual pattern.

Marian gave him no reason to suspect, however, that he was not supremely welcome. 'How good to hear your voice. I was hoping that you'd call tonight. When are we going to see you? Not this weekend, I guess. You'll want to organise yourself. The weekend after then? That'll be wonderful. And you'll come down on the Friday before dinner. There's a good train that gets in around half past six; leaves Paddington at four o'clock and if you're travelling second class as I expect you are, it's as well to book a place. There's a cricket match at Taunton on the Saturday. Somerset are playing Notts. You'd like to watch that, wouldn't you? And we'll have some people round for dinner. Is there anyone you particularly don't want to meet? That'll be fine, we *are* looking forward to it.'

She could not have been more welcoming. But he wished that he could have overheard that morning's conversation between his mother and his sister. Had they been upset at his not having given them longer warning? 'Now don't be fanciful,' he rebuked himself. 'Don't get self-conscious.'

'All settled then?' his mother was adding brightly. 'Now we can relax and enjoy ourselves. I've got a casserole simmering, so I haven't to keep rushing into the kitchen. You must tell me everything. Does this interview mean that you've got some promotion coming?'

'I wish it did. I wish I knew. I expect it's only a routine check-up. But one always hopes.'

'I wish that you were in the army, or the navy, where you had real promotions, so that I could say, "my son Adrian's got his majority".'

'I wish that too.'

'I suppose that you are the equivalent of a major.'

'I suppose so, yes.'

'The same kind of pay?'

'It's hard to say. My pay is tax free.'

'I know so little of what you really do.'

'Beryl complains of that.'

74

'It makes it difficult for wives and mothers.'

'You don't have worries of that kind with your son-in-law.'

'No, no I'm lucky there. Partner in an old family business. He knows where he is, and so do his children. You'll be delighted with them. Susan is quite a young lady now. Look, I must show you.'

There was a photograph of Susan on the mantlepiece. She was wearing a tightly-fitted sweater and a short sports skirt. She was thirteen and looked seventeen. What a change had come over her in the last year. 'I don't suppose I'll recognise her,' he said.

'I don't suppose you will, and Eric is becoming such a little man.'

She prattled away with the liveliest animation. There's no need for me to worry about her, he thought. She's got her grandchildren. They fill her life. And it was not only her grandchildren. Her nephews and nieces had their share of progeny. 'I'm very lucky to have this flat to myself,' she said. 'They're always wanting one or two of their children put up for a day or two. Dentists or nets at Lord's, that kind of thing. A lot of my friends tell me that they feel useless; that they aren't doing anything, that they're just spending money that other members of the family would be glad to use. But as for me, well frankly I don't know how they would manage without me. I'm a godsend to them.'

Maybe this was the most contented period of her life.

The telephone rang again, but this time the call was for him. 'A Mrs Littlejohn,' his mother told him. A Mrs Littlejohn? The CG's wife. What could she be wanting? 'I'm sorry to disturb you the moment you arrive,' she said, 'but I know how busy you are going to become. Mark told me you were coming over. I do want to hear all the gossip and I have to be away next week. I don't suppose you will be over here for long.'

'Only three weeks.'

'Then it would be best if we could manage something right away. What about your coming round for a drink tomorrow evening?'

'That would be fine by me.'

'Wonderful. I'll expect you about six. I'm in Chiltern Court: that's by Baker Street Tube Station. No. 536.'

Next morning Adrian sat beside the telephone attempting to work out his programme for the next ten days. He rang up first the secretary of the Stoics, a touring cricket side which he had joined when he was at Oxford. The secretary's voice was cheerful.

'Good to hear from you, welcome home. I suppose you want to fix up a game or two.'

'That's the idea.'

'How long will you be over?'

'Three weeks.'

'That isn't long. Let's see what we can do. There's a match on Friday against Hampstead. Stewart's managing the side.'

'Stewart's an old friend of mine.'

'I know he is. But he's overbooked. He was talking to me last night. I wish you could have given longer notice.'

'I wish so too, but this was a last-minute command.'

'Too bad. Now what about next week? Richmond on Wednesday. We might be able to manage that. The side is full, but there's always a chance of someone dropping out. I've got your telephone number. I'll call you if anyone does.'

'What about the week after?'

'We haven't a fixture that week. But in the following one we're playing Surbiton. I'm managing that match. I know I can fit you in.'

'Alas, I'll have gone by then.'

'You will, too bad. I wish you'd given us longer notice, but I'll try and fix you into that Richmond game.'

He then tried one of his oldest school friends, John Wilson, an exact contemporary. Wilson was equally warm and welcoming.

'Wonderful to hear your voice. Too long since we've met. We must get together. I'm going abroad on Saturday, but I'll be back by the end of the month.'

'That's just when I'm going back to Tangier.'

76

'You are, too bad. And I've so much to tell you. We've got another baby: did you know? a boy. Such a relief after those two girls. Daphne's thrilled. Not, of course, that she isn't delighted with the girls. Next time you're over, you must come in and see them. Too bad our going away. Better luck next time.'

He rang another old friend. There was no reply. His fourth attempt was more successful—a man who had been at Oxford with him was not only home, but just back from his holiday.

'What about lunching with me one day?' said Adrian.

'Nothing I'd like more.'

'What about one day next week?'

'I'll have a look in my book.' There was a pause. His friend regretted that he was full up all next week.

'What about the week after?'

'I think I can manage that, yes, let me see, what about the Thursday?'

'The Thursday will be fine. Simpson's at one o'clock.'

'I look forward to it.'

After another half hour, he found himself with three engagements in which he would act as host for the week after next but with the immediate next week completely blank. It was by now quarter to eleven and the day stretched ahead of him. It was a clear, sunny day, a good day to watch cricket; Hampshire was playing Middlesex at Lord's. Hampshire had batted first and made 312 for 5. They would presumably declare this morning. There would be a struggle after lunch for bonus points. How many runs could Middlesex make and how many wickets could Hampshire take in eighty-five overs? Eighty-five overs would take about five hours; it might be exciting in the early afternoon. He would aim to get to the ground about half past twelve: that would give him time to stop at the travel agents at Golders Green and get some theatre tickets for next week.

'Expect me about half past seven,' he told his mother.

As he had expected, the ground was not very full. No one in the Warner stand or in the grandstand; only a sprinkling in

77

the free seats in the mound, but as always there was a large group in front of the tavern, with beer mugs in their hands. Every now and again there would be a shout of encouragement, applause, or obloquy. Adrian as a member of Middlesex took a seat on the second gallery, behind the bowler's arm. The gallery was almost empty. He did not see anyone he knew. On his right several members of the Middlesex XI were on the dressing room balcony. Titmus was there with his pads on; Murray too. What a couple they were. They seemed to defy the almanack. He hoped that one or other of them, preferably both, got runs this afternoon. It was probably the last time he would see them. He remembered them twenty years ago when he had been an ardent fan. As a boy he had thought that he would spend a lot of time at Lord's when he retired. He wondered if he would.

He lunched off a pint of Watney's Red Barrel, accompanied by a scotch egg and a ham roll. The beer was very good. That was one of the things he missed in Tangier. The local Pilsener, the flag Pils was well enough, but it had not the flavour and authority of full-bodied draught beer. He took a long deep pull at it. He stood up at one of the tables that ran down the centre of the room. His legs were stiff after the hard seat on the balcony. The beer warmed his blood. He was tempted to take an extra half pint, and a roll and cheese, but if he did, he would feel drowsy. He didn't want to fall asleep on a hard seat. He returned to the long room. Sixteen minutes to two. Twenty-four minutes before play re-started. He walked along the wall: looking at the trophies, the old signed bats, the balls with the silver disks commemorating the particular feat that had justified their survival 'off this ball such and such a player had scored his three thousandth run', the eighteenth and nineteenth century pictures. Some twenty other members and their guests were similarly occupied. Half of them wore club ties that were familiar, Incogs, Old Uppinghamians, Cryptics. He ought to know someone here. He didn't though. Most of them seemed to know each other.

He began to feel a little sorry for himself.

* * *

Adrian barely knew Vera Littlejohn. He and Beryl had not been invited to a formal meal at the consulate: there was no reason why they should have been. And Vera had been away on the two occasions when there had been parties for a ship. They had been in the same room at one or two mountain cocktail parties, but they had only exchanged local gossip. She had made no particular impression on him, nor he fancied, had he on her. She was a tall, rather heavy, not unhandsome woman. He wondered whether her husband had suggested that she contact him. He was inclined to doubt it. He presumed that she had wanted to hear some Tangier gossip.

That at any rate for the first half hour of his visit was the way it seemed to be. 'It's very good of you to have come round,' she said. 'I feel so starved for gossip. Mark's very good about writing, but he has to be careful about what he says. He can never be sure that his letters won't be steamed open. Tell me about everyone. Has Mabel Stanley managed to sell her house?'

She chattered briskly on, so briskly that he began to wonder whether she had not another reason for having invited him. Was there something special that she wanted to know, something special that she wanted done? That was one of the disadvantages of being in his kind of racket. One was always suspecting people, imagining that they had *arrière pensées*, that everyone had an axe to grind.

'Now tell me about Mark,' she was continuing, 'I suppose you're seeing him all the time.'

'Not all the time. I'm not really on his staff, you know.'

'I know. I know. You're one of the cloak-and-dagger boys. That's why we've seen so little of you. I've complained to Mark about it: "If we don't ask the Simms up more often, people will suspect that there's something fishy somewhere." '

'Of course we'd like to be invited, but we don't expect to be.'

'That's very sweet of you. All the same . . .' she paused. 'When did you see Mark last?' she asked.

'Two, three days ago. I can't be sure . . . and when I do see

79

him, I'm not really seeing him. I have a message for him to transmit or he has one for me. We don't communicate, if I'm using the right word. The messages are in code.'

'I see.' There was another pause, and this time, or so it seemed to him, there was a tension in the air. She had something on her mind. That's why she had asked him round. She was worrying about something.

'Mark's quite well, isn't he?' she said.

'Perfectly, as far as I know.'

'Things *are* going all right?'

'I've no reason to believe they aren't.'

'And you are more likely than anyone else to know if they weren't.'

'I wouldn't say that.'

'You have your ear to the ground, in the way the others haven't. I always feel nowadays that we are all of us sitting on a volcano, that may explode at any moment. He can't tell me what's on his mind; maybe I'm fancying things, but I can't help worrying. Things are difficult for me. I ought to be out there, I know; my duty is to my husband, my first duty, but at the same time I've a duty to my daughter, and that duty is the more . . . Well, how shall I put it? Mark isn't her father, you see. Did you know that?'

'I did.'

'But I tend to think of her as his daughter. We've been together, the three of us, so long. Her father was—is for that matter—completely irresponsible. He ran away when she was two years old. She's hardly ever seen him. But he is her father, and I'm always afraid that she will feel cheated because she's never had a father. Probably I put her first, more than I should. Which isn't fair to Mark. I ought to be in Tangier, but Tangier can't give Julia what she needs, not at the moment. She needs to be in London, to meet the right kind of people, in particular the right kinds of men. Would you say that in Tangier she'd be meeting the kind of young men that a young woman should be taking seriously?'

He shook his head. He could answer that question very definitely. Tangier was full of elderly retired men, some

bachelors some widowers. 'Occasionally there's an unattached American,' he said.

'I'm not sure that I'd want her to get mixed up with an
American. Not yet, anyhow. Are there any youngish un-
married Englishmen?'

'There are one or two.'

'But they are not the marrying type.'

'They're not.'

'Exactly. And what's the alternative—a young Moroccan?'

'There are plenty of them. They're very handsome.'

'Which is why so many young Swedish girls go there?'

'They don't seem to waste their time.'

'Exactly. And I don't see why they should. But it isn't what
one wants for one's own daughter, at the age of nineteen. I
don't feel that it would be fair to Julia not to let her have this
summer, this so crucial summer, here in England. I believe
she needs me here in England, more than Mark needs me in
Tangier. At least, that's how I see it. That's why it's so
helpful for me, having this talk with you. Everything is all
right, isn't it, as far as he's concerned?'

There was a note of pleading in her voice. She was begging
to be reassured, and once again he had that same suspicion
that he had had with Marshall, that somewhere along the
course, Littlejohn had put up a black. Marshall had been
apprehensive on that account, just as his wife was now. But
once again he was himself completely in the dark. He did not
know what kind of black Littlejohn had put up. How could he
tell whether or not his boss was in danger now of putting up
another. He had seen nothing. No one had whispered anything. There was only this suspicion. That the two people
who knew most about him were worried on his behalf. And
that was not evidence.

'As far as I know,' he said, 'you haven't any cause for
worry.'

'I haven't? It's such a relief to have you say that. I can't
help worrying with these divided loyalties. It's very good of
you to have come round. To have set my mind at rest.' He
must be all right she thought. He must have learnt his lesson.

81

That night she cabled Tangier to say that it would be impossible for her to come out this summer.

The cable reached Littlejohn shortly before ten o'clock next morning. He stared at the slip of grey-green paper. 'Desperately sorry cannot change plans at time so crucial for Julia Please understand Will come out October Deep love from us both.'

'Well,' he thought, 'that's that.' He pushed back his chair; was he going to look back on this moment as the decisive step. The last moment when it had been possible for him to draw back? The step once taken, it would be too late. He walked down the passage. He paused outside Frieda's door. He hesitated before he tapped.

Come on, pull yourself together, he adjured himself. In two minutes you'll be back in the passage, and one way or another, it will be settled.

As he opened the door, he heard the sound of typing. Frieda's desk faced the window; though she had answered his knock she had not interrupted her typing. How punctilious she was, not breaking off in the middle of a sentence. She swung round in her chair, and surprise crossed her features. He always summoned her to his study.

'No, don't get up' he said as she pushed back her chair. He walked over to her table and stood beside her.

'Have you ever been to Rabat?' he asked.

'I never have.'

'I have to go there next week. There are a couple of conferences I should attend. It would be a help to me if you came too.'

She bent her head.

'I thought of going on the Wednesday, coming back on the Saturday. On the Friday the King attends the mosque. I've never been to that. I think I should.'

'Shall I book seats on the evening plane?'

He shook his head. 'Let's go by train. It's a pleasant journey, one sees the country. And book rooms at the Hilton.'

'That sounds very self-indulgent'. There was a half twinkle in her eye. 'I believe in being comfortable. I also believe on certain occasions in going to a hotel or restaurant where I'm certain not to meet anyone I know.'

'I see.'

'That's settled then.'

'That's settled.'

The twinkle in her eye became a smile: almost a congratulatory smile, as though she were saying, 'don't you feel much better now you've got that off your chest.'

Back at his desk, he drew his writing pad towards him.

Dear Frank. His letter started.

The Rabat train left Tangier at half past three. It was an elegant red and yellow painted pullman type. It had only one first class compartment, with a bar attached to it. It had long well-padded seats. It was not unlike the first class compartment on a luxury flight. There were less than half a dozen other passengers.

'Let's sit on the right hand side,' he said, 'so that we can get a good view of Azilah.'

He had brought with him a pile of the day's papers. 'Which of these haven't you seen,' he asked. In point of fact she had not seen any of them. 'If you've got a copy of *The Telegraph* I'd like that,' she said.

He handed it across to her. Himself, he opened out *The Times*. He clearly did not want to talk. She was grateful to him for that. This thing was going to work out all right, she thought.

She began to read *The Telegraph*. She had already heard two instalments of the news that were later than it was. She searched for a section of London gossip.

The train swung and jolted over the uneven track. The countryside was beginning to look dry. The spring flowers had withered, the general effect was one of brown, rather than of green. The sea on the right was calm. As she turned the page of her paper, she glanced at Littlejohn. *The Times* had fallen forward on his lap. The sight of him asleep stirred her. He looked so unguarded and unarmed. It gave her a sense of responsibility. She could not see herself as a frail damsel being cajoled into a dubious adventure. She was the stronger of the two. She knew what she was doing. She was going into this with her eyes open. She had no sense of guilt. She did not like his wife, a woman who in her opinion had taken on a job as wife to a Consul General and had fallen down on it. She deserved what she was getting, or what she was going to get, if this came to anything, and she did not think it would.

Herself, she was not out for anything—anything for herself, that was to say. But she had a sense of kinship with this man, lonely, not unimportant in his way, who had been denied the assistance, the encouragement to which, through his post, he was entitled. She was a 'loner' too. They might have something to give each other. If that was so, well, then the better for them both.

Whatever it was, there were no snags attached. He couldn't be a nuisance to her, as so often an unattached man could be—she was familiar with that problem. And she would make no demands on him. 'Good luck to both of us,' she thought.

9

The department which Adrian had to visit off Whitehall had
once been a hotel, and had the run-down air of a building
that had been constructed for another purpose. It all seemed
just as temporary as it had fourteen years ago when he had
paid his first visit there. That half-worn carpet, that substantial desk, the half-filled book shelves, the straight-backed
chairs, the framed photographs of Royalty that had been
hastily assembled from a dump to which they would one day
be as casually resigned: the only permanent effect was the
distinguished personage at the desk, an ample, middle-aged
man in a well cut, not quite new dark blue pin-stripe suit,
with an off blue shirt in whose collar was knotted neatly, an
Old Etonian tie. That kind of man had always sat at that
desk; the room and furniture had been assembled to give
him the appropriate background of official and important
competence.

He rose as Adrian crossed the room.

'Come in, my dear fellow, come in. I'm very glad to see
you. It's very good of you to give up a morning of your hard-
earned leave to putting me in the picture. We so depend on
that, for being kept up to date. I haven't been to Tangier
since the late 1940s. It must be a quite different place, yet I
go on thinking of it as being just the same: I don't suppose I
should recognise where I was, if I were to be dropped there
in a parachute.'

'You would if they dropped you in the centre, sir.'

'Ah, the old Place de France. That's still there is it? And
the Café de Paris with all the tourists sitting on the terrace in
the sun; and the Minzah hotel, with its Moorish courtyard
and the Villa de France. I saw a film of it the other day. Yes, I
recognised that. I had three days there once: when it was still
an international zone and you could get whisky at a pound a
bottle. Tell me how everyone is. Not that any of my old
friends can be still alive.'

'I expect some are. You remember George, the Australian journalist?'

'What—is he still there?'

'A very patriarchal figure now; he's grown a long white beard.'

'George, with a beard; and what about that Spanish dowager, a countess of some kind, who had a small white poodle.'

'I haven't seen a poodle.'

'Then she's probably checked out. Can't picture her without a poodle.'

Name followed name. They were like two old school friends meeting after fifteen years.

'I'm so glad you've come,' Sonning was continuing. 'I've been wondering about Tangier. How's it working out? all this Moroccanisation.'

Sonning was probably as well informed on that score as he was himself: he made his account brief and factual. 'Every business has to be owned fifty-one per cent by a Moroccan, a great many of the French and Spanish don't want to work on these conditions. They are selling out and leaving. Their only problem is getting their money out.'

'What about the British?'

'Not many of them have businesses. They are grumbling about inflation and the falling pound.'

'Who isn't? Are many of them having to leave?'

'Not many. They haven't anywhere to go.'

'Of course. Of course.'

It was a cosy conversation, but it was not the kind of conversation that he had come back to London for; he did not want to discuss the British expatriates' reaction to the falling pound, but whether HMG was going to need an intelligence desk there any longer.

'I suppose,' Adrian said, 'that Tangier isn't of very much importance to us as an organisation any longer.'

'Not the importance that it was, when the French and Spanish had protectorates.'

'But the Basque nationalists . . .'

86

Sonning cut him short. 'You're as well informed on that as I am. Gibraltar is still worried about that. By the way did you know that Marshall had been replaced?'

'He never told me.'

'When did you see him last.'

'Three weeks ago.'

'He wouldn't have known for certain then. A chap called John Groves is taking over. In fact he's there already. A younger chap; very much on the ball. You'll get on with him I'm sure. You go over pretty regularly to Gibraltar, I suppose.'

'I'm a Mason which gives me a useful alibi for going over.'

'A pleasant one too, I expect.'

'It's a nice excuse for going over at HMG's expense, and filling up my larder.'

'What is it you're short of, mostly?'

'In my case, Kelloggs's cornflakes.'

'You'd think you could get them anywhere. What about English cheeses?'

Adrian talked about the difficulty with English cheeses. This isn't getting me anywhere, he thought.

'One thing about Tangier that's very satisfactory for me, is that there is a quite large American group there. You knew, didn't you, that I was married to an American?'

'Did I? Yes, of course I did. Somebody was talking about her the other day, told me she was delightful.'

'I find her so.'

'That's lucky. And she's liking Tangier all right?'

'She seems to. In addition to the consulate staff, and the Voice of America, there's the American School. That's quite important.'

'So I've been told.'

'In some of the places I've been, there were hardly any Americans at all. That would have made it rather lonely for her.'

'I expect that our posting department had that in mind when they sent you to Tangier.'

There was a twinkle in his eye. Adrian recognised that he

had been forestalled. The old boy was on the ball. If he was not, he would have been sitting in that chair, looking so very much the right man in the right job. Sonning knew exactly why he had come to see him, to sound out the ground, to see whether the situation that made his own presence in Tangier necessary was likely to continue; and to make the point that if he were going to be re-posted, he would prefer because of Beryl to be sent to a post where there was an American colony. I've made my point. He knows I've made it, and he's let me see that he knows I know I've made it. No need to linger here. Adrian stood up.

'It's very good of you to have found the time to see me.'

'On the contrary, it's very good of you to have given me a half hour of your leave.'

I've done what I was advised to do, Adrian thought.

It was ten to twelve: too late to go home for lunch. He turned to the left up Cockspur Street, then to the right up Whitcomb Street: there was a pub halfway up which had an Edwardian atmosphere of red plush and gilt. He ordered himself half a pint of Watney's Red Barrel and a cheese and tomato sandwich. How well they did this kind of thing in London now. He took his time. He would probably follow this up with a glass of port; then he might take in a cinema at cine-centre. They opened at one o'clock. That would take him to three o'clock. What would he do then. Go up to Lord's? There was only a minor match on. He wished he belonged to a club, so that he could sit at a long table next to someone with whom he could establish some point in common; then he could sit in a long chair and read the weeklies, or else find a library novel that he couldn't afford to buy but would be glad to read. Doze perhaps after it. Yes, he should have joined a club fifteen years ago.

The bar was filling up, mostly with young men, half of them long-haired and bearded: there were two or three girls in jeans, with shirts hanging loose over their hips; they were untidy, yet they looked clean and prosperous. Most of them were drinking beer. They were making quite a little noise. They seemed at ease with one another: did they know each other or had they come in independently, or in groups of twos and threes, availing themselves of the freemasonry of the public house; as he himself would have done fifteen years ago. He felt shy now of doing that.

He finished his half tankard and returned to the bar. 'A large tawny port,' he asked, 'and a cheese sandwich.'

He sipped the port appreciatively. The rich full wine sent a glow along his veins, it also sent courage along his nerves. He knew now what he had to do. Staffs were being reduced. He had to prove his worth. He must be the initiator; devise devices of his own—and right away.

He finished his port, left the pub, and turned left into Lower Regent Street. The BEA offices were fairly empty. 'I have a return ticket to Tangier,' he said, 'for Thursday week. I want to leave instead as soon as possible. Is there a flight tomorrow?'

The assistant consulted his list. 'Tomorrow at thirteen fifty.'

'Is there a vacancy on it?'

'There are several vacancies.'

'I haven't my ticket with me. If I get to Heathrow two hours ahead of time, will that be all right?'

'That will be all right.'

He got out to Highgate shortly after three. His mother was watching television. 'I hadn't expected you so soon,' she said.

'There's been a complication.'

'Nothing serious, I hope.'

'Nothing that time won't cure; I've got to go back to Tangier sooner than I expected.'

'How much sooner?'

'Tomorrow morning.'

'Oh.'

In the past he had felt guilty when he had to change his plans at the last moment. He hated having to disappoint his mother; so much of her life was built round him. At least that was what he had thought when he was at school and Oxford, and probably that was how it had been then, but she did not seem so very disappointed now. Perhaps she wasn't.

89

Her life was filled with other people, other interests. If he had brought her grandchildren, that would have been another matter, but he hadn't and how could he expect her to be interested in an American daughter-in-law whom she had never seen?

'Will you be dining at home?' she asked.

'Of course.'

'That's very nice of you.'

'I wondered if you'd like to go out somewhere.'

'No, I don't think so, dear. Unless you particularly want to. There's a Simenon play on the box that I was looking forward to.'

'Then let's watch that. And I think that I should ring up Beryl right away. It'll be breakfast time over there.'

'Fancy that. That's one of the things that I can't get used to, the different times at which things happen in different countries. Beryl only just waking up.'

As a matter of fact she was not yet awake. She had been to a party the night before, and she had asked her mother to let her sleep on late. When her mother woke her, she protested, 'No, really, I can't. I must sleep on.'

'But it's long distance. It's Transatlantic. It must be important. You have to come.'

'Oh well, oh well.' She pulled on a bed-jacket, splashed cold water across her face, staggered, still half asleep, to the telephone in the living room. 'Yes,' she said. 'Yes. This is Beryl Simms.'

There started the interminable cross examination that attends transatlantic calls. 'Yes, this is Beryl Simms.' 'Mrs Beryl Simms. Please hold on.' There were pauses; there were interpolations. There were repetitions, voices, 'Yes, London, this is Oklahoma.' Pause after pause. Imploring injunctions to hold on a little longer. She was still half asleep. She found herself dozing off. At last, at last, there was her husband's voice. 'Yes, this is me. How are you, Beryl, this is me.'

She was barely conscious. 'I've just woken up,' she said.

'You have? I'm sorry. This time lag. It's difficult. Listen now, I've changed my plans. That Whitehall interview. I told you about it, didn't I? I have to go back to Tangier right away.'

'Right away?'

'Tomorrow, yes. It needn't affect you though. You must do what you want. Come when you feel like it. Don't alter your plans.'

She could scarcely follow him. Three minutes ago, she had been asleep. Adrian going back to Tangier. He would be there tomorrow. Should she go at once? There was that dance at the Country Club.

'Don't let this worry you,' he was saying: 'It's nothing serious. Nothing I can't take in my stride. Come when you're ready to come. Don't alter anything on my account. No, it isn't important, of course it isn't. I just felt I had to warn you.'

'I see. I see,' she said. She did not see at all. She was still half asleep and there he was, burbling away, saying the kind of thing that you did say on a long distance call, asking what the weather was like, how her parents were, was she having fun. And she kept on answering 'Yes, yes, of course,' and 'no, of course not,' when a negative was required.

'I must ring off now,' he was concluding. 'It *has* been good to hear your voice.' There was a click. Then silence. Then there was her mother coming in. 'Is everything all right?'

'Of course, why not?'

'A long distance telephone call all the way from England. One feels it has to be important.'

'It wasn't though.'

'Adrian all right?'

'Perfectly.'

If only her mother would desist, would let her go back to sleep. But she went on and on. 'I know you did not want to be disturbed. That's what I told Daphne.'

'Daphne, what did she want?'

'I don't know. She didn't tell me. She seemed to think it was important. But I told her you wanted to sleep on. I promised to let you know as soon as you woke up, so that you could call her back. You'll do that, won't you.'

'Yes, yes, I'll do it. Yes, of course.'

She was by now, thoroughly awake. She had missed the chance of that last half hour of sleep, that was so heavy and so refreshing; that made all the difference to you later in the day. I'd better get up, she thought. Shower, and start the day, and hear what Daphne had upon her mind. Daphne was her closest confidante. They had told each other everything from their days in high school, in fourth grade; Daphne the one person to whom she wrote real letters.

Ten minutes later she called back. 'I hear you've news for me.'

'Who do you think's coming into town?'

'Who?'

'You'll never guess.'

'Tell me, if I'll never guess.'

'No, no, not right away. You've got to have your three guesses first. I want to hear the surprise in your voice, when you hear who it really is.'

It was a silly game, but it was Daphne's favourite game; she had to play along with her. She couldn't deny Daphne her little giggle.

'I'll tell you who it is,' she said. 'It's Francis Rankin.'

There was a splutter of laughter from the other end. 'Francis. I wouldn't have called you up on his account. Francis, that stuffed shirt. Try again.' Beryl had another shot. Again there was a splutter of incredulity. So was there for her third shot.

'Now that I've earned it. You can tell me.'

'Right then: prepare for cavalry. McCrudden: Eric McCrudden.'

'What?'

Her 'what' hit exactly the note of excitement that Daphne had counted on. She chuckled. 'I told you, didn't I, that that would take your breath away.' And Daphne was right. It had taken her breath away.

McCrudden, she always thought of him as McCrudden, not as Eric. She had met him, just before she had left for Europe, at one of the monthly dances at the Country Club. He was the tall, rangy type. She had noticed him the moment he came into the room. Not exactly good looking, but with an air of having been around. He was dark, clean-shaven, with his hair cut short. She had not seen him about before. Who was he? And just as she was wondering that, she noticed that he had noticed her. They looked at one another. The stranger in the crowded room. He walked across to her. 'Who are you?' he asked.

She told him, but did not ask who he was. Instead she asked 'What are you?' He was at Dallas; he had just finished his dissertation for his Ph.D. That was one of the reasons he had told her, later, why he was not married. Unless you were rich, and he was not rich, a wife had a dreary time while her husband was working on a dissertation. The first three years of marriage which should be a halcyon period was a time of drudgery. 'You seem to have thought things out,' she said.

'One needs to, doesn't one?'

'A great many don't.'

But though he had thought things out, he did not seem stodgy, pompous, a careerist. Certainly there was nothing pompous about his dancing. There was a purposeful vibrancy about it. He did not indulge in tricky steps. She found it easy to follow him, easy to respond. She closed her eyes, conscious of the music, but even more of him. He did not hold her close, but she was conscious of his hand, of his fingers on her shoulder. She was conscious of his legs moving against hers: every so often he slid his right leg between hers, pressing against her, then retreating only to return again. When the music stopped, he said, 'Could I persuade you to dine with me one night?'

'Why not?'

'When?'

She hesitated. It was Tuesday. What was wrong with Friday? Friday would be fine, he said. That night she lay awake for a long while, her hands clasped under her head. Friday. A week from Monday she was taking off for Europe. That would give them ten days together. Time for them to get to know each other, to learn about each other, to achieve a genuine harmony; but not long enough for it to go too deep. The very thing that she was looking for.

She was not without experience. There had been, two years ago, the first experiment, undertaken in a spirit of curiosity, a resolve to find out 'what that was all about' so that she could meet her contemporaries on equal terms. It had not been too satisfactory. But she had been warned that she must not expect to enjoy herself 'the first few times'. She had, though, got a kick out of the actual adventure. It might, she had thought, be better with someone else. There had been a few more experiments. Then there had been something that had been altogether different. He was in his third year at O.C.U. He was in the football side. He was handsome. He was a local hero. She had been thrilled when he had asked her on a date. Her individual status had gone up several points. Her friends envied her. 'This is it,' she had thought, 'this is what they write about in books.'

For a month, for two months, she had gone on thinking that. Then he began to bore her. He only talked about himself: about his football and the jobs he was being promised because of his prowess on the field. She was irritated, too, by the strict training that he imposed upon himself; no revels in the days before a match, then a couple of days to recover from a match. And because they were going steady, she could not have other dates. That would have damaged his *persona*. She was his girl and should be proud of it. She was limited by him. She did not want promiscuous affairs, but she did want to see as much of the world as she could and the various people that composed it. She was relieved when one of the smart jobs that he had been offered in the East materialised. She acted as though she were heart-broken, but she rejoiced.

She had then subjected herself to a strict interrogation. No more going steady unless there was a probability of marriage at the end of it. A brief affair was something different. Two people bound in different directions, who found themselves isolated by chance in the same beach hotel for a week or two, that was something altogether different. And was not that

94

exactly what this McCrudden offered her: the perfect last fling before she went away. And it was now five minutes to two on the Wednesday morning. The day after tomorrow, she would be seeing him.

But she did not have to wait until the Friday evening. On that very same evening she was to see him at the Golf Club. He had gone out a little while before she had. He was a couple of holes ahead of her. As she came up the sixteenth fairway, she saw him putting out on the last green. The sight of him sent a shiver along her nerves. Had he noticed her, she wondered. If he had, he would be surely waiting on the terrace. She was impatient to finish her last holes. Thank heavens she was playing a foursome, not a four ball. She prayed that she and her partner would keep their balls in the centre of the fairway, that they would not have to waste time hunting in the rough. Please keep straight, she adjured her ball. It did; so did her opponent's; and when they came up the rise to the last green, she could see him on the terrace, sitting beside a tall half-filled glass. He was alone. He rose as she came off the green. 'What can I get you,' he asked, 'to set beside my scotch and soda?'

He did not include her companion in the invitation. She felt he should have done, but was grateful to him for not doing so. He had the character to be rude, on her behalf, and after all, he was a stranger here. She would like a Schweppes stone ginger beer, she said, with a slice of lemon.

'I've got to be away in forty minutes time,' he told her. She was grateful to him for warning her.

Forty minutes over a drink, on the golf club terrace, was ideal as the prelude to what should be a decisive meeting in two days time. Forty minutes just gave you the right time to get something said.

'What are you going to do with your Ph.D.?' she asked. 'Are you going in for teaching?'

He shook his head. 'Not for the moment.'

He told her the ideas he had. He had connections in Dallas. He was going to call himself a consultant: business openings, investments, property, that kind of thing. 'I'm going to keep my eyes and my ears open. I'll give myself three years. By the end of those three years, I should be on my way—or rather I should see my way.' He spoke not boastfully but with confidence. It would be exciting to be beside him during those three years. But that was something that it was not going to be possible for her to be. She would have these ten crowded days, then it would be all over. Again at the end of the day, she lay on her back with her hands clasped behind her head. Ten crowded days and then a memory. Was that what she really wanted—with him? She and her friends had brooded over marriage. Each knew that she wanted to be married some day, but each was scared of it. So few marriages seemed to last these days. None of them wanted a divorce. They would move with their eyes open. They would not marry in ignorance, as their grandparents had done. In theory they had believed in trial marriages, yet they had not liked the idea of being put on trial, of having a man say, 'I think I'd like you to be my wife, but I'd like to see how you suit me before I make up my mind.'

It would be all right for her to say that to a man, but not for a man to say that to her. It would diminish her. What each would prefer, what each had hoped for in their hearts of hearts had been an affair that had begun light-heartedly, but that had suddenly become serious, that had grown deeper, tenderer. Of which the man would say suddenly, 'Don't you think that this is too good to be let go? I don't want to lose you, ever.'

And that was just how it would not be with McCrudden, if she went out to dinner with him in two nights time and started a rumbustious ten day affair.

She knew what she had to do: she had to give herself a chance of seeing if it was the real thing with this McCrudden.

Next morning at breakfast she would tell her mother that she felt she should see her father before she went to Europe. She did not want to hurt his feelings. 'Why don't I go on tomorrow?' she would say, 'spend a week with him, then go straight to Europe?' Then she would ring up McCrudden. She would herself sound heartbroken. But she would be chuckling inside. How she would relish the disappointment in his voice. He would beg her to let them meet once, at least once before she went. His pleading would send a glow along her veins but because this was her own doing, she would not feel a qualm. It was her own planning. The way she wanted it: and she would not be away so long. Six months, not more.

She would write to him while she was away: fond little notes that would assure him that she was looking forward to their next meeting. And the fact that he would be here awaiting her return would make a subtle difference to her time in Europe. It would give her something to look forward to; so that her return would be the opening not the closing of a chapter. It would also be a check on her: he would be a guardian, a watchdog, to prevent her getting too involved in Europe. She hoped that she would have some romance in Europe. It would be a feather in her cap—an Oklahoman to have a love affair with a Frenchman or an Italian—perhaps both, but McCrudden's presence in the background would prevent her from getting too involved. She would not want to think of a European in terms of marriage. She wanted to marry an American, to centre her life in America. She could think of this European trip as her last fling. The future stretched before her, radiant with promise.

The telephone call next morning went the way she wanted. He had been disappointed. The 'Oh' in his voice had made up for any disappointment that she felt herself. And she had sent him a letter from New York, and a postcard from Paris— another one from London. But then there had been Florence, Adrian—her carelessness, so that it had ended with a note from Venice: 'My dear. I was married yesterday, to an Englishman, please wish me luck.' She had not given him an address to which he could wish it her. And now and again, quite often when it came to that, she had wondered what would have happened if she had not been careless. If her thing with Adrian had been what they had both planned for it, a three weeks 'bit of nonsense,' might it not have been better for all three of them?

When she read of McCrudden's marriage, she had had an

97

irritating sense of being cheated. And now here was Daphne with news about him.

'McCrudden?' she said. 'What about him?'

'Coming here next week. He's staying with the Fergusons. They're taking him to the dance.'

'*Him*, not *them*?'

'*Him* was the way I heard it.'

'So he's not bringing her.'

'I gather not.'

'Are they at outs?'

'I wouldn't know.'

'They might be, wouldn't you think?'

'It's unusual for men to come on visits without their wives, if everything is fine at home.'

'Thank you anyhow for warning me.'

'It's worth a TL isn't it?'

'You bet it is.'

There was a thoughtful expression on her face as she hung up. She was fully awake now and her thoughts were racing. McCrudden and without his wife and with herself alone here.

Beryl's cable to Tangier announcing that for family reasons she had decided to stay on the full forty-five days of her ticket, awaited Adrian's return on the Tuesday evening. There were only four other envelopes in his letter box. He had not expected more. His business mail went to his office. He had practically no personal mail. 'I have no personal life,' he thought, 'apart from Beryl.' And now he would be here for the best part of three weeks without her. Well, he must make the most of a bad job.

He turned his key in the lock, once, but at the second turn it stopped. He pressed and the door opened. That's funny. He could have sworn he had left it double locked. He had a mental picture of himself standing on the doorstep, with Beryl having gone ahead, with the two suitcases beside him, and Beryl calling up to him. Had he remembered to turn off the pilot light under the water heater? Hadn't he better check, she'd called. And he'd gone back into the flat to see, although he had been certain that he had, as that was the kind of thing he never did forget. He had been rather impatient with her, he remembered. Perhaps because he had been impatient with her, he had not bothered to double lock the door; just shut it, picking up the suitcases and hurrying after her. That's how it must have been. Otherwise the door would have been double locked. Of course it would. Of course.

The flat had a musty smell. Two weeks, after all. He swung the windows open: stood on the balcony breathing in the cool fresh air. An east wind was blowing. The palm trees were swaying. He closed the windows before he opened those on the other side, otherwise the cross wind would blow the screen over, which was something that Beryl had never learnt. Papers were always being blown across the floor, flower vases being overturned. He stood in the centre of the flat looking round him. It was good to be back. But it would be better in three weeks' time.

He left his own study till the last. In the doorway he checked, surprised. There was a curious smell in it, a stale and heavy smell. He did not smoke and had in consequence an acute sense of smell. He sniffed suspiciously. Somebody's been in here, he thought. He sat down at his desk. The smell was stronger here. It was not actually unpleasant. It was a masculine smell: the kind of smell that was advertised in magazines for men. He walked back into the other rooms, one after another. In none of them was the smell apparent.

He opened Beryl's wardrobe, this was where she kept her jewellery. No, not there. He went back to his own study: yes it was here that the smell lingered. It was here that the intruder had staged his visit. He sat down at his desk; he looked round him carefully. Nothing seemed to have been disturbed; everything was the way it was, the photographs and booklets on the shelves. On his desk the usual litter of envelopes, papers, ink bottles, calendar, paperweights, paper knife. The familiar disorder. He pulled at the top drawer. It was still locked. He opened it. Everything looked the same. The cheque books in their separate section. The cancelled cheques. The receipts. His diary in the middle. He took it

99

out; laid it on the desk; opened it. His heart bounded. The cotton that he always stretched across the fourth page had been disturbed. There *had* been an intruder.

'Now, keep your head,' Adrian adjured himself, 'keep your head. In your absence someone has broken into your flat, has forced the lock of your desk and read your diary. The diary won't have told him anything. No secrets have passed into interested hands. You knew that something like this might happen and you were on your guard. That's not the point. The point is, that somebody in Tangier is sufficiently interested in what you are about to organise an extremely skilful subversive operation.' He examined the keyhole of his desk. There was nothing particular about it. A common-place standardised model. There were a hundred such in Tangier. Anybody in this racket would have a skeleton key capable of coping with it. There was no need for him to worry about that. Any locksmith could deal with such a lock. But how had the intruder got inside the flat? That was the problem.

He made a reconnaissance. He examined the shutters and the windows, one by one. Any agile person could have swarmed up on the balcony on either side; but how could the windows have been forced without showing some sign of illegal entry: there was no sign. Nor could the intruder have entered from the roof: there was no open air shaft: simply a stone chimney stack above the lavatory with narrow slits: adequate for ventilation but impossible for anything but a small marmoset; the intruder must have come in through the front door, with a key.

The knowledge sent a thrill along his nerves. Something was happening here after all. How little that prim ass Sonning really knew. He stood up. He began to pace the living room. His excitement mounted. He was in the middle of real drama. He wasn't in a backwater, after all. He'd got to make the most of this. He'd show them. He was at the start of a whole new career. He would surprise them all. It was nine o'clock. He had eaten on the plane. He had planned to have an early, quiet evening: to have a single whisky, go to bed, and wake up fresh. But his mind was racing. He couldn't sit here alone. He had to get out, where people were: to feel himself a part of the human drama. He couldn't think things out here. The Parade was the place. He'd sit out in the garden; collect his thoughts. He couldn't be bothered to unpack. He'd get out right away.

In the roadway outside, he paused. The road in front was badly lit. Beryl refused to walk down it alone. Her bag might get snatched, she said. He had laughed at her qualms, but he wondered now if they were not justified. Was it safe for him to walk down that road? He remembered that car collision in the Place de France: that young Moroccan in the roadway. Was he himself in danger? The idea excited him. Suppose someone were to leap at him from the shadows. What a fool Sonning would look. He crossed the street. He strode firmly down the dark, clustered roadway. This would teach Sonning a lesson.

The Parade was crowded, as he had known it would be, at this hour, or this time of year.

He looked about him. Ah yes, as he had suspected. There at a large table was a group of the very people that he was most glad to meet, but that he was in point of fact surprised to meet here. Sarita was the first one that he recognised and with her Jurgensen, James Murray from the American Consulate, and Pablo Monterey, the last person he would have expected to meet in that group. What were they all doing at one table? Then he got the clue—Frieda Fitzgerald, of course, of course. The Tangier players; they had come on after a rehearsal, and there along with them was Littlejohn. That did surprise him. What was *he* doing here?

He hesitated. Should he join them? Littlejohn's presence made him wonder whether he should, without a special invitation. Littlejohn was in three-quarter profile. He would not recognise him unless someone called his attention to his being here. And that was not likely. He had better move away, and then next morning he could make some reference to having seen him at the Parade, thereby getting some credit for not having forced himself upon the group, a point up to himself with somebody like Littlejohn. He was just about to turn, when Sarita saw him. Her arm went above her head. Her hand beckoned to him in an imperious wave. He could not but come across.

'What on earth are you doing here and without Beryl?' she demanded.

Littlejohn looked over his shoulder.

'I hadn't expected him. I'm not responsible.' He said.

'It does not matter who's responsible. The fact is that he's here, and without his wife. He took her away. He's upset our whole production. We may even have to postpone it until the autumn. The call of duty, that's how he explained it, and we're all very susceptible to that. At least I am. And now here he is back without any warning, and without our heroine.'

Adrian explained, or rather endeavoured to explain the situation.

She shook her head. 'To me that all sounds unconvincing, highly unconvincing. What does our host think of it?'

Littlejohn shrugged. 'I am perplexed too, but . . .' he paused. 'I haven't the control over my staff that I suspect your father-in-law has over his. Come and sit down with us and tell us what you know or at least as much of what you know as you feel you're entitled to let us know.'

It was the first indication, the first public indication that Littlejohn had ever given that Adrian was not an ordinary routine member of his staff. Littlejohn off his guard. That was unusual.

Littlejohn was sitting between Sarita and Frieda, Pablo Monterey was on the other side of Sarita. Adrian took a chair and was about to put it next to Sarita, but Littlejohn checked him, 'No, on the other side of Frieda.' Frieda was sitting next to Murray. Perhaps Littlejohn wanted him to have a talk with Murray. Littlejohn never did anything without a reason.

Frieda made room for him and Adrian sat next to her. It was actually the first time that he had sat next to her at a table. They had gossiped at cocktail parties, they had passed the time of day at the office, but in view of his own anomalous position, he had thought it better to maintain a distance. He and Beryl had never invited her to their own parties. Ordinarily if he had found himself seated next to her by chance, he would have kept the talk on the level of local gossip, but now since Littlejohn had insisted on his sitting next to her, he felt he might as well presume on her familiarity with his position. After all, apart from Littlejohn, she was the only person in Tangier who knew the precise nature of his posting. He might as well take advantage of it. His was a lonely role. It would be a relief to let his hair down sometimes.

'Perhaps you were surprised at my coming back so soon,' he said.

'I'm never surprised at anything that anyone in your racket does.'

'You know what that racket is?'

'When I was in Vienna, I was a very good friend of one of your men there.'

Adrian half-closed his eyes. Vienna, four years ago, who would that have been? It might be a clue. 'It's a funny game,' he said.

'That's how it strikes an outsider sometimes.'

'And the tricky thing is that it isn't meant to be.'

'That's one of the things I've guessed.'

She was smiling, in a friendly, understanding way. He had the sudden, unexpected feeling that they understood each other, that they could talk in shorthand. I might do worse than concentrate on her, he thought. I'm going to need all the allies I can find.

'I was wondering,' he said. But before he could tell her what he had been wondering, Littlejohn had turned towards her.

'Now, about this next rehearsal . . .' Which was as far as he himself was concerned, the equivalent of a royal command. Adrian turned to Murray.

'Are your smugglers and dope runners keeping you from getting lazy?'

'As much as they always do. They're the background to my existence here. Whenever I think I have a quiet afternoon ahead and that I might be able to linger late at the Yacht Club after lunch, I have to hurry round to the police to interview some wretched creature who was caught at the docks with his pockets full of kif. Only this morning, as a matter of fact . . .' he paused and looked at Adrian thoughtfully, '. . . something happened that made me wish that you were here.'

'What was that?'

'I can't tell you here.'

'Then why don't we meet where we can talk. What about lunch tomorrow at the Grenouille?'

'I can see nothing wrong with that.'

'At one o'clock then?'

'At one o'clock.'

The party broke up early. It was Littlejohn who broke it up.

'I have to keep earlier hours than you young people. Can I drive you back, Frieda, or do you want to make a night of it?'

'I have to keep early hours too.'

'Then let's be on our way.'

On his way back into the bar to settle the account, he paused by Adrian.

'You'll be coming in tomorrow, I suppose,' he said.

'Of course, sir.'

'Good. I've got something for you. I'll let you know when I'll be free. I expect it'll be rather early. Can I give anyone else a lift? What about you, James?'

Murray shook his head.

'No, thank you, sir. I prefer to walk, but I'll be on my way as well. I'm for early hours.'

Young Jurgensen too excused himself. That left only Sarita and young Monterey. 'Don't hurry,' Sarita said. 'It isn't late for us.' That meant that he had to stay on too. Sarita could not be left alone with Monterey.

'In that case, what would you like to drink?'

'Coffee would be fine for me.'

'Coffee would be fine for me, too,' said Pablo.

'It wouldn't be for me.' He caught the waiter's eye and ordered himself a beer. 'Now tell me all about the play. How is it going?'

'Not as well as it would be with Beryl here. When will she be back?'

'She's got a forty-five day ticket. That marks the limit.'

'She may not stay that time.'

'She may not, but once she's there, she will be tempted.'

'We may have to postpone it till the autumn. It's so hot, in August.

'She'll come back full of energy.'

'She'd better.'

'And how's young Jurgensen?'

'He's not the world's greatest actor.'

'But he's agreeable, isn't he.'

'He's more than that, much more.'

'He enjoys it, doesn't he.'

'Oh, yes, he enjoys himself.'

'He's had a strange history.'

'So I've been told.'

'Do you know much about it?'

'Only what he's told me.'

'And was that much?'

'Enough to tell me what's most on his mind.'

'And what is that?'

'The need to justify himself in the eyes of his home town. He thinks he's in disgrace, and probably he is. He wants to do something over here that will make it possible for him to go back as a hero.'

It was what Beryl had already told him.

'He's not going to find that very easy, is he?'

'All the same I envy him,' said the Moroccan.

'What for?'

'For having a country that means that much to him.'

'Don't we all have that?'

'I don't.'

That astonished Adrian. It astonished Sarita even more.

'How can you say that, you of all people, you that at last have a country of your own, you with your own King.'

'I preferred it the way it was.'

'Under Spanish rule?'

'I never thought of myself as being under Spanish rule. I thought of myself as a Spaniard. My grandfather served with the Moroccan contingent in the Civil War. He was killed at Teruel. I was proud of him. It was the Moroccan contingent that saved Spain from the communists. I was brought up as a Catholic. I used to look at those inscriptions on the barracks at Tetouan. All for the country. *Todo por la Patria.* They made my heart beat faster. They were my grandfather's memorial. You can't guess how I felt when those inscriptions were torn down. When the Spanish troops went home, I felt that Franco had betrayed us, that my grandfather had died in vain. The Moroccans saved Spain, and Spain abandoned us. I can never forgive Franco, never.'

His eyes shone, his voice glowed with indignation. It was the first time that Adrian had been alone with Pablo. It was the first time that he had thought of him as a separate, distinct individual. He had not realised that there were Moroccans who felt like this. If this was how he felt, there must be many other Moroccans who felt in the same way. There was more afoot than he had suspected, much more.

10

Early next morning Adrian spread out his diary. This might well prove to be a valuable weapon. Through this diary he would be able to pass on to whomsoever his adversary was the kind of information that he wanted him to have. He would give accurate information that would convince that adversary of his veracity. Then he could give false information that would mislead, that might entrap that adversary, that might overthrow that adversary's plans. He might even discover who had broken into his flat. 'Returned late last night. Found a cable announcing that Beryl will not be back until her forty-five-day ticket is exhausted. A disappointment, but I have plenty to do here in light of the new instructions I received in London. Went to the Parade and found the C.G. there with members of the theatre club. After he had left Sarita and I discussed Jurgensen with Pablo Monterey. Sarita said he would do anything that would make it possible for him to return to Utah as a hero. I feel that he is vulnerable . . .'

That should do the trick, he thought. His first impulse when he had realised that his flat had been broken into had been to change the lock. But that would be a mistake. It would warn his adversary that he had been discovered. Far better to keep him in the dark till the last moment.

Half an hour later he was once again at the Café de Paris. It was good to be welcomed back by the newspaper man and the waiter who brought him, without being prompted his orange juice, his soft-boiled egg, and a small cup of black coffee, and it was good to open *Le Matin* at its second page. It was twelve days since he had seen 'Juliette de mon Cœur'. An instalment had begun only a few days before he had flown to England. They should be on that same section still. Yes, there was Juliette's venal father, with his long ended bow tie and flabby cheeks. He had got involved with some northern gangsters who wanted to install a gambling saloon in a new tourist complex. One of the gangsters was paying court to Juliette in the hope of securing her co-operation. It seemed from the current instalment that he was on a fair way to achieving his fell purpose. At any rate Juliette was wearing a ring with a diamond so large that it would be difficult to draw a glove on over it. Tomorrow or the day after, he should be right back again in the story. He turned to the back page and read the football news. He did not follow the local matches carefully. Perhaps he should. It would be a distraction for him, and it might be useful to go out to the stadium on the Marshan. A man in his job should see as many sides as he could of the life that he was supposed to be interpreting. In October, when it was too cool for swimming, he might begin.

He read through the list of the results, mainly to give the impression that he was interested. He read them for as long as a casual fan might be expected to. Then he folded up the paper. As he did, he noticed a tall, elegant, well dressed young Moroccan coming in from the street. Adrian had not seen him anywhere before. Was he the new cut-out? He was carrying a copy of *L'Opinion*. He looked across in his direction, noticing him without appearing to, sat down at a table, opened the paper and began to read. A waiter brought him a small black coffee, and a *croissant*. He sipped at the coffee right away. He broke off a very small piece of the *croissant*. He caught the waiter's eye and pointed to his coffee cup. He's making a meal of this, Adrian thought, I can't wait here for ever. Perhaps he's not my man after all. He stretched out his hand towards his hat. As he did so, the Moroccan stood up, and came across. 'I wonder, sir, if you could be so kind as to exchange your copy of *Le Matin* for my *L'Opinion*.'

'Of course, I shall be delighted.'

He studied *L'Opinion* then later watched the young man cross the Place de France and turn up the Rue de Fez. If there were the need for a person to play a certain role in a plot that he was hatching, this was the right man for it. There was a very reasonable chance that such a plot would be undertaken.

Within a few minutes of his arrival at the Consulate, Adrian was summoned by the Consul General. He was handed a sheet of paper on which was typed: 'John Groves taking over from Marshall Gibraltar Arriving Tangier Friday August seven. spend weekend. Simms meet airport provide accommodation.'

Littlejohn watched Adrian read it. 'Is that quite clear?' he asked.

'Yes, sir.'

'It arrived two days ago. I did not quite know what to do. I might have had to meet him myself.'

'I'm sorry to have been a nuisance.'

'You haven't been; you might have been, which is a very different thing.'

He smiled benignly. He seemed in a good humour.

'I hope that nothing went wrong in England to bring you back sooner than you expected.'

'No, sir, nothing. I did all I needed to. I thought I could make better use of the unexpired portion of my leave later.'

Littlejohn shook his head. 'My first company commander said to me, "Never postpone a leave. Leave is a privilege and not a right. Leave has a way of getting cancelled." '

The CG was singularly jovial.

'Is there anything you want to ask?'

'I don't suppose you know anything about John Groves.'

'How should I? We move in different worlds.'

'Of course, sir. Will you want to see him?'

'I presume that he will want to pay his respects to me. Your people usually do, just for the drill of it. Except that, well, this time . . . I've always wanted to have your wife to lunch or dinner, and I've never got around to it. This might be a good opportunity.'

'I'm very sorry, sir, but I don't think Beryl will be back by then.'

'She won't? I'm sorry. I'd have enjoyed that. Another time, another time.'

He seemed fifteen years younger. Adrian stood up. He hesitated. Was the CG going to make no reference to his subordinate's visit to his home? Perhaps he didn't know about it. At any rate, it was no business of Adrian's to raise it. He returned to his own office in a puzzled mood. Too much was happening too fast, and in two weeks' time he would be serving a new master. Was this the first step towards demotion? Marshall had tried to warn him, but had sheered off the decisive act, leaving it to a stranger. He shrugged. There was no point in worrying, yet. He'd take it in his stride. He'd do the fellow well, find out the form. Whom should he ask to meet him? A female. What kind of female. Frieda perhaps. He had to know what the man was like before deciding. Best take him to the Parade and see how he reacted.

He sat back in his chair, staring at his desk—at his 'out' tray that was empty, at his 'in' tray that contained only a few routine reports. Too much was happening too fast. Four weeks ago when he had watched that young Moroccan walking across the Place de France with a copy of *Le Matin* underneath his arm, he had felt that he had not a worry in the world, but thirty seconds later there had been that crunch of brakes, that elegant figure spreadeagled in the roadway and his whole life had been turned upside down. He had not recognised it at the time, but that was what had happened.

What would happen to him if he lost his job? How could he find another? He had lost touch with England. No one knew about him there. He had felt so lost on this last leave that he had cut his leave short. Who had ever heard of a man cutting his leave short? What would he do if he lost his job? There was only one answer to that. He must not lose it.

There are some fifty restaurants listed in the Tangier telephone directory; only six of these are patronised by residents of the community. There was no means by which a visitor could tell from outside that the Grenouille was one of these. It is no more than a window in a narrow street running from the Rue de France towards the sea. It had the sign of a frog hanging over its main entrance, but it had no sidewalk café, no row of tables to suggest elegance and comfort. But once you had climbed its short flight of steps, pushing open its front door, you recognised by the second sight that experienced travellers possess, that it was a real place and likely to be good. It was small, it was on two levels, it had wicker chairs and tables. It was very clean. The waiters were smiling, smartly-dressed Moroccans. It was run by an Englishman in his middle fifties who had made his home here. He ran the bar himself and had kept the prices low.

When Adrian arrived, Murray was already at a corner table on the lower level. He was sipping at what appeared to be a dry martini on the rocks. 'Let's do ourselves well,' he said. 'What'll you have? I've arranged to put you on my expense account.'

'In that case, I'll have what you are having, if it's what I think it is.'

'It is what you think it is.'

'Fine, I'll have it.'

'And, while you are waiting for it, I'll explain how you've earned it. Am I right in thinking that one of your chief jobs here is keeping an eye on the Basque separatists?'

'You're right.'

'Then I think I may have something up your street. A young American has been pulled in trying to smuggle kif on to the Algeciras ferry; there's nothing unusual in that, of course. We had three last week. But this one is somehow different. He doesn't look a hippy. He shaves and he washes, and he has excellent clothes. He's an only child; his grandfather was killed in the Spanish Civil War.'

'On which side?'

'The Loyalists, one of the volunteers. His father seems to be an aimless kind of person, married two or three times, never made any money; this chap quarrelled with his mother, or rather, with his stepmother. He never went to college: graduated from Senior High, but that's about all. He's not incompetent, not by any means. He gets jobs and then gives them up. Has no ambitions that I can see, no tangible ambition, but he seems to have some objective on his mind. That's what puzzles me about him. I can't guess what it is. He was caught by the Moroccan customs on his way to the Algeciras ferry. He had ten thousands dollars' worth of kif in a belt under his shirt. But he does not smoke kif himself. He says he wanted the ready cash. He could live on that for two years, he said. But I don't believe him. I don't know why I don't, but I don't. I don't think he wants it for himself, but he is sending it to someone for a purpose, some purpose that he has at heart, and that's where you can help me. It's easier for you than for me to find out what that purpose is.'

'How do you make that out?'

'Because you're one of the funnies, you're cloak and dagger.'

Adrian got his point. He had access to agents whereas Murray had not. Murray was a straightforward diplomat. 'What makes you think he has this purpose?' Adrian asked.

'A hunch. I've learned to trust my hunches.'

'You have to have a clue first before you get your hunch.'

'I have a clue.'

'What is it?'

'His hatred of the Franco régime.'

'Because his grandfather was killed in the Civil War?'

'Exactly. He thinks that his father made such a mess of things because he had not got a father. He blames Franco for everything.'

This was the second man who had resentment against Franco because his grandfather had been killed in the Civil War—one as a loyalist, the other as a rebel. There could not be any link between them, or could there? Was there any greater loyalty, any tighter bond than that of a shared hatred?

Adrian could see what Murray had on his mind.

'You're suggesting that I should introduce one of my boys to your delinquent and see if he can't wheedle out his story.'

'That's about it.'

'What's likely to happen to him?'

'A long term in prison unless we can work a deal.'

'Are you anxious to work out a deal?'

'I don't want to have an American boy mouldering in a Moroccan gaol.'

'At the same time if you do get him out of gaol, you want to know what kind of citizen you're repatriating.'

'Precisely.'

'Does this chap speak Spanish?'

'Of a kind.'

'If I send you round someone who might seem suitable, can you arrange for him to interview the prisoner?'

'Of course.'

'Is your fellow worried about his future?'

'That's the odd thing about it. He does not seem to be. He does not want to go back to America. There's nothing for him there, he says. He would not be allowed into Spain. He's at a loose end. The oddest thing about him is that he doesn't seem in any hurry to get out of prison. It can't be true, I tell myself, but I believe he's plotting something and feels that he can go on plotting it inside his cell. So if you can find someone who can help me to find out what's making him tick, I'll be very, very grateful. And now let's see about ordering some lunch.'

Two days later there was another rehearsal. This time it was at Murray's flat. Adrian had got himself invited. 'I think it would be advisable if I made opportunities for our meeting each other casually. Couldn't you enroll me as deputy stage manager?'

'You'd be invaluable.'

'Then in that case I hope that I'll have something to report to you. I'll arrive ten minutes early.'

'You'll be most welcome.'

He did have something to report. 'The day after tomorrow at ten-fifteen, a young Moroccan will call on you. He will give the name Majid Abdul Khamas. Will you arrange for him to see the prisoner?'

'I will and thank you.'

They were rehearsing the scene in which the husband Stanley, the part taken by Pablo Monterey, seduces his sister-in-law Blanche, Sarita's part. It was the key scene in the play, and the two had got their words perfect now. 'I've been on to you from the start,' Stanley was saying. 'Not once did you pull any wool over this boy's eyes. You come in here and sprinkle the place with powder and spray perfume and cover the lamp bulb with a paper lantern, and lo and behold, the place has turned into Egypt, and you are the queen sitting on your throne and swilling down my liquor.'

His dark eyes flashed. There was fire in his voice. He had entered into the role. He was talking with the same wrath that he had at the Parade when he had been abusing Franco; he was a handsome creature. Adrian wished he knew him better, wished he knew more about him. He must see more of him. He must get to see more Moroccans. He needed to professionally. He had been negligent in the past. He had taken his job for granted. He had taken everything for granted, as Englishmen of his father's generation had, men who had been bred to believe that all would go well, must go well, if you lived in the traditions of the establishment. You were heirs of the Empire. You went to a certain kind of school; you passed a certain kind of exam, and you were safe for life. Some had more brains than others, some had more diligence than others, but nothing could go really wrong with you. Himself he had lived in terms of the establishment: he had done fairly well at school, fairly well at Oxford. He had got a reasonable job—and there he was, fixed for life. It wasn't the kind of job that was rewarded with a knighthood. But it was a job that brought you respect and supplied you with a satisfactory standard of living. You did what you were told to do, and all was well. That was what he had been told, but the schoolmasters who had told him that were back numbers now. The Empire had gone, and there was no guarantee of employment. He wasn't safe for life. He would have to pull up his socks, or he would be in trouble. He could not drift any longer. He had to work at this job of his. He had got to get acquainted with men like Pablo Monterey.

And there was Sarita now, alone on the stage, desperately telephoning for an imagined rescuer, 'Operator, operator, give me long distance please. I want to get in touch with Mr Shep Huntleigh of Dallas. He's so well known he doesn't require any address. Just ask anybody who—wait——No, I

114

couldn't find it right now . . . Please understand, I—no wait—one moment. Someone is—nothing. Hold on please.' There was a real note of terror in her voice. She was trapped and she knew it. It was the first time he had seen this scene rehearsed. He waited impatiently for the final moment, for Stanley's savage spring as he overturned the table, catching her by the wrist.

'Tiger, tiger, drop the bottle top. Drop it. We've had this date with each other from the beginning.'

How would Sarita feel when he caught her in his arms, carried her towards the bed. Surely there would be some direct emotional response. She couldn't be insensitive to his animal attraction. Beryl had said that she was attracted by young Jurgensen. But there could be no comparison surely between the two—not when she had seen what Monterey could be, when he had revealed by his acting his potentiality as a lover.

Sven was sitting in a hard, straight-backed chair; he was still dressed like a Mormon missionary, in a neat dark suit, with a white shirt and a black tie. He was not unattractive, not by any means. But in comparison with Monterey . . . Adrian shrugged. How could one tell? Perhaps Sarita pictured herself as the huntress casting herself in an aggressive role.

There she was now, slim and lax, caught up in Pablo's arms; she seemed completely absorbed in the part she was portraying, but perhaps out of the corner of her eye, she was appraising Sven's air of innocence. It took all sorts to make a world.

'Excellent, excellent,' Murray was saying, 'couldn't be better. Now I think we all deserve refreshment.'

That was Adrian's duty. As deputy stage-manager. He went round taking orders. 'What can I get you?' he said to Sven.

'Scotch, please.'

'So you're beginning to find yourself at home with alcohol?'

'I'm beginning to wonder how I managed all those years without it.'

Sven was sitting next to Sarita. He brought Sven his scotch and Sarita a campari soda.

'Have you got around yet to one of Madame Porte's martinis?' he asked Sven.

'I thought Porte's was a tea and cake shop.'

'So it is, but it's something else besides.'

He made a story of it. Madame Porte sold the best chocolates, the best cakes, she served the best tea, coffee, and chocolate in Tangier. Her shop had at the start been largely patronised by elderly British ladies, but such ladies, she discovered, liked to have their morning tea laced with gin. This was a taste that could be developed into a profitable and convenient side line, but it had to be a legitimate side line. She acquired a license to sell liquor, and because she insisted on everything she did, being served supremely well, she installed a first class Spanish barman. His speciality was the dry martini. He served it in a plain German wine glass. It was a lagoon-sized beverage—the equal of two ordinary martinis. One martini at a session was as much as most of his clients could take. He kept the glass very cold. A sliver of lemon peel curved inside its rim; the first sip sent a shiver along one's nerves. Its special flavour was his secret. He put something in. There were those who said it was distilled olive juice. 'You've tried it of course,' he said to Sarita.

'Of course.'

'Is there anything you haven't tried?'

'If anyone could introduce me to it, I'd be his slave for life. Or hers,' she added.

'Don't you think it would be a good idea if we introduced this young man to one?'

'I think it would be a very excellent idea.'

'What about next Sunday after church?'

'At half past twelve?'

'Just the right time for it.'

And that should start the ball rolling, Adrian thought. If there was a ball to roll.

Next Sunday Adrian arrived in Porte's at quarter past twelve. The young Moroccan—to Adrian he was known as

Hassoun—was seated at a table in the window. Adrian joined him. 'I am not going to tell you what any of this is about, at present. But there is an important change of method that I learnt about in London. I am myself going to take a far more active part in our work. I am in fact going to direct a cell of my own. In a quarter of an hour, I shall be joined by a young Spanish woman whom perhaps you know by sight. She is the daughter-in-law of the Spanish Consul General. You do not need to bother about her. The young man is called Sven Jurgensen. He is an American working at the American school. I want you to try to become his friend. I shall introduce you to him as Majid Abdul Khamas. Do not stay with us at the table. I shall ask you to stay with us, but you must say that you have an engagement somewhere else. You should not find it difficult to get to know Sven. He goes to the film shows that the American Consulate gives. You can easily join that. Now tell me about that prisoner. What did you make of him?'

'Nothing much so far.'

'Do you think you are likely to?'

'We got on quite well. There's a girl in Tangier that he wanted me to talk to.'

'Have you seen her yet?'

'I'm seeing her tonight.'

'Good. By the way, I'm not happy about those meetings of ours at the Café de Paris. They're risky. You know that shop in the Rue Bruxelles that's run by a Russian. It's called Italico. I buy my papers there. I'll go there every morning when my office closes. There's a bookshelf that's screened from the manager's desk. If you have anything for me you can meet me there any afternoon just after one. Ah, here they come now. They are early; just as well.'

Both he and the Moroccan stood up as the young couple came across. 'May I present to you Abdul Majid Khamas,' he said, 'a lifelong resident of this city. Señora Jerez and Mr Sven Jurgensen.'

Hassoun bowed, but did not shake hands. 'Enchanted,' he said. 'I must now be on my way. I must thank you Monsieur Simms for granting me this interview.'

'Don't let us drive you away,' Sarita said. 'We are early.'

The Moroccan smiled. 'I have already had my little talk with Monsieur Simms. I have another interview this morning.'

He bowed from the waist and he was gone. Sarita watched him. 'A handsome creature, that,' she said. She said it on a note of slight interrogation, as though she would appreciate some information about him. But Adrian did not give it. He turned to the bar. He raised three fingers. 'I don't need to give orders here,' he said, 'they know what I take. Unless, Sarita, you'd like something different. The cocktail maisons are very good.'

'They are more than very good. They are supreme in their own way. But I want to be a part of Sven's new experience. I want to share it with him, sip by sip. Your first Porte's martini, Sven. This is something that you will not forget.'

11

The following week in Oklahoma, Beryl prepared for the dance at the Country Club. She was joining her sister's party. There would be no special beau for her. It was the kind of dance where parties mixed. The Fergusons were taking seven or eight guests. There would be more men than women.

'Does he know that I'll be there?' she had asked Daphne. Daphne had shrugged. 'As likely to be "no" as "yes".'

Quite definitely it was 'no'. She recognised that the moment that he saw her. He started; his eyes widened; he stared, then smiled; hesitated, then came across. She had seen him first standing behind a group seated at a table. She could only see his chest and shoulders; now, she recognised that he had not put on weight. He moved with his former, feline grace.

'This is a surprise,' he said.

'Not to me. I'd heard that you would be here.'

'Why didn't you warn me?'

'I wanted to see how surprised you'd look.'

'In that case, let's dance.'

The first time they had danced together, he had not talked. Nor did he now. He danced with the same confidence, the same authority. He did not hold her close, but she was conscious of his fingers on her shoulder; his long, lean fingers. She remembered how that first time he had slid his right leg between hers. That was four years ago. She was now a married woman, entitled to experience, with the right to be audacious. He slid his long leg between hers, just as he had then, but now she responded to its pressure. The music stopped. He stood away. 'Four years ago we had a dinner date,' he said. 'Don't you think it would be a good idea if I took up my rain check?'

'A very good idea.'

'What about tomorrow?'

'Tomorrow would be fine.'

They were right back to where they had been four years before.

He took her to the Round Tower revolving restaurant.

'What can I offer you,' he asked, 'what do you miss in Tangier?'

'There's a dearth of Bourbon. A whisky sour to start with.'

'And what in the way of food?'

'Morocco's a Moslem country. I'd like pork chops.'

'What about wine?'

'Any red French wine. Moroccan wines are plentiful and cheap and wholesome. But that's where it ends.'

'You're making it very easy for me.'

She sipped the whisky sour with appreciation. What a relief after all those gin and tonics and those sangrias.

They were twelve stories up. No other tall building interfered with the view past city sprawl to a far skyline. Out there were the shapes an Oklahoman knew, oil derricks and the ever-nodding monsters beneath them. Scallops of telegraph wires narrowed to the horizon where now the sun was sinking.

'That's what I really miss most, I think. The vast slow sunsets here.'

'Our Big Sky,' he said. 'It makes you feel there's no one else in the whole world. It's an injunction to concentrate upon ourselves.'

That should not be difficult, she thought. 'Tell me about yourself,' he said.

'There isn't much to tell.'

Adrian, she said, was in the Foreign Office. That meant a move every three years or so.

'That means not having a home, doesn't it?'

'For the time being.'

'Don't you miss a home?'

'Not yet.'

'How old is he?'

'Thirty-five.'

'He may start missing one in a year or two.'

'He may.'

'How did you meet?'

She told him.

'That sounds romantic.'

'These things usually are, aren't they?'

'They ought to be.'

'Wasn't yours?'

He answered that obliquely. 'Your letter was a great shock to me,' he said.

'I'm sorry.'

'I had been in Houston for an interview that I'd hoped would lead to something, and that hadn't. I was despondent. When I got back there was your letter, lying on the table by my bed. Oh, well, I thought, this will make up for everything. I propped it on the mantlepiece. I unpacked my suitcase. I looked at it while I hung up my suit. I postponed the opening in the way a schoolboy leaves the best cake till last. Then, when I did open it . . .' He paused.

'When did you open it?' she asked.

'I quoted a line of poetry, I've forgotten whose. Something about the pillared firmament being rottenness and earth's base built on stubble.'

'All that on the strength of a single dance?'

'But such a dance. I knew how I was feeling. I thought it would be the same with you. During those three months other women had not existed for me. I hardly noticed them.'

She smiled. 'You were able to console yourself pretty quickly, so I've been told,' she said.

'That was a gesture I made for myself.'

'On the rebound, like the hero in a novel.'

'More or less.'

'I hope it turned out all right.'

'She's in Reno now.'

'I see.'

There was a pause. 'Is there anyone else?' she asked.

'Not on my side. Maybe there is on hers.'

'What makes you suspect that?'

'She was so ready to get divorced.'

'It was your suggestion then?'

'Yes.'

'Why?'

'There seemed no point in going on. We hadn't any children. We were meaning less and less to each other.'

'Did you quarrel much?'

He shook his head. 'Hardly ever. There wasn't enough electricity for that.'

'I see.'

She was glad that was how it was. She wouldn't be interfering with someone else. Whatever there was between her and McCrudden, it would be their own. She had sometimes, no, she had often wondered how she would feel, how she would act if she found herself attracted by another man. Sooner or later she was bound to be. The need for novelty, the thrill of the untried, of the unexpected, the wondering 'What would it be like with him?' Of having new sides of herself explored. Was anything in life more exciting? She could not believe that she had done with that forever, at the age of twenty-four. He leaned forward across the table. The look in his eyes was tender.

'Seeing you again like this,' he said, 'it seems as though those four years hadn't happened, that we are just where we were then.'

The pork chops were set before them. They looked excellent. They were excellent. She had forgotten how good they could be. He had ordered a half bottle of Burgundy. 'We can have a sweet German wine with the dessert,' he said.

She had forgotten how good a good Burgundy could be. She took a second deeper sip. The world seemed a very pleasant place.

'Are your chops all right?' he asked.

'They're fine.'

'You're going very slowly with them.'

'I don't feel very hungry.'

'Neither do I.'

Each had left one of the chops untouched by the time the wine was finished.

'What about that dessert?' he asked.

'I'm not sure I need one.'

'Just coffee then?'

'Just coffee.'

'And a liqueur?'

'No, thank you. No.'

They had finished their coffee by half past nine. 'On our way?' he asked.

She nodded. What now? she wondered. It was up to him. Sooner or later something like this had been bound to happen. She was glad it was happening like this.

He swung the car northwards on to the Edmund road. Where was he taking her? She was curious, excited, and expectant. This was new, something really new. To be driving beside him in the night, each knowing what was in the other's mind, with no word said. Before they had even kissed.

'There's a lover's lane down here,' he said.

So he was not going to take her to a motel, not right away. She was grateful to him for that. It carried her back to college days. Petting in a parked car. Then after a time he'd say, 'I can't stand any more of this . . .' It was going to be good. It was going to be very good.

He took his right hand from the wheel, put his arm round her shoulders, his fingers caressing the soft skin of her upper arm. She leaned toward him. 'Is it far?' she asked.

'The next crossroad. Not half a mile.'

Half a mile. Two minutes and she would be in his arms. She closed her eyes. Two minutes and the most exciting passage of her life would have begun. She leaned against him as his arm tightened round her. Two minutes, less now, and then . . .

It happened so quickly that she did not know what had happened. There was a jerk as he swung the car to the left, a crash as they struck a car parked without lights, as they reeled off the road into a post.

As accidents go it was not a serious one. The car was not a total wreck. Beryl herself was not more than bruised and shaken, but McCrudden had his left leg broken above the knee. He would be in hospital for at least a week.

Two afternoons later Beryl sat beside him. 'The dice have been loaded against us, haven't they?' he said. No need to elaborate the point. She was grateful to him that he recognised they could talk in shorthand. 'I've been trying to console myself with the thought that maybe it was providential.'

'How did you work that out?'

'Suppose that we had had nine days together, they would have been wonderful, I'm sure of that. But when they were over there'd have been nothing left. A chapter that closed. That is true, isn't it?'

'That's true.'

'Whereas with things the way they are . . . We might, who knows, meet under quite different conditions in ten years' time.'

'That's a long way off.'

'It seems so now. But in ten years you'll be only thirty-four, I won't be forty. We'll have the best of everything ahead of us, and that sense of unfinished business.'

He was thinking about her in very much the same way that four years back she had been thinking about him. She had not wanted to spoil for the sake of a few hectic days the possibility of something that might prove durable.

'It isn't likely, I know that,' he said. 'But I need to console myself.'

And indeed he did look pathetic, he who was so strong and vigorous, lying there helpless, strapped and bandaged. He needed to be consoled. She leaned across him and bent her head. Their first kiss. Maybe it would not be their last.

On the way back she stopped at Western Union. There was no point in her staying on . . .

Adrian's second thought when he opened her cable was, 'Friday, the day that new man arrives. We can have that dinner at the Consulate.'

PART TWO

PART TWO

12

Beryl had a corner seat on the evening Iberia plane. Through the window she could see the white and blue towers and minarets of Tangier. It was half-past seven. The sun was sinking and there was an ochre-red haze over the sun-scorched countryside. She was feeling good and rested. Arriving in Madrid at eight she had left the airport and booked herself a single room at the Ritz, which was conveniently close to the Prado. She had had a bath, four hours' sleep, a sandwich lunch, spent two hours at the Prado; then had her hair fixed at the airport. She had had a reasonable supper on the plane and was now in the mood for anything. It was good to be back in Tangier. It was good to be back with Adrian. She had brought him a couple of amusing sport shirts. She had chosen him—instead of sherry, which he could get at a price in Tangier—a bottle of Spanish Red Wine, Marquis de Riscal, which he could only get by driving all the way to Ceuta. She was in a receptive mood, ready to be warmly welcomed.

The plane had not been crowded. She should get through Customs quickly. She could see him over the heads of her fellow passengers. He was standing beside a man whom she did not recognise; a tall, thin English-looking man, moustached, otherwise clean-shaven; slightly older, it seemed, than Adrian. Adrian left him as she came through immigration. His arms were firm about her shoulders. She noticed that he had been drinking whisky. 'Be careful of my packages,' she said.

'I'm afraid we've got a guest,' he said.

'Oh.' That explained the smell of whisky.

'He's my new boss from Gibraltar. He came across this evening. There wasn't time to get him into town between the arrival of his plane and yours. So we stayed out here.'

'Is he staying in the flat?'

'No. At the Villa de France.'

'How long will he be here?'

'Only two days. He's going back Sunday morning. It's a fiendish nuisance. But it was all fixed up before I knew that you were coming.'

'Of course. Of course. What are our plans now?'

'To check him into the Villa de France, go back and dump your suitcase, then take him out to dinner.'

'Where?'

'The Himaldi. He should have Moroccan cooking.'

'Fine. Fine. What do you know about him?'

'Only what I've picked up over two whisky sodas. Which isn't much. Isn't that your suitcase?'

'You ought to know it by this time.'

It was the same carpet-covered case that she had brought to Florence. He had never seen one like it. It was easily recognisable at Customs. 'Have you anything to declare?' he asked.

'Only a nonsense or two for you.'

They were through the Customs in three minutes. The officials were unpredictable. Once in so many times they opened every package. This was not one of them. 'Have I to be on my guard against anything?' she asked.

'Not as far as I can see.'

She looked at Adrian's new boss cautiously. He had an accent that she could not place. It might have been cockney. It might have been Australian. He made himself agreeable. 'It's an infliction to have an unexpected guest thrust on you after a trip like that. I'll do my best to be unexacting.'

He sat in the front of the car with Adrian. 'It's my first visit to Morocco,' he said. 'It's my first visit to an Arab country, for that matter. I shall exhaust you with my questions. What are those large hats some women wear?'

'They're Berbers.'

'I know about them.' He did not neglect Beryl. 'Your husband tells me you're from Oklahoma. That's one of the states I somehow didn't get to. I had my chance. I was stationed in Albuquerque once. I flew over your state several times. It looked very flat.'

128

'It is very flat.'

'That put me off.'

'It puts a lot of people off.' They laughed together. 'He's OK,' she thought. 'He's got the same sense of humour as myself.'

'I hope you'll be comfortable at the Villa. You ought to stay with us, of course. But when you see our flat, you'll realise why. We don't have a spare bedroom.'

'To protect yourselves against house guests.'

'Exactly.'

'Isn't that carrying security to an extreme?'

'That's not the main reason. They keep cutting off the water. The two of us can manage on our own, just; but with a house guest, no.'

'I see your point.'

Again they chuckled. 'I can manage him,' she thought.

They passed the Boulevard de Paris on the way to the Villa de France. 'Within walking distance,' she said as they deposited him and his suitcase. 'We'll be back within fifteen minutes.'

They were back in less. She did not want to unpack now. 'He seems all right,' she said.

'I'm glad that you're getting on with him.'

'Does that mean you're not?'

'I'm playing this with my cards very close against my chest.'

The Himaldi was one of the town's best Moroccan restaurants. It was inside the Medina; registered as a hotel, first floor was set out with low banquette tables. It had high stained-glass windows. It was hung with rugs. In the centre against a wall four musicians sat on a raised dais. It was patronised by package tours. 'It won't be crowded tonight,' Adrian reassured them. 'Only two smallish groups.' They had a table facing the orchestra. They sat side by side, with Groves between them. They were each handed a large wooden platter with the menu inscribed on it in English, French, and Spanish. 'You'll have to tell me what to choose,' he said.

'With the clock going forward, it's only about lunch-time for me,' said Beryl, 'I've had four meals in the space of time in which I normally have three, including a very pleasant supper-snack on the plane. A pastella will be all that I can manage.'

'I am less fortunately placed, or rather I should say more fortunately placed. I'm hungry and ready to indulge myself. What are all these things? Harira, for example.'

Adrian explained. 'A hot thick spiced soup; lentils is the chief ingredient. The Moroccans take it during Ramadan, when the gun goes at the end of the day. They eat it with honey cakes and dates. It is very good but very filling. If I had it, my appetite would be destroyed.'

'Then I'll just have three spoonfuls, but I've got to try it. What's this Pastella that your wife recommends?'

'A pancake stuffed with pigeons and almonds. It's fairly light.'

'Then let's have that next. What about Couscous?'

'That's very filling too.'

'Then don't let's worry about that. What about those things on skewers.'

'Kebabs—Brochettes. Let's divide four between us. Then let's have a Tajine. That's their main meat dish. A sort of stew, they put prunes in it. If we have that and then some cakes, with tea to follow——'

'And am I supposed to eat this with my fingers?'

'No, not a Tajine.'

'That's a relief. And what do we have to drink. Mohammed issued a ban on wine.'

'But the Moroccans make wine and like to have us drink it.'

'Then that's what we'll do, won't we?'

'And the red wine is better than the white.'

'It usually is as you get nearer the equator.'

The waiter produced a bottle of Chaudsoleil. 'That's a name that can mean anything,' Adrian said. 'Some of it is reasonable.'

Groves took a sip. 'This is something to quaff, not sip,'

he said, and took a substantial swallow. 'Yes, that's better, that's a good deal better. We'll be having another bottle, I presume?'

'If this chap wasn't my boss, I could quite like him,' Adrian thought.

As it was, he was grateful for having Beryl on the other side of him to monopolise his conversation. It was impossible to have a general conversation between three when they were sitting side by side and most of the time leaning back. Beryl seemed to be enjoying herself. The conversation was lively. She was laughing half the time. She was also looking very pretty. He wished that Groves was not here. He wished he was alone with her. He had a lot, more than a lot, to tell her, and always after a separation it took them a little while to find their way back to one another. Tomorrow there was that dinner at the Consulate, and he would have to spend the whole of the day with Groves. He would have to find out what Groves had upon his mind. Groves was not an easy man to place. In his early forties, he was a north countryman. He had not been to a University, called up with 'A' levels for military service, he had got a commission, had volunteered for extra service. He had been seconded to intelligence. He was presumably highly intelligent, but he hadn't—in the way that Marshall had—been raised in the same stable as himself.

Groves had, during that forty minutes at the airport, talked exclusively about himself. It was as though he had been saying, 'I'm the chap you have to deal with now, and it's best for all of us if you realise the kind of chap I am.'

Marshall had not needed to explain himself, but Groves had, and that to Adrian made sense. They would meet tomorrow, each knowing who the other was. Marshall had been a member of the pre-war Establishment; he had known from the start that the worst could not happen to him, unless he put up the kind of black that a man of his type had not the right to do. Groves was different. He was a lone wolf. He would help to the limits of his capacity anyone who was in the same category. He was capable of loyalty, but he would be merciless to anyone who got in the way of his ambitions.

And that was restful, Adrian thought.

He let himself drift out of the conversation. The Pastella had been followed by brochettes. They were now taking their share of the Tajine. It was a good Tajine. The second bottle of Chaudsoleil was almost empty. A third was needed. If a quarter of it was returned to stock, what did that matter, when wine was at ten dirhams a bottle. He waved to the waiter.

There was a clap of hands. This was the signal for the Moroccan dancer carrying on his head a large brass tray laden with candles and cups of tea. Adrian nudged Groves' elbow. 'This is what we came to see.'

The Moroccan dancer had grace and charm. He was clad in a long gilt caftan. He swayed. He undulated. He lowered himself upon his heels. He had an ambivalent sexuality. Women could respond to him, and so could men. It was a difficult dance to execute. There was always a slight danger of the tray with all its candles slipping. It did, every now and again; perhaps designedly to create an atmosphere of suspense. 'This is incredible. I've seen nothing like this,' said Groves.

Mint tea was served. 'If you drink this after a Moroccan meal,' said Adrian, 'your digestion will survive. Don't risk coffee.'

'I'll be glad not to.'

The orchestra was active still, but there was a sudden and instantaneous movement from three-quarters of the tables. The two package tours had exhausted their sponsor's hospitality. The four remaining tables were occupied by independent tourists.

'Time for us to pack up, isn't it?' said Groves. It was ten past eleven.

'And now for home,' said Adrian after they had dropped him at the Villa de France.

He glanced at Beryl. She was crouched in the corner of the car. Yesterday afternoon, he could not be bothered to work out how long ago that was in terms of altered hours, she had been in Oklahoma. She was now in a different universe.

He swung the car towards the garage. The guardian of the street, a self-appointed mercenary who was supposed to keep watch against intruders, came galloping up the Avenue. He fancied that by opening the door of the garage, he justified the fortnightly payment of ten dirhams that Adrian accorded him. He never seemed to be around when there was luggage to be loaded or unloaded. 'I wonder if he is responsible for that key,' thought Adrian.

'And now to get unpacked,' said Beryl. She looked tired. She must be very tired—yes, but even so . . . He hadn't seen her for a month and such a month. 'One little drink first,' he said.

'Oh no, too late.'

'Please, please,' he urged. She hesitated. 'I haven't seen you for a month,' he pleaded. 'I haven't seen you this evening for a second.'

'OK.'

She sat on the long sofa in the living room. She picked up a copy of *Le Matin*. She turned to the second page. 'Juliette de Mon Coeur' had introduced a new situation. She must get Adrian to put her in the picture.

He was beside her with a tall glass, filled with an orange-coloured liquid. 'It looks cool and strong,' she said.

'It is. It's got whisky in it. Quite a lot.'

She took a long slow sip.

'It's very good,' she said. During her stay in Madrid, she had bought some Maja perfume. The open window drove its fragrance across the sofa. It was a month since he had sat beside her. He leant across. He took the glass from her hands. 'That can wait,' he said. He slid on to his knees beside her, slid his arms under her knees and swung her legs on to the sofa. 'Oh, no,' she said, 'Oh, no.'

He slid a cushion underneath her hips. He took her face between his hands. She tried to pull away, to turn her head from side to side; there was a fierce, brief struggle, then suddenly she gave way; turning to meet him, vibrant and responsive. In ninety seconds it was over. Their heavy gasps sank to an even breathing. 'Thank you,' she said. 'Thank you.'

Next morning, on his way back home to breakfast, Adrian called in at the Villa de France. Groves was sitting on the terrace. 'Exactly the right hotel for me. Exactly. Thank you. Now what are you planning for this morning?'

'That depends on what you want yourself.'

'Does it? I suppose it does. What I need is an all-in picture of the place.'

'You haven't given yourself much time for that.'

'Haven't I? Perhaps I haven't, but I'm not a journalist writing an article on "How Tangier's changed". I'm trying to see how the boys we're watching are seeing it, as a base for what they want to do.'

'I'd find it easier to do that if I knew whom we were watching and for what.'

'Didn't Marshall explain that?'

'Not in any detail.'

'I see. Yes, I think I see. He belongs to the Old School who held that you only need to know as much as you require to carry out your immediate job. That's sound enough, but it gives the man above you too much authority. You can never be sure that he may not be operating strategically on information that you don't possess. How has your job been explained?'

'To see what the Basques are plotting, whether they are using Ceuta as a base for their operations. From that incident a few weeks ago, it looks as though they were.'

'I gather that you played a very useful part in that exercise.'

'It was a piece of luck for me.'

'It's always luck when the coin comes up the way you've called. The point is that you made the right use of that luck. What did your wife make of that?'

It was the question that Adrian had known was bound to come. He had his answer ready. 'I had to tell her something of what was in the air.'

134

'What did you tell her?'

'That it was part of my job to watch the Basque separatists.'

'Why did you have to tell her that?'

'She began to be suspicious.'

'Why?'

He explained why. 'I see, I see.'

There was a pause. 'Your wife could be very useful to you, couldn't she?' Groves said.

'She is very useful.'

He changed the subject.

'My chief difficulty,' he said, 'is that I don't know what our people in Whitehall want to have happen here.'

'Is that something that you need to know?'

'I'd like to know whose side I'm on.'

'I can see that. We'll have another talk about all this tomorrow. In the meantime, we can sign the Consulate book.'

They stood outside the main gate of the Consulate. Groves looked down the hill. 'That leads to the Grand Socco, doesn't it?'

'Yes.'

'I'll want to go there, and I want to see the Petit Socco. I've heard so much about it. We'll have a mint tea there. But first I want to see where that man of ours was killed.'

They turned left towards the Place de France.

'I like to be able to picture everything,' Groves said. 'You remember, don't you, how in the Western Desert Montgomery kept a picture of Rommel on the door of his caravan to remind him of the kind of man that he was up against. I've never forgotten that. It's so easy for us sitting at a desk, surrounded with files and folders to forget that we're dealing with human beings, not entries in a ledger. Now let's reconstruct it. This is the Café de Paris. Right. You are sitting at that corner table. The fellow comes across, and you change papers. Then he crosses the Place. I want to follow his route exactly. He crosses here. Now that's a one-way street coming down past the Café de France. There couldn't be any danger there. Then there's this other Café. Now we come to the two-way street. The Rue de Fez. There's a taxi rank on the

135

left. There'll be cars coming down past the rank. Now from the other side, on the south-bound road, there are cars coming into it. You say in two directions. That can be, yes, I can see that it's confusing.'

'You have to look two ways. There are the cars coming up over your right shoulder, from the Place de France. Then there are the cars coming down the hill that you think are going on across the place but that suddenly swing left into the Rue de Fez.'

'Let's stand here and watch a minute.'

'It doesn't happen every time. Not once in a dozen times, perhaps. That's why it's dangerous. You forget that you've got to be on your guard.'

They stood on the east side of the road, below the taxi rank. Car after car went by. 'I see your point,' said Groves. They went on waiting. Car after car. Then, at last, two cars, one from the Rue Belgique and one from the Rue Pasteur turned simultaneously into the Rue de Fez. 'Yes, yes, I see,' Groves said. 'You're looking over your right shoulder, and then suddenly there's a car coming at you straight. If one was off one's guard . . .'

They watched a little longer. Groves looked at his watch. 'Five minutes, and only once those two cars side by side. It would have to be a considerable coincidence. If I was planning to bump a man off by riding over him, I don't think that this is the way I'd choose. What happened at the Inquest?'

'Both had insurance. No one took much interest.'

'Did you find out anything about the drivers?'

'One was from Tetouan.'

'That's nearer danger. Has a tab been kept on him?'

'We can't give orders to the Moroccan police.'

'I know. I know. Wait a second. I'll walk across there on my own.' At that very moment, once again, two cars swung simultaneously into the Rue de Fez. On his return he shook his head. 'It might be,' he said, 'and again, it mightn't.'

He crossed the Place de France and looked into the Café de Paris. 'Which is your table?'

136

Adrian pointed it out.

'Do they know who you are?' Groves asked.

'I've no idea. They call me Monsieur Adrian.'

'Monsieur Adrian, I like that. Yes, that's good.'

'There's a good view of the Kasbah from just down the street,' said Adrian.

There was a short, seventy-yard promenade, from which the ground sloped steeply to the lower town. It was planted with red oleanders. Boot-boys plied their trade along it. Across the valley you could see the stout Portuguese bastions of the Medina and above them the turrets of the Kasbah. 'They built things that were meant to last in those days,' Adrian said.

The hillside was crowded with small buildings, some blue, but the majority of them white. 'I'd suggest,' said Adrian, 'that we take a taxi to the Kasbah, then walk down through the old town; that will land us into the Petit Socco for our mint tea. It should be about half past ten by then; we can think out our plans.'

'Let's stand here for a minute first. I want to absorb this.'

There was a mist across the Straits, blurring the Spanish hills. 'How often can you see Gibraltar?'

'More often than not.'

'Yet we don't see you. At least I never have. Hi, there's a taxi.'

It was a roundabout drive. They went through the Marshan, the original residential sector. There were square-built, dignified Victorian-style houses. The streets were narrow, then suddenly through a gap, twenty feet above them were the fortifications and the narrow fortress gate. 'That's one of the things I was resolved to see,' said Groves. 'Dela-croix painted it.'

'He knows more about this place than I do,' Adrian thought.

Later they sat in the Petit Socco sipping a mint tea. It was not more than six yards wide. It had cafés on each side of it. 'In 1938 during the Spanish Civil War, both sides used to come here on leave,' Groves said. 'The Loyalists sat on the right hand side, the rebels on the left. They never spoke to one another, though now and again some of them would recognise each other. There were no incidents. They respected each other's leave, then with their leave over, they went back to kill each other. There's something very civilised about the Spanish.'

The west side of the Place was now in sunshine, and the café tables were packed with long-haired hippies, male and female. 'I'm glad they're not our problem,' Groves said.

'Can we be sure they aren't?'

'I think we can. They aren't out to cause trouble, though they may become troublesome because of "pot". They aren't the people who drive into agents in the Place de France.'

'Who are our problem?'

'That's what I wish we knew. Some of them are genuine patriots, but half of them, at least the way I see it, are nihilists. They are at outs with the world. They don't believe in anything. They feel that things as they are couldn't be any worse, and that if they smash up what exists, someone may build up something better. Make a political happening of it. Not that I think they really go that far. Do you remember what Byron said about having simplified his politics into a detestation of all existing governments? I believe that's how most of the people with whom we are dealing operate.'

'Some of them are in it for the money surely?'

'Chaps like the one who was knocked over by the car. Yes certainly. What about the man who's come to take his place?'

'I can't place him, quite. He's a Gibraltarian. I've an idea that he may be working for the Spanish.'

'A double agent?'

'In a sense.'

'But we are not working against the Spanish.'

'We're not?'

'Not so as you'd notice it, as people used to say.'

We're not getting very far, thought Adrian. 'I'm wondering what to do next,' he said.

'What would you do yourself if I weren't here?'

138

'Lunch at the Yacht Club.'

'Then why don't we do that?'

'It wouldn't show you much of Tangier, of the life of Tangier, that's to say.'

'What's the alternative?'

'A picnic.'

'What's the idea of that?'

'Most of us go on picnics now. It would give you an idea of how we restore ourselves.'

'A picnic? I'd never have thought of that. It's something I never do. Something that I've not done since I was a schoolboy, staying with my aunts. Would it mean going far?'

'Fifteen minutes drive.'

'Well . . .'

'We could go back to the flat and warn Beryl. She can fix up part of it. Then we can go into town, pick up a thing or two. Have a martini at Porte's. That's something you mustn't miss. Beryl could pick us up there. Martinis are too strong for her. Then after lunch you could have a long siesta to prepare you for his Nibs tonight.'

'Now this is making sense.' Groves looked appreciatively round Porte's coffee room. 'Those murals, the ladies and gentlemen of *La Belle Epoque*. Paris in 1890. That's when I'd liked to have lived; twenty-five years old, with enough pocket money to keep myself amused. There's always a snag though. If I had, I'd have probably contracted syphilis.'

'What a thing to say.'

'Obvious, my dear Watson. Have you read the Goncourt Journals?'

'No.'

'If you do, you'll see the way it was. They all had it, Daudet, Maupassant, Baudelaire. There weren't any free-hearted amateurs. Only ladies of the chorus and the corridors, and they had no proper cure. Probably the world we live in isn't all that bad.'

'You're married?'

'Naturally, I don't see how one avoids it, if one likes women and can afford to. Not that I want not to be, I can assure you.'

Adrian wondered how that marriage was working out. Not too well perhaps.

'This *is* the goods,' Groves said. 'I'm glad you brought me here. It fills in the picture. Do you meet your agents here?'

'Now and again. I don't like to do anything unusual that might seem suspicious.'

'I guess you're right. You remember that story of Poe's where the man on the run hid a letter in the most obvious place. In a torn envelope in a letter rack.'

If I'm going to tell him about my flat being broken into, now's the time, Adrian thought. But he wasn't certain that he wanted to tell him, yet. He wanted to keep something up his sleeve. To play this in his own way, in his own time. He would relish the opportunity of surprising Groves. You had to be careful with ambitious men, who played the game by their own rules—who made up the rules as they went along, to suit their interests.

'It makes one wonder,' Adrian said.

'Makes one wonder what?'

'When the next real thing will happen.'

'Not knowing is what makes this job fun.'

'You find it fun?'

'If I didn't, I wouldn't stay in. There's not all that money, and there's no fame attached. You won't get a *Times* obituary when you check out. But you wake up every morning thinking that something new may happen. My, but this martini's good.'

By the time the glass was empty, the effect of its contents on Groves was obvious. He was warmer, more expansive, more talkative, but he still showed no temptation to be confidential.

On Beryl's arrival, however, his manner appreciably changed.

'We've missed you,' he said, 'but maybe it's as well not to have had you here distracting my attention from the martini. One thing at a time. When I was young I used to find that being with an attractive female made me lose my appetite. It was the test I applied to myself, if I found myself enjoying my lunch, I'd say to myself, "No, this isn't the real thing," but if I found myself leaving a grilled sole untouched, I'd think, "Ho, ho, here we are again." '

'He's not a man's man at all,' Adrian thought. He's only at his ease with a woman. I don't think we're going to have a very easy evening with his nibs.

As the night before at the Himaldi, Groves concentrated his entire attention on Beryl. He was an appreciative and co-operative guest. He was clearly enjoying himself.

They took him to a small patch of ground on the edge of town that had been bought some twenty years back by a French–American who had arranged it as a picnic spot. Trees and flowers had been planted. There were three small ponds; there were four round, cement tables with cement stools beside them. There was an oven. It was still a private property, and there was a guardian who watched over any cars that were parked beside his hut. Only friends of the owner were supposed to use it and, in fact, not so many residents of Tangier were aware of its existence. Adrian regarded his knowledge of it as one of the pleasant requisites of his job.

Groves was enthusiastic. 'I begin to think your husband is a far more effective operator than I had supposed. I don't think that Marshall had an idea how good he is.'

'In that case,' said Beryl, 'I hope that you're going to recommend him for a raise.'

'Now that's how I like to hear a wife talk. That's because you're an American, perhaps.'

'In America, before they give a man a job, they have a look at his wife to see how she'll fit the part.'

'Didn't Marshall come across to check you over?'

'Is that why you came?'

'It's why I'll want to come again.'

Beryl was good at picnics. She had prepared a chicken salad. The cheese was fresh. She had a bowl of strawberries. The coffee was hot and strong. She had also a special ice bag for keeping the white wine cool. 'This,' she said, 'is my special contribution to the household. Adrian hasn't seen it yet. I only found it on my last day.'

It was very quiet in the wood. They were completely shut in by trees and flowers; they were unconscious of the wind that, as nearly always in Tangier, was rustling the palm fronds, yet you only had to walk a few yards up the path to see, between the trees and across a valley, the spires of the Marshan.

'How often do you come here?' Groves asked.

'Every other weekend in the summer. Every week in the spring and autumn.'

'I'll certainly be finding excuses for coming over here. What do they think in Oklahoma when you tell them about all this?'

'They never ask me. They are not curious; they are only interested in themselves. They want to tell me their latest gossip and how much the Smiths have spent on their new swimming pool. Isn't that how you find it when you get back to England?'

The talk moved briskly, lightly, easily. Beryl was a wonderful wife in ways like this. What luck he had had to find her. What a fluke after all. Marriage was the last thing he had had in mind that day in Florence. Suppose she had been another kind of woman. What a mess their life together would have become in a job like this.

'What about going down to the beach now for our siesta. Then a swim afterwards,' he said.

'Will you be wearing a black tie tonight?' Groves asked.

'Everyone's very casual about dress here, but I think Littlejohn prefers it.'

'It seems no extra trouble, since one has to change.'

'We'll probably be dining out of doors. It may get cool later on. Personally I like to have something round my neck.'

'Will it be a large party?'

'As far as I know, only the Spanish Consul General and his daughter-in-law.'

They did dine out of doors, on the terrace, in a protected corner, where they were not conscious of the wind. The table was alight with flowers. Littlejohn had Beryl on his right, with the Spanish Consul General on his left. Sarita was at the

142

foot, with Groves on her left and Adrian on her right. Littlejohn raised his glass to Jerez. 'How I wish I could offer you as good wines as you offer me.'

'I have no complaints against Moroccan wines.'

'They are not as good as Spanish.'

'Ah, well.'

'Whisky and gin are the only commodities that I can, as one says, import in the "diplomatic bag".'

'My guests would prefer to have more whisky and less wine.'

'Not you and I though.'

'As you say, not you and I.'

Adrian had assured Groves that the dinner would be good. It was, and it was rounded off with a robust tawny port. 'Now at last,' said Littlejohn, 'I am able to give you a glass of something that is not only good, but English, and I think that in terms of the tradition that it represents, I can say to these young ladies that the time has come for them to leave the gentlemen.'

Sarita and Beryl took their glasses to the lawn.

'Now tell me everything,' Sarita said.

Beryl smiled wryly. 'It was just a family visit.'

'Not a single heart throb?'

'Only half a one.'

'Beryl, I'm ashamed of you.'

'What about yourself?'

'Nothing of much consequence.'

'What about your Mormon?'

'The kettle's simmering.'

'When are you going to bring it to the boil?'

'That's what I ask myself.'

'How is he settling down?'

'Well enough, I'd say.'

'He's an adjunct to the Tangier Theatre?'

'Decidedly.'

'Not worrying about his fellow missionary?'

'What did you think about that, by the way?'

'What did I think about what?'

143

'About his confession.'

'More or less what you'd think I'd think.'

'And what was that?'

'That it was a terrible thing to happen to a boy like that.'

'And what did you feel about the way he behaved?'

'What else could he have done?'

'You didn't ask yourself how you'd have behaved if you'd been in his position.'

'How could I? I'm a woman.'

'Yes, but suppose it had happened to you as a woman. Suppose that you had gone out on a mission with another woman, and after a while that woman made a similar suggestion; what would you have done. What Sven did?'

'Naturally, of course.'

'You wouldn't have been tempted by the thought "this is something that I've never tried. This is my best chance of learning what it's like." '

'Good Heavens, no.'

'Are you quite sure?'

There was a mischievous, conspiratorial twinkle in Sarita's eyes. 'Is that what you'd have done?' asked Beryl.

'I reckon so.'

'You say that now, for the hell of it, but if you had actually been in that position?'

'Perhaps I have been in that position.'

'You haven't been a Mormon missionary.'

'I know, but I can have been, can't I, in a position where that particular pistol was held against my head.'

'And you thought . . .?'

'I thought exactly what I said. I thought, "This is the best opportunity I'll ever have of finding out what this is all about." And what I'm now asking myself is this, "Why didn't Sven ask himself that question?" '

They stared at one another. Sarita laughed. 'What a little innocent you are,' she said. She raised her hand and laid it against Beryl's cheek.

From the other side of the terrace came the interruption of Adrian's voice. 'The men are missing you,' he said. 'But they like sitting over the table. Won't you come back and join us?'

The evening broke up early. 'If you're catching a plane tomorrow,' said Littlejohn, 'you'll be grateful for a full night's sleep.'

'Thank you, sir. I shall.'

Adrian drove him out in the morning. Only twenty minutes, but Groves said all he had to within ten of them. 'I can guess how you feel,' he said, 'but there's no need to worry. You're not being kept in the dark. We're concerned, you and I, with tactics, not with strategy. We don't know how long Franco will be there. He's an old man, everything may change overnight. Whitehall wants the facts. We want to know what the Basque boys are plotting. They may be plotting nothing, and Whitehall may call it a day. But in the meantime, we've got to find out all we can, in any way we can. That's what I've come over to say. I wanted to see you first; to get a picture of the general set-up; to see if you're the kind of person to whom I can say that, and I find I can. Find out all you can, and in any way you can. I give you a free hand. You don't need to refer everything back to me, and don't worry about money. If you've someone you want to subsidize, you can trust your judgment.'

That day Adrian lunched with Beryl at the Yacht Club. 'This is the first time we've been alone,' he said.

'I know, and there's such a lot I want to hear.'

'There's a lot *I* want to hear.'

'Nothing that can't wait. It was just seeing old friends, chatting about old times; times and friends that you don't know about. I want to hear about London. That's us. What happened with Sonning?'

He told her what had happened with Sonning. 'That's what decided me to come back right away. I was wasting time; the sooner I got to work on the issue here the better. I've got to initiate something, and I believe I've found the way. There's another man too about whom I'm curious. That good-looking, young Tangerine Pablo Monterey.'

145

'Him, why him?'

'He's got a grouch against Franco. I only learnt that the other night. Have you seen much of him?'

'Hardly anything.'

'Then try and see something more of him. The next rehearsal is on Tuesday, isn't it; did you know, by the way, that I'm now the deputy stage manager.'

'I didn't, and I think that's fine.'

'Then let's keep one or two of them back afterwards. I want to see how they are with one another.'

'And does young Sven work into this?'

He hesitated. He had promised not to keep her in the dark, but he was more than a little in the dark himself. So much was suspicion, so much conjecture. He prevaricated, 'I've an idea that these Basque boys might think that he was someone they could use.'

'We don't want to get him into any kind of trouble.'

'On the contrary, we are trying to protect him.'

'I'm not too happy about this.'

'Neither am I. This isn't a pretty game. You remember that bomb in Ceuta?'

'I know, I know, but all the same . . .'

He leant across the table. He put his hand over hers. 'I've promised you, haven't I, that I won't keep you in the dark.'

Was he keeping that promise? He was telling her more than he would have done six months ago. He was telling her more probably than Groves was telling him. But was he telling her everything? He had not told her about that intruder into his study. Hadn't she the right to know that her house might be entered at any moment? He shrugged. How could he tell her everything. No wife could be expected to know everything. He did not know everything himself.

Next morning he took out the journal from his locked drawer. The thread lay across it in exactly the same position that it had the day before.

His pen hovered about the paper. He had to make more use now of this journal. 'Visit from Groves,' he wrote, 'have been given a free hand.' Was that enough, he asked himself.

Probably, why not. It gave the journal for the first time an air of authenticity. Groves had only just made an entrance in his life. He could use that entrance as an excuse for a change of tempo. He could start entering soon the news that he wanted the other side to have. But he must, to start with, convince the other side that the entries were genuine.

The rehearsal on the Tuesday evening was a full one.

'Let's start at the beginning,' Murray said.

'Scene one. That's Beryl, Pablo, Frieda, Margaret, Sven. This is a most important scene, it's the one that establishes the characters. It has to go right from the start. On your toes now, go.'

Pablo, the husband was on the stage alone. 'Hey there, Stella Baby,' he called out.

It was the cue for Beryl's entrance. The stage directions described her as being a gentle young woman of about twenty-five and of a background obviously quite different from her husband's. Simply by walking on to the stage she established herself as that. How pretty she was, how graceful, and her voice, 'Don't holler at me like that.' It was the right sentence to establish her as what she was. Of a different class from the others in the play.

Frieda came on in the part of Eunice. It was an important part, in the sense that it had to be done right, but it was a subsidiary role. It did not bring the actress herself into prominence. She had been promised something more impressive in the next production. But even so she looked highly decorative. She spoke clearly and her voice had an agreeable warmth. Watching her now in her part, an idea that had half-occurred to him the other night returned.

When she came off the set, he crossed to her, 'It's a hot night; you must feel thirsty. Can't I get you something?'

'I'd love a glass of red wine with some ice and rather more than a splash of soda.'

'It's on its way to you.'

He mixed himself one at the same time. 'You're going to be very good in this,' he said.

147

'Thank you.'

'There's something I rather want to say to you.'

'Yes?'

'When the rehearsal's over and we get into a series of small huddles, could you get into one with me?'

'I'll manage that.'

From the way she manoeuvred herself into a position in a corner where it would not be practical for anyone to sit on the other side of her, he suspected that she had often found herself in a situation of this kind.

'Yes?' she said.

From her tone of voice he knew that he had not to explain himself in any detail.

'That man from Gibraltar has given me a free hand,' he said.

'Ah.'

'As regards expenses.'

'That's pleasant for you.'

'I wondered if you would care to have a cut.'

'I don't see why not, do you?'

There was no need for details.

'There are one or two people here about whom I'm curious,' he said. 'In particular Pablo Monterey.'

'What do you want to know?'

'As much as you can find out. He spoke so violently about Franco the other evening. A man who speaks as violently as that might be ready to take action of some kind. Anything you can find out would be of help.'

'I'll do what I can.'

Each knew exactly what was in the other's mind.

On the following morning he tapped on her office door. He handed her an envelope. She put it into the top drawer of her desk. 'Thank you,' she said.

She opened the envelope as the door closed behind him. It contained twenty fifty-dirham notes. It was more than she had expected. She pursed her lips. Later in the morning she passed him in the passage. 'Thank you very much,' she said. She stressed the 'very'.

Adrian had told Beryl that he might be late for lunch. He called in at Italico's.

'Is the *Herald-Tribune* in?' he asked.

'Not yet.'

'Too bad.'

'Maybe later.'

'I'll be round later.' He looked at the magazines and the shelf of Penguins. His elegant Moroccan was examining them too.

'I think I should have something for you in a day or two,' the Moroccan said.

'I shall be here every morning.'

With a light step, he set out for the beach. Things were starting to develop in the way that he had hoped.

Two mornings later, Beryl was called up by Sarita. 'Something rather special for you,' she said. 'I need to bring it round when we shall be alone. When would be convenient?'

'That sounds mysterious.'

'That's how it strikes me.'

'In that case you'd better come round right away.'

Sarita was round within ten minutes. She handed across an air-mail letter with an American stamp on it. The envelope was addressed, in a handwriting that was unfamiliar to Beryl, to the niece of the Spanish Consul General. 'Go on, open it,' Sarita said. An unaddressed envelope was wrapped in a covering letter. 'Read it,' Sarita ordered.

'Dear Madam,' the letter read. 'Could you please give this letter to Mrs Adrian Simms. I do not know her address. Please could you give it to her when she is alone.'

'If that isn't mysterious, what is?' Sarita said.

Beryl looked at the postmark on the envelope. 'Oklahoma.' She smiled. It could not be from anyone but McCrudden. He had known her address all right, but he hadn't wanted her to get a letter under her husband's roof that she would find difficult to explain. He had not known Sarita's name, but she had told him that her best friend in Tangier was the Spanish

Consul General's daughter-in-law. It was rather clever of him, she thought.

'Would you like me to go away so that you can read it by yourself?'

'I'm sure there'll be nothing in it that you couldn't read.'

'Then I'll watch, waiting for that tell-tale blush.'

It was a short letter. Beryl was very conscious, as she read, of Sarita's eyes upon her. 'Dearest,' it began, 'I've just called up your house, to learn that you are leaving tomorrow; which means that I shan't be seeing you again; a disappointment. But perhaps. I don't know. There really isn't more to say. You know how I feel. And how I expect to be feeling in ten years' time. Don't forget me—not altogether. And if a change were to come into your life—You will remember, won't you? And good luck.'

A short letter, a very short one. But it touched her. In ten years' time. Who could tell how things would be in ten years' time? She refolded the letter into its envelope and put it in her bag.

'The moment I've left you'll take it out and read it all over again,' Sarita said.

'I suppose I shall.' But she did not want to discuss Mc-Crudden, not now at any rate. She changed the subject.

'Adrian interrupted us the other night,' she said. 'You were telling me about that woman who held a pistol at your head. Did you make the experiment?'

'I did.'

'And how did it work out?'

'The way that you'd expect it to.'

'You were pleased with the experiment?'

'Enough to make me decide that one day I'd myself hold a pistol at someone's head.'

'Which is what you did?'

'What do you think?'

Next morning just before lunch Adrian found his Moroccan at Italico's. 'I have news for you,' he said.

'Can you tell me here?'

'It's rather long.'

'Then I think I would prefer that we met at Porte's. As we have met there once, it will not look surprising. Half past seven is the best time for me. It is very crowded then. There would be an excuse for your sitting at my table.'

'Very well. I will be there tonight.'

'I look forward to it.'

At seven-thirty Porte's was very crowded. It always was at this time in the summer, but it was far from being a profitable time for the management: the tables were occupied not by rich local Tangerines or affluent tourists, but by penurious Moroccans on excursions from Rabat and Casablanca, who would sit for an hour over a bottle of Coca-Cola which they would divide among a family. A good customer like Adrian had difficulty in finding himself a chair. When he at last did, it would surprise no one that he should be sharing his table with a Moroccan.

'Well?' Adrian asked.

'As far as I can gather,' the Moroccan said, 'the prisoner was trying to smuggle kif into Spain to provide funds for a guerilla movement.'

'What is the purpose of this movement.'

'It is anti-Franco.'

'But it must be for someone.'

'I do not think so. He simply wants to do harm to Franco.'

'How was he recruited?'

'It's hard to tell. He came over as a tourist. He has a little money. I don't know how much. You know what these student tourists are like. They sit around in cafés. They pick up and are picked up. Anyone could take advantage of them. He hoped, as far as I can tell, that he would find someone over here who shares his ideas.'

'What are his plans now?'

'What plans could he have, at the moment?'

'I'm told he isn't so very anxious to be repatriated to America.'

'He feels that he can do more here than he can there.'

'Was he recruited in Spain or here?'

'There.'

'I suppose that he's in touch with the people who recruited him.'

'They must have representatives over here.'

'I'd like to know who he's seeing.'

That evening there was a rehearsal. Adrian missed the beginning, but he had an opportunity for a few minutes of conversation with Murray at the end.

'Have you any idea,' he asked, 'when that American will be coming up for trial?'

'Your guess is as good as mine. You know how dilatory these fellows are.'

'Do you know who sees him?'

'I could find out.'

'I'd be glad to know.'

He and Beryl had made no plans for themselves that evening.

'Why not a quiet evening, just ourselves,' he said.

'Why not.'

'Did you have any talk with Pablo?'

'A little.'

'How does he strike you.'

'I like his hair oil.'

'What a thing to say.'

'Why not. It was strong but not offensively.'

'As the advertisements claim?'

'Exactly.'

'Would you recognise it on someone else?'

'Most likely.'

'You'd recognise a strong scent that wasn't his?'

'I think I would. Yes, I'm sure I would. What would you like to eat?'

'What have you in the frig?'

'Not much.'

She had been back such a little time that she had not built up an anthology of odds and ends.

'I've bacon,' she said.

'Why not scrambled eggs and bacon.'

'Why not?'

'We've got beer and there's still some aquavit.'

'A Danish supper, in fact.'

'What's wrong with that?'

'I can see nothing wrong with that.'

They had very happy memories of their two years in Copenhagen. They had brought back a Danish glass decanter, shaped like a pig; they had a set of small glasses for aquavit. They toasted each other across the table. 'Skol,' they said.

It was several weeks since he had tasted aquavit. It made him feel reminiscent.

'We had a wonderful time there, didn't we,' he said. 'It was our real honeymoon.'

'Florence was good.'

'But in Florence we didn't know that it would last. We were both thinking of a time when we'd not be together. You were talking of going back to college in September.'

'You were thinking of your next posting.'

'We'd be talking of a time, we'd be thinking of a time when we wouldn't be together.'

'We'd talk of how we'd have to keep in touch.'

'One day our paths might cross again, we'd say.'

'We'd wonder if we'd still feel in the same way about each other.'

'I'll probably be married then, you'd say.'

'That was how I felt. "This is my last fling before I settle down," I think. I wanted it to be a good last fling.'

'And it was that, wasn't it?'

'It certainly was that.'

'But Copenhagen wasn't an anticlimax.'

'Oh, no, no, no.'

They had arrived there in December, the tourist season was over. Tivoli was closed, but for the Danes themselves, this was the Copenhagen season, with the ballet and the opera open and the little country chalets shuttered up. They had stayed in the Codan while they were looking for a flat: their room had looked out on to a harbour; they had watched the ferry boat leave at midnight for Aarhus. The red lights of the DFDS had shone upon the ceiling.

'And wasn't it exciting when spring came—with the beech trees that brilliant green and the lights going on in Tivoli and all those excursions.'

'Why don't we take more excursions here?'

'Why don't we?'

'We mustn't get into a rut.'

'As soon as the play's over, let's go to Xauen.'

'Why wait till the play's over. Let's go the moment we see thirty-six hours clear.'

'Let's do.'

'Let's look at our diaries and take the first free chance. We can leave after lunch, then drive back the next day after breakfast. I'll only miss an afternoon and a morning at my office, and I'm not someone who has to check in on the dot.'

They spread open the long desk diary that was divided into months. It was black with entries. Either he or she had something or they both had.

'Next week and the week after are impossible.'

'Perhaps we're looking too far ahead. What's wrong with tomorrow?'

They had nothing on that evening. There was no lunch party the next day. There was a rehearsal in the evening. They could easily get back for that; why not?

Adrian was awake early the next morning. He opened his desk and took out his diary. 'Have arranged with Beryl to go to Xauen. I would have preferred to go to Ceuta. But I learn that the frontier is going to be closed for the next three days.'

I mustn't be always right, he thought. This spy has got to think me human.

Beryl was waiting for him in the car outside the Consulate, their suitcase in the back. A picnic basket was beside it.

'Now, isn't this fun?' she said.

They opened their basket at the point on the road to Tetuan where the Spanish customs shed had stood. It was a frugal meal: a salad, a cake, a thermos of coffee. The fields surrounding the deserted sheds had been as desolate as the sheds when they took out the basket, but no sooner had they set it on the ground, than from nowhere a quartet of Arab urchins had emerged—in the way that they always did. 'Heaven knows where they come from,' Adrian said. They stood silent, twenty or so yards away. They had, for Europeans and Americans, spoiled the pleasure of picnicking.

'I'm glad we had that place to take Groves to,' Beryl said.

They were on their way within a quarter of an hour, having left half a cake behind them.

'We'll have an appetite for dinner,' Beryl said.

They reached Xauen shortly before five. There were three charabancs in the square, but two of them were surrounded with embarking passengers. 'It should not be too crowded tonight,' said Adrian. They booked into the main hotel, changed into bathing things and sat beside the pool. There were only three other couples there; the tables on the terrace had been cleared, and the restaurant was being prepared for dinner. Up the hill facing them a thin stream of white-clothed females were making their way to the white mosque at its summit. Along the road that curved round its base, a stream of peasants passed; most of them carried bundles on their heads. It was very peaceful.

'I'm going to have my swim now,' he said, 'before the tourists who're taking their siesta crowd the pool.'

The water was cold enough to be refreshing. He swam six lengths then climbed out and sat beside her. 'We ought to do this sort of thing more often, very much more often.'

They took a short stroll before dinner, along the stream that ran up to the pool where in the morning the women washed their clothes. On the mountain to the left a large barrack-like hotel was in process of construction. For centuries this had been a holy city. Abdul Karim in the early 1920s had made it his headquarters during the Rif war. It had been out of sight of the main road that ran from Tetuan to Fez. The Spaniards had been scarcely aware of its existence till their planes flew over it. Now it had become one of the chief tourist attractions in the country. It would soon have lost its identity, but it was still a very charming place with its blue and white houses, its red roofs, its narrow wind-

155

ing streets, its massive heavily studded doors, its shops, its weavers, its cobbled market square, and the red-brown battlements and square tower of its fortress.

It was here that Beryl and Adrian invariably brought out visitors, but it was the first time they had come out alone together for a long, long time. For that matter, it was a long time since they had been out anywhere alone.

'This is the first time we've been out alone since you got back,' he said, as they sat down to dinner.

'And we haven't had a real talk since your man from Gibraltar came across.'

'I know.'

'Have you heard from him since he got back?'

'Only routine correspondence.'

'Did he seem satisfied with what he found?'

'I think so. I hope so, yes.'

'Have you been worrying about it?'

'Of course, a little.'

'You never talk about it.'

'I've been trained not to talk about my work.'

'You can discuss it with your wife.'

'That's the one person with whom I'm not supposed to.'

'In details, yes. I can see that, but not when it's a case of a personal worry. You can share your worries, can't you?'

'Some of them.'

'Those that affect her, surely.'

'I know. I know.' He shook his head. 'One gets into the habit of not talking. That's the problem.'

'But you have been worried, haven't you?'

'Yes, I've been worried.'

'In that case . . .' she paused. There was a question in her look. 'Surely there must be something . . .' she paused. 'It makes me feel so useless.'

He shook his head. 'You mustn't feel that . . . It's, you know, the difference between strategy and tactics, strategy is the all-in plan of campaign, tactics are the intermediate details. You know the strategy of what it's all about. I've told you that; but it's the tactics, the day to day details that I

156

have to be discreet about. The trouble is that sometimes tactics and strategy get confused. That's what is happening now.' He hesitated; then in a rush he blurted the whole thing out. 'I'm worried because I'm afraid that I might lose my job, and if I lose it, I don't know what I'd do.'

She stared at him. She had not expected this. She had not dreamed of anything like this.

'Is it likely?'

'It's not impossible.'

'How far is not impossible from likely?'

He shrugged. 'I've no idea: that's what worries me. It's the kind of thing that I didn't think happened to an Englishman, at least my kind of Englishman. We qualify for a job, and after all it's a tough training—four years in a prep school, four or five in a public school, three or four at a university—you ought to be all right after that, and that's what I thought I was, but now I'm beginning to wonder if I am. I don't know where I'd find a job now if I had to . . . I guess it's different with you.'

'I suppose it is. I don't know. People lose jobs, but they always get another one. In America you could always teach.'

'Teach . . . me?'

'You've a degree, what we call a master's. You speak three languages.'

'You mean to say that I could turn up in America and get a job.'

'There'd be complications, you'd have to get a certain kind of visa; you'd have to have a job on offer; a permit to work, but as the husband of an American, oh, you'd have no problem.'

'You mean that?'

'Why shouldn't I? It's the kind of thing Americans are doing all the time.'

'How lucky I was to marry an American. Let's celebrate. Let's see if they haven't anything better on their wine list than Chaudsoleil.'

They were back at their flat by half past one. As always after a shuttered night there was a musty atmosphere in the

157

place. 'Windows, windows,' he shouted, 'let us have fresh air.'

He opened the main windows in the sitting room, walked out on to the balcony, and breathed in the clean, fresh air. It was good to live in a place like this. He crossed to his small study. As he opened the door, he checked. He sniffed. He sniffed a second time, then called to Beryl.

'One minute, honey, please.' He led her into his study, holding her by the hand. He closed the door behind them. 'Does this remind you of anything?' he asked.

'Does what remind me of what?'

'Isn't there anything here that strikes you as peculiar?'

'What should strike me as peculiar?'

'The smell of something?'

She sniffed, then nodded. 'Yes, you're right—I get it—Pablo's hair oil.'

He sat in front of his desk, turned his key in the lock of his outer drawer, drew out the diary, turned the page and stared. The thread was displaced, for the first time since he had come back from England. The spy had been on his guard. Someone must have warned him that he would be away. Someone who had known his plans. Who could have known them? His Fatima of course. She could have told the guardian; she could have told the postman. They had known at the Consulate that he would be away. But he had made the decision late the previous evening; that had left only six hours in which to have spread the news.

Whom had he told? He had not seen any of his agents, no, but there had been a telephone call that morning. He had arranged to meet his man at Porte's that evening. They had a routine for confirming or cancelling appointments. His agent would ring him at the Consulate and ask if he were free for golf that evening. He would answer 'yes' or 'no' and ring right off. He had said 'no' that morning. He had not given a reason for not being available for golf. He had not said he was going to be out of town. On that telephone call alone his agent would not have assumed his absence. Whom else had he told? Had he left a note for Littlejohn; not as far as he remembered. But of course, he had told Frieda. Yes, that was what he had done. He remembered now. He had put his head round her door. He had said, 'I'll be leaving at lunch-time. I'll be back by tomorrow afternoon. Could you warn the boss?'

Had he told anyone else? He did not think he had. Who else had called during the morning? He did not think any-body had. It was ridiculous that he could not remember. But it was not easy to remember something by which you set no store. Could Beryl remember?

He rearranged the thread across his diary and shut away the book, locking the drawer. He crossed the drawing room, Beryl was laying the plates for lunch.

'Don't bother,' he said, 'I'll do that.'

'It isn't any bother.'

'All the same, let it be my bother. Can you remember, by the way, whether you told anyone yesterday that we were going to Xauen yesterday.'

'I told Sarita.'

'You tell Sarita everything.'

'There has to be someone to whom one tells everything.'

'I'd like to be invisible and hear what you two talk about.'

'Isn't that what every man would like.'

'I've an idea that you two might be rather special.'

'Maybe you'd not be wrong.'

'Did you tell anyone else?'

'Not that I can remember.'

Yet, it must have been something said by one or other of them during that six hours that had reached the ears of the interloper. He was in the dark, exasperatingly in the dark.

'By the way, where's the rehearsal tonight?' he asked.

'At the Simonds.'

The Simonds were an American couple who had been in the Foreign Service. As a young man he had been stationed in Casablanca; he had come over to Tangier for weekend leaves. In the days when it was international, he had main-tained that you got more fun there at a reasonable cost than anywhere in the world. Now that he was retired and had made his home there, he still maintained that there was more fun to be got there than anywhere he knew, and even if the cost was no longer reasonable, it was less unreasonable than most places that were equally agreeable. He was an important and valued member of the community. He was a generous host. And new societies were always anxious to get the Simonds on their committee.

'There'll be no need to make arrangements for a meal tonight,' said Adrian, 'there's always plenty to eat up there.'

Before the rehearsal, Murray addressed the company, 'Things are going so well now,' he said, 'that I think we can definitely decide to have our performance at the end of August. The Spanish College has offered us their theatre for the last week-end, that's to say the 27th, 28th, and 29th. The committee have agreed to accept those days. That means that we shall have to work exceptionally hard these next two weeks. And I'm happy to announce that a very generous and helpful proposition has been put to us. Pablo Monterey has invited us to his house near Tetuan next Sunday. We can get there early; those of us who don't go to church, or who go to an early service, can get there by eleven. We could have a two-hour rehearsal before the buffet lunch that we are very generously being offered. We can then have a full series of rehearsals during the afternoon. It is very generous of Pablo, and we are extremely grateful. Now, let's get started; as we're not all here, we'll open with the scene between Sarita and Sven. That's scene six. Just the two of you. Now then, Sarita.'

Beryl sat apart from the others, watching them. It was an effective scene: the scene where the elder sister breaks down the reserve of the young man. For Beryl it had a dramatic irony. A scene was going on beneath the scene. Was Sarita throwing herself so completely into the part that Sven could have no doubt of her intention? Beryl had not seen the rehearsal of this scene since her own return from Oklahoma. Had it changed its tempo and its temper?

'Can I kiss you good night?' the young man was saying.

'Why do you always ask me if you may?'

Was there a new glow in that? Did she want there to be, Beryl asked herself.

There was no doubt that Sven was acting with less reserve. He was letting himself go. How attractive Sarita looked. She could not imagine any man not wanting to make love to her. She waited impatiently for the kiss that would conclude the scene. Would it be a real kiss? She remembered the position that they took for that embrace. She did not want his head to be in the way. She shifted to the end of the sofa so that she could see their faces. She felt her own excitement rising.

'You need somebody,' Sven was saying, 'and I need somebody too. Could it be—you and me, Blanche?'

With a little cry, Sarita huddled into his embrace, with real abandonment; she tried to speak but could not. She seemed to be overcome by her emotion. She had realised completely the author's idea of the scene and character. Sven was kissing her gently, timidly, her forehead, then her eyes, and then . . . it was a real kiss, for both of them. Beryl found herself trembling. It was as though she were in the scene herself; which was she, though? Sven or Sarita, or was she both?

Sarita came across to her when the scene broke up.

'You were wonderful, you were wonderful,' she said.

Sarita laughed, 'It's hard not to be wonderful with a scene like that.'

'And you made him wonderful too.'

'He's improved, hasn't he, since you went away.'

'He's really in the part.'

'He ought to be.'

Her eyes were twinkling. What did their twinkle mean? Did it mean what Beryl thought it did?

'Come along now. Let's go back to the beginning,' Murray was announcing; 'Scene I, that's Beryl, Sarita, Pablo, Sven again—you were fine in that last scene, fine. Now then, off we go. You open, Pablo.'

It was a long rehearsal and as soon as it was over there was, as Adrian had known there would be, a plentiful supply of nourishment. There was no lack of help in Morocco, and three elegant young Moroccans with baggy red trousers, white jackets, white shirts, red sashes, and red turbans were passing round dishes of drinks and trays of sandwiches. Beryl and Sarita sat together on a secluded seat.

'I keep thinking of our talk after that Consulate dinner,' Beryl said.

'That's what you were meant to do.'

'You're the first person that I've known like that.'

'I'm the first person that you've known was like that.'

'I'll have met them, you mean, and haven't known it?'

'That's what I mean.'

'Why haven't I recognised them?'

'Perhaps they didn't want you to.'

'And you did want me to?'

'That's what I mean.'

There was a pause. There was a teasing look in Sarita's eyes. She was half smiling. 'I'm puzzled,' Beryl said.

'Why are you puzzled, my sweet innocent?'

'You like men, don't you, in that way, I mean?' Beryl said.

'I like them very much.'

'But you like women more?'

'I like women differently.'

'In what way differently?'

'Have you ever read Maupassant's *La Femme de Paul*?'

'I haven't. Should I?'

'Yes. It's the first story in that genre; and Maupassant was a man who was crazy about women, who killed himself through women and for women. In *La Femme de Paul* a man's mistress deserts him for a woman. The man commits suicide. The story explains what it is that makes the woman prefer a woman, a relationship that is "plus intime". That is the key phrase "plus intime".' Sarita paused. 'With another woman one can be *intime*, in a way that one can't be with a man. A woman knows what one likes and how one likes it.'

'You said that after that first time, you were curious to make the experiment on someone else. Which do you prefer, being the aggressor?'

'It all depends. But you must not think, you know, that

162

I've had all that experience. You mustn't think that there've been dozens.'

'But there have been several?'

'There have been several.'

'And you're saying that they're quite different, the passive and the aggressive, and you're saying that they are both exciting, in a different way. In which way is the one different from the other?'

'With the aggressive ones, it's in a rather bitchy way. You meet an experienced woman. You can tell at a glance that you've attracted her, but she can't tell how experienced you are. You flirt with her. You keep her dangling. She's on her guard. She won't commit herself until she's sure. You drop her little hints, but not too obvious hints. It's the chase, from the other way about. And it's fun saying to yourself, "When we exchange notes afterwards, how I'll tease her. I'll say, surely you could have guessed from that. How slow you were, how dangerously slow." Because she has to be the aggressor, in the final instance. If she isn't, it won't be any fun for her. And the more fun it is for her, the more fun it will be for me.'

Beryl shook her head. 'You've got me confused. You've got me thoroughly confused. And now here's Adrian coming across to interrupt us.'

'He's always doing that.'

'I know; that's the worst of husbands.'

He stood above them, smiling down. 'On our way?' he asked.

'On our way.'

They walked across to Mrs Simonds. 'A wonderful party, Susan,' he said. 'You always manage to get the most wonderful cold cuts for your sandwiches.'

'Not nearly so good as I had hoped to get.'

'How so?'

'I had planned to go into Ceuta, but the Frontier's closed.'

'How did you learn that?'

'From Pablo Monterey. We were going to have driven in together. But he rang me up this morning to tell me that it was closed for the next three days.'

163

Next morning Adrian looked in on Frieda. 'Is anyone giving you a lift to Pablo's place?' he asked.

'Yes, our boss.'

'Too bad. If you had come with us, you could have shared the driving.

'I thought there was a snag.'

'Have you managed to see anything of Pablo?'

'I dined with him last night, after the rehearsal.'

'Where did he take you?'

'Claridge's.'

'Did you well, in fact.'

'I don't think he needs to worry about money.'

'What do you make of him?'

'I wonder sometimes if he's completely sane.'

'Why?'

'His hatred of Franco. It's almost mental.'

'In what way?'

'He drags it into everything.'

'Give me an example.'

'He'll be talking about English politics. Suddenly he'll say, "I suppose some of your Britishers wish you had a Franco running your country for you." '

'I gather that a number of them do.'

'Then he'll say, "If I were one of them, I'd bribe the IRA to blow up your Prime Minister." '

'I wouldn't say that made him mental.'

'Not that one remark. But when he's saying that kind of thing all the time.'

'I see.' Adrian paused. 'The more you can manage to see of him, the better.'

'You wouldn't like to give me an idea of why.'

He shook his head. He gave her the same answer that he had given Beryl when he had asked her to keep an eye on the young Mormon.

'If I told you why I was interested in him, I should be putting ideas into your head. You'd be looking along certain lines. And you might miss something important that I'm not myself aware of.'

She nodded, 'You're quite right. You'd be putting me in blinkers.'

Even so, he wished he could tell her. He wished he could tell Beryl. He wished he could compare notes with someone. And he ought, he knew very well that he ought, to tell John Groves. It was his duty to tell John Groves. He ran the risk of losing his job by not telling John Groves. Why did he feel that Groves was the kind of man who, when the showdown came, would appropriate all the credit to himself. If he was going to trust his hunches, shouldn't he trust them all the way? He could not sit here twiddling his thumbs. He must attack.

That morning he left his office early. Pablo had several commercial irons in his fire. One of them was the directorship of a small housing agency that operated on the second floor of a building on the south side of the Place de France. Pablo would almost certainly be there this morning. Murray's announcement that the performance would be held in August, gave him an excuse for calling. He was, after all, the deputy stage manager.

As he had expected, Pablo was at his desk.

'I've brought round,' he said, 'a list of the various properties that we will be wanting for this show. I've an idea that we might be able to find quite a few of them in your house.'

'I suppose you could.'

'I don't know why I hadn't thought of it before. As I'd never seen your house, it simply hadn't occurred to me, but as you've so kindly invited us out on Sunday, it seems too good an opportunity to miss. You and I could go round together while the others are having a siesta.'

'I'll be delighted. Anything I can do to help. Let's have a look at that list of yours.'

There was a table in the window place. He brought up two chairs, set them side by side, and spread the list out on it.

'Let's see now what you'll be wanting; as you'll realise on Sunday, there's a good deal of junk about the place. Let's read the stage directions. What do they say? "The place has a raffish charm." I daresay that that's how you'd describe my home. "Rickety outside stairs," it says, and "ornamental gables". Have you ever been to New Orleans?'

'I've never been to the USA.'

'You haven't, that's funny. Being married to an American. New Orleans is Spanish more than French, and my home is more Spanish than Moroccan. We ought to be able to find exactly what you want. Chairs and tables that are starting to fall apart. Plenty of that I'd say.'

They went over the list item by item. It took them half an hour.

'I'll be going down there on the Saturday,' Pablo said. 'I'll check my furniture against your list, then on Sunday we can see what you want, and I can arrange to have it moved up on the Monday.'

'That'll be fine.'

They stood up. Adrian looked across the Straits. It was a cloudless day. Gibraltar stood out clearly on the horizon. It was shortly before one, and the two ferry boats, the Spanish one with its red and yellow funnels from Algeciras, and the squat British *Mons Calpe* from Gibraltar, were approaching the harbour. On the terrace across the street, there was the usual crowd of tourists, loiterers, pedestrians, shoe-blacks, looking out to sea just as they did every day. So peaceful, so serene. A thought flashed across his mind.

'It looks so peaceful,' he said, 'so exactly the way it is every day of the week. Can you imagine what a sensation there would be if there was an explosion there, if the *Mons Calpe* blew up and sank.'

Pablo started, 'What a thing to say.'

Adrian laughed, 'It's the kind of thing that's happening all the time.'

'All the time. How do you mean?'

'What I say. All the time. Sabotage. Kidnapping. Reprisals.'

'But who would want to blow up the *Mons Calpe*?'

'The Basque Liberation group.'

'What good would it do them?'

166

'It would weaken Franco. It would encourage his enemies. Another nail in his coffin. It would worsen his relationship with Britain.'

'Do you really believe that?'

'Why not? You remember those terrorists before World War One. Nihilists, they called themselves. They were always murdering or trying to murder crowned heads and premiers. At the time the conservatives would say, "What good do they think they are doing, murdering one minister, one king. Someone else will take his place." But we know now that the nihilists were right; we can see now that those bombs, those bullets did achieve their purpose. There are not many crowned heads left today.'

Adrian paused. He was watching Pablo closely. Pablo looked pensive. 'If I were one of the big boys in the Basque Liberation Movement,' Adrian said, 'I should give very serious attention to the idea of blowing up either the *Mons Calpe* or the Algeciras ferry. I think I'd go for the *Mons Calpe*. Easier, less strict security; and it would annoy the British, the better for the Basques.' Pablo did not reply. But his pensive look grew more serious. I've planted a seed, thought Adrian.

13

Pablo's house was on the northeast side of Tetuan, a hundred or so yards up the slope. From the outside it was not particularly impressive. A high wall ran beside a roadway. In the middle of the wall was an iron gate that gave the impression of being the entrance to a warehouse. You could not see through the gate or over it, but once inside you recognised that you had entered a solid residence. A two-storied house, wide and long, with rectangular shuttered windows. The first impression was of bleakness and of blankness. There was a driveway that branched at the front door leading on one side to an ample garage and on the other side to the trades-man's entrance. The front door opened on to a dark, large hall that led into a courtyard. There was a passage round the courtyard, off which a succession of doors opened. A gallery ran round the upper story, off which a further succession of doors opened. The courtyard was open to the sky. A fountain played in its centre. There were brightly tiled paths leading between the flowerbeds. A broad path led to a second garden on the other side. This garden was shaded by palm trees. And there was a swimming pool. This second garden had been prepared for the rehearsal. The centre had been cleared and two rows of chairs had been arranged. There was a general atmosphere of dignity and colour.

'I don't know what you meant by talking about "raffish charm",' said Adrian.

Pablo laughed. He made a deprecatory gesture. 'I think that's how it would strike my grandfather, I'm glad he did not live to see the change. I cannot remember him, alas. I am only thirty years old, but my father showed me photographs of him. I have one in my bedroom. I will show it to you.'

It was the photograph of a handsome tall man in uniform, with a colonel's epaulettes; he had a trim, rather long moustache, with the ends curled. 'The photograph was taken on my grandfather's last morning here. He said to my father, "My son, I am going to fight to preserve your heritage." I am glad that he did not live to see what had happened to this house, what has happened to this country. To think that the man for whom my father gave his life should hand over this country to the infidel. A great Christian gentleman, that is what they called Franco then, a great Christian gentleman who handed over this country to the Moslems.'

His eyes glistened. His voice shook. Adrian could understand why Frieda had described him as being not quite sane.

'I will show you round the house,' he said, 'and if anything strikes you as being suitable for our production, I will make a note of it. Now here is the dining room—the banqueting hall, as my grandfather named it.'

It was a long room, opening on to a garden on each side. The windows ran almost to the ceiling. They were set well apart, so that the room was light in daytime, but the curtains were of heavy, gold-shot damask. Between the windows gilt-framed family portraits alternated with suits of armour.

'I wish we could see it as it was in his day. The party he gave for my father's coming of age—all that is over, but still, when we have this table laid out for our buffet lunch you will see. It will not be what it was, but you will see.'

He was very proud of his house, and it was something to be proud of. It would have an effect on one to be brought up in a home like this.

'How did your father die?' asked Adrian.

'He was lucky. He went the way he would have chosen; killed hunting. He did not live to see the Moroccan take-over. It would have broken his heart.'

Adrian felt himself warm to Pablo. They had something in common. Himself, he had never seen his father. This young man had barely known his. They had both lacked a father's guidance. And, here they were now in conflict with one another; though Pablo did not know they were, or rather Pablo did not know that Adrian knew they were. To Pablo, he was a dupe. Pablo had acquired the key to his flat, had broken into his flat, had read his papers. It must be strange for

Pablo to be the host now of the man whose photographs he had seen on the shelves of the room that he had rifled. 'Now here is the main drawing room,' he was saying. 'There's something that I particularly want to have you notice.'

It was a lavatory that had been built into the angle of the library wall. 'The Duke of Wellington, the Great Duke had one built into his English house in Stratfieldsaye. I wondered if he copied it from a Spanish model that he saw in the Peninsular Campaign, and whether my ancestors who built this house copied it from the same model.'

'It's very possible,' said Adrian.

'I wonder if Franco has any sense of guilt,' he said. 'I wonder how Garibaldi felt when Nice became a part of France. Franco had spent so much time in Morocco. He must have seen this house. He may well have dined here, have sat at this table under these pictures, under this armour. He owes everything to Morocco. And yet when it suits his interests, he can hand Morocco back to the Moroccans.'

It was not difficult to see how Pablo could have allied himself with an organisation that was opposed to Franco. He had youth and vigour. What scope had he for ambition here? 'I must find out more about him,' Adrian thought. 'I wonder how reliable this new agent is. I might do worse than go across on Wednesday to Gibraltar.'

'Sooner or later the Spaniards will find out the truth about him,' Pablo said. 'He won't live forever, and once his hand is off the wheel, you'll see. He's a strong man. I'll say that for him. And because he's strong, his followers imagine they are strong too. But they aren't, they're men of straw. The revolutionaries can afford to wait.'

The wild look had come back into his eyes. 'Frieda may well be right,' thought Adrian. 'He may be halfway round the bend.'

Pablo had not expected more than half the company to arrive before eleven. But he had overrated the Anglican influence among the American and European members of the cast. Only Frieda and the British Consul General were not there. Frieda had rung up that morning to explain, 'It's his turn to read the lessons. He's got a sense of duty. But we'll be there by lunch time. That I promise.'

But they were not there by lunch time.

Adrian and Beryl exchanged a glance.

'Are you thinking what I'm thinking?' she asked.

'I expect I am.'

'Good luck to them.'

They raised their glasses in a toast. The glasses they raised contained a rich red wine.

'I suppose this is Moroccan wine,' Adrian said to Pablo. 'But it does seem to me exceptionally good.'

'I've kept it for six years; that's the important thing, letting it age, and most people don't bother to do that.'

'You don't make any wine yourself?'

He shook his head. 'It isn't that the Spaniards didn't care, but the soil is much better on the French side, near Casablanca, and you must remember that the Spaniards never colonised their part of Africa in the way the French did in Algeria. The Moslems don't drink wine, and the Spaniards could get all the wine they wanted from Andalucia. But I'm glad that you like this. I do think it's good.'

And it was certainly a sumptuous buffet that had been arranged in the old banqueting hall. There were dishes o Pastella, there was a Tajine served in a large wicker basket with a conical cover. A servant kept replenishing the supply of brochettes. There were two dishes of Royal Prawns, which also were constantly replenished. There were dishes of sliced oranges, sprinkled with cinnamon; there were almond cakes.

'I wonder how rich he really is,' Beryl said to Adrian.

He shrugged, 'I shouldn't think he knows himself. And I don't imagine that he cares.'

'He's certainly put himself out for us today.'

So generously indeed that no one was tempted not to linger over it. Murray stood up. 'I must say one little word of thanks for the generosity of our host. I have been, we all have been, very amply entertained in this gracious and hospitable country, but I cannot recall a single occasion on

which I have been so—how shall I put it—so sumptuously
spoilt. So sumptuously indeed that I think we should best
show our appreciation by not resuming our duties right
away, but indulging in the national custom of a siesta. Let us
start again at three-fifteen.'

Beryl and Sarita, as was their custom at rehearsals,
curled up in a pile of cushions. As always, they returned to
their perennial topic. It had become a serial conversation,
continually interrupted, to be resumed at the point where it
had been abandoned. 'You remember what you were saying
the other day, about the other situation, when you were the
aggressor. Tell me how it is that way?'

Sarita laughed. 'It's almost more fun that way. You'll
see a girl; no, not a girl, a young woman, someone in her
early twenties; and there's an unripe look about her. She
may have had affairs with men. She probably has, because
girls nowadays are ashamed of being virgins, but it hasn't
really worked with her. She hasn't been aroused, and you
guess that why she hasn't been aroused is because it isn't
men she really likes; with her you have to be very tactful,
very adroit. You have to reveal her to herself. You have to be
very careful not to frighten her. You have to move step by
step. It's so exciting that often you go slower than you need.
You tantalise her. She begins to realise what you are doing.
She's impatient. She's angry with you. "Why won't she come
to the point," she thinks. At last you put her out of her
misery.

'But sometimes, of course,' she went on, 'the woman has
been aroused; she likes men as you yourself do, but she
hasn't realised that she has this other side to herself.'

'And then you show her that she has?'

'Exactly.'

'And is that difficult?'

'It's not too easy.'

'How do you set about it?'

'By making her inquisitive; by making her wonder if she
may not be like that herself, if she's not missing something.'

Is this what she's doing with me? Beryl wondered.

172

She remembered almost the first thing that Sarita had said to her, when she herself had said, 'You're the first person that I've known like that,' and Sarita had answered, 'I'm the first person who you've known's like that.' And she had said, 'I've met them, you mean, and haven't recognised it.' She could remember each section of the dialogue. She could remember the sound in Sarita's voice, the mocking look in Sarita's eyes. 'Why haven't I recognised it?' she had said.

'Perhaps they didn't want you to recognise it.'

'And you wanted me to recognise it?'

'That's what I mean.'

And it was at that very moment—that unpropitious moment that, as it alway did, an interruption came. This time it was Frieda and the Consul General. Littlejohn was profuse with apologies.

'You know how it is—or at least you don't know how it is—shall I say how you *should* know how it is, but after church on Sundays at St. Andrews, there is something of a—well—I suppose "get-together" is the right phrase. One of the church wardens is a most efficient and public-spirited man, and also a man of means—a desirable addition for a church warden. He runs what is, in its own way, the best hotel in Tangier—small, intimate, French and Moroccan specialities, this admirable fellow provides for the congregation a cookie and a cup repast. What goes into that cup, I do not know, it is delicious and it is strong, it has a mandatory taste, and when, after the second of these potations, a member of the congregation asked me to look in at his apartment for what he called—I'm afraid for what he called—"a final noggin", I lacked the authority—once again I suggest that authority is the word—I lacked the authority to resist, so that Frieda and I found ourselves on the road eighty minutes later than we had expected. By that time we were feeling a little hungry, in spite of the generous supply of—I think they are called canapés—with which our, to me, still unidentified host supplied us. I was feeling in need of substantial sustenance; I did not know how Frieda might be feeling, but I did think that a plate of soup would be beneficial. It is not, alas, the

173

time for the rescuing mercy of Harira, but there might be somewhere some kind of soup du jour, as they call it on the *Mons Calpe*, that would achieve a similar result. It proved there was—at a wayside restaurant, and so salutary did it prove, that when the maitre d'—I felt from his presence that he could not be less than a maitre d'—suggested that we should sample his plat du jour, we could not refuse. As a result, ladies and gentlemen, I apologise. We are one hundred and thirty minutes late. It does not matter that I am late: I am partless in this party. But that Frieda should be late, that is another matter. I am responsible, and I apologise.'

Adrian stared at him. He had never seen his boss in this mood before. He looked at Frieda. Was there or did he only fancy that there was a glow about her?

The afternoon wore on. After the strenuous rehearsal of the morning, and the ample lunch there was a general absence of animation. Murray recognised this. There was a gap between the scenes. Beryl curled up among the cushions, watched Sarita drowsily across the room. Why had that interruption come, just at a crucial moment. Why had Sarita wanted her to know. Was that the first step in the game of courtship? Why had she wanted her to know. Next time she would ask. Had Sarita wondered if she was herself that kind of woman. Is she playing a game with me? Beryl wondered. Is she tantalising me, the way she said?

'And now, ladies and gentlemen,' Murray was announcing, 'It is six o'clock. I don't feel that we can encroach any longer . . .'

But he was interrupted, 'No, no, please,' Pablo was interjecting, 'one last surprise, one last little surprise. Not more than an hour, not more I promise you . . .'

There was a clash of cymbals, and in from the garden trotted a small four piece band; Moroccans, in scarlet tunics and white trousers, taking their place against the centre of the wall. 'Now, ladies and gentlemen, please one last hour—to put us in the mood for a strenuous two weeks of rehearsals—and yes, let me see, oh, here they come. The bottles that will restore our flagging energies.'

A young Moroccan, also in red jacket and white trousers, was wheeling in a tray on which were set three steaming ice buckets from which protruded gold foiled bottles. 'I will open the first,' said Pablo.

The cork exploded with a lively 'pop'. He poured the foaming liquid into a tall tulip-shaped glass. He sipped, then half-filled a second glass. He handed it to Littlejohn. He raised his own, clinking it. 'My house is honoured by your presence here.' He sipped, then put down his glass, raised his hands, and clapped again, 'On with the dance!' he cried.

The band broke into a fox trot. Littlejohn put down his glass. Frieda was standing beside them. Littlejohn turned towards her. 'This is my privilege, I fancy.'

Pablo laughed, 'No, no. It is my *droit de seigneur*. The host chooses the most attractive woman in the room for the first dance.' He stretched out his hand; he took Frieda by the wrist. As he drew her to the centre of the floor, a frown creased Littlejohn's forehead. Beryl and Adrian were standing side by side a few yards away.

'Did you notice that?' he asked.

'I'll say I did.'

'That speech when he arrived, it was peculiar, wasn't it?'

'I'll say it was.'

'Something unusual's in the air.'

'Something very unusual.'

'Look at him now.'

Littlejohn's eyes were following Pablo and Frieda as they danced. They made a striking couple, and it was clear that they were enjoying themselves. They were the right height and the right weight for one another. They were not indulging in elaborate steps. They were not dancing ostentatiously. They were not conscious of the onlookers. They were not dancing to be looked at. They were dancing for each other, to give pleasure to one another.

The music stopped, but Pablo clapped his hands.

'No, no, once more,' he called.

The music became more vibrant. Pablo held Frieda closer. His fingers pressed against her shoulder. Littlejohn had not moved from his position by the sideboard. His glass was empty. His frown was deeper. The music stopped again.

'You dance divinely,' Pablo said. She smiled. There was encouragement in her smile. 'It would be heaven to make love to you,' he said.

'You should try some time and see.'

Daylight was visible round the curtain next morning when Adrian woke. He picked up the clock. Twenty past six. Time to be up. He switched on the light over the telephone table. He looked at the calendar. The day was a blank except for a rehearsal that evening. It was at their flat; at six o'clock. He wondered how Pablo felt when he came as a guest into the house that he had entered clandestinely so often. He opened up the window. He set the garbage outside the door. The guardian waved at him and hurried up the street. He wished the guardian's Spanish were better and his own Arabic more colloquial. He would like to entrap the guardian into some admission. The guardian very likely knew a lot. But did he know what he knew; did he understand what he knew? When he had talked to his Fatima about him, she had tapped the side of her head with her finger, indicating that he was mad. The guardian of an adjacent block of flats, one morning when his own guardian was not on morning duty, had put two folded hands against his cheek and closed his eyes suggesting that the guardian was asleep. Then he raised his hand to his mouth and made a sign of drinking, suggesting that he was sleeping it off; he did not himself feel that the man made much sense.

The guardian was breaking now into a kind of trot. He had something on his mind. Money, presumably; though he had been paid less than a week ago. He was not entitled to any more for several days. When he wanted money, he pointed to his mouth, suggesting he was hungry. Then he would raise five or ten fingers, to explain that five or ten dirhams would solve his problem for the moment. When his need was greater, he would bring a letter written in French to explain that his child needed clothes or that he himself would have to go to the hospital. But this time his need was simpler. He pointed to his feet; he tapped his shoes, then he said, 'Madame.'

Which meant that his wife needed shoes. Well, it was sometime since she had had any. Beryl could probably do something about that. She had replenished her wardrobe in the USA.

'OK,' he said, 'OK', and patted the guardian on the shoulder.

It was quarter to seven. He opened the door of his desk and took out his diary. He wrote up a description of the previous day's party. 'Everything superb. Pablo a super host. What a beautiful house. No wonder he resents the loss of his Spanish nationality. Had a long talk with the British C.G. He is going to a conference in Rabat next week.' That was quite true; it was still top secret, but there was no harm in Pablo knowing it. Then he wrote, 'C.G. is planning a visit to Gibraltar to discuss the new British policy about Spain.' That was not true, but it would do no harm to maintain Pablo's interest in Gibraltar. One day soon, he might give a definite date for the visit—to provide Pablo with a target.

At the office he learnt that a destitute British subject had to be sent back to England. He would be shipped by the Algeciras ferry, steerage class; he would be given a second-class rail ticket via Madrid and Paris. Himself he would have to see him on the ferry. That meant he would not be able to lunch with Beryl at the Yacht Club. Damn, he thought. He wanted a talk with Beryl. He did not quite know what he wanted to say, but he needed to be with her.

He felt restless, sitting here at his desk with so much about to happen, but with nothing that he needed to do immediately. He might as well go round to the American Consulate and see Murray. The production of *A Streetcar Named Desire* supplied him with an excuse.

He found Murray alone. He spread out the list of possible

properties that he had made out the day before. They agreed on the things that they would need.

'Pablo can transport them himself, can't he?'

'It doesn't look as though there was any lack of funds there,' said Adrian.

'I'd say there wasn't. It's the biggest party I've been to in this tourist's paradise.'

They exchanged notes about various aspects of their work. 'By the way,' said Adrian, 'have you any news for me about that kif smuggler of yours?'

'He's still in jug.'

'Does he have any visitors?'

'Oddly enough, our host of yesterday.'

Pablo had acted quickly. He'd have to see Hassoun and see him quickly. And, as he had to be down at the docks to see his DBS on to the Algeciras ferry, he would not be able to meet him at Italico's. That would mean his using the alternative route. If he had needed to see him, and had failed to do so, he would be in Porte's at seven-thirty. Hassoun would look inside the door and if he was there join him. If he was not there, he would presume it was unimportant and present himself the next day at Italico's. 'I must see him tonight,' thought Adrian. Even if it would mean missing the rehearsal.

On his return to the office, he rang up his flat. He was answered by the Fatima.

'Madame dort?' he asked.

'Non, madame bain.'

'OK'

He did not want to interrupt her in her bath.

Half an hour later she called back. 'I'm sorry I slept late,' she said.

'I'm not surprised.'

'I don't know how you manage with such little sleep.'

'I doze at my office.'

'You do?'

'Couldn't you tell from my tone of voice that your call woke me up?'

They laughed together. We do get on well, he thought. 'Shall I be seeing you on the beach?' she asked.

'No, I'm afraid you won't.'

'I won't?'

'No, that's what I rang up about. I've got to see off one of our bad hats on the Algeciras ferry.'

'Then I'll see you at the rehearsal.'

'Now there's another thing gone wrong. There's someone that I've got to see, and the only time that I can see him is about eight.'

'The rehearsal will be over before then.'

'That's what I was thinking; where you will be going afterwards. To the Parade?'

'Maybe. You'd better look in there anyhow if it's on your way back from where you're going.'

'It is.'

'Then let's leave it that way, vague.'

Which was the way she liked to leave things, provided they were the kind of things she liked. She'd be seeing Sarita. That was what mattered most. On days when she was not meeting Sarita, she felt listless. The day had no point. There was no point in getting up. But, as it was . . . and with Adrian getting back late. They'd have time alone together. I'll ask her that question today. I will, I will.

Porte's was crowded. There was not a table vacant. 'Do you mind sharing a table, Monsieur Adrian?' he was asked. He hesitated. He could scarcely say no, because he was expecting in a few minutes to be saying, "No, of course not," when he was asked if he minded a Moroccan sitting at his table. At last he noticed what seemed to be a table that was about to empty itself; two plump little girls beside a plump mother who had only one mouthful of cake left on her plate. He walked across and bowed. Might he take a seat? he asked. He could see no other table. But of course, of course.

One of the little girls stood up. She lifted her plate. 'What shall I get you this time, Mummy?'

Her mother dramatised her deliberation. She wanted to make it an adventure for her daughter. She raised her left hand, extended her forefinger, laid it against her temple. 'Let me see now, what shall it be, a chocolate éclair or a coffee éclair, or one of these cream buns. I can't decide; they're all so good.'

'But you must decide, really you must, Mummy. The tables are all full up.'

The mother shook her head. 'It's no good. I can't decide. I will leave it to you. Then it will be a surprise for me. Off you go.'

This would mean another half hour at least. He looked around the room. No, there was no other table. He would have to make do with this. Across the room he could see the barman already at work on his martini, peeling the thin sliver of lemon peel that would run round the inside of his glass. He did not need to give an order here. Always the dry martini in the tall, thin stemmed hock glass. He could see his 'man in Tangier' coming up the stairs, pausing at the head of the stairs, looking round him, noticing Adrian, taking in the situation and walking over to the bar. There were always two or three Moroccan men standing there. Hassoun would have quite a little wait, but he would not worry. He would be quite happy there, gossiping with friends.

The waitress from the bar had already arrived with his martini. She had also brought him a glass of iced water and a small plate containing four minute, triangular ham sandwiches. At the same time the small girl returned from the cake counter: she had brought a round open cherry tart, a slice of strawberry shortcake, and a meringue. She had to clear a place for them. 'What a lot of food,' she said.

'I'm as hungry as you are,' Adrian said. 'But we like different things.'

'That's what makes the world go round.'

He took a sip at his martini. As always that first sip sent a shiver along his veins. How good it was. It would take a full half hour to drink. The French trio would have barely finished their cakes by then. That would mean a second martini for him. That was not a fate worse than death.

He was right. There were only two sips left in his glass when the family finally collected their belongings. Within half a minute the waitress was busily clearing away the dishes.

'Yes,' he said, 'I'd like a second.'

'Of course, Monsieur Adrian, of course. And do you mind if a gentleman who has been waiting a long time joins you?'

'Of course not.'

She did not say 'he has sat with you before'. Was that tact on her part, or had she not noticed that he had sat before with Hassoun? How much did they realise here in Porte's of who he was and for what he stood? Sometimes one was surprised at how much they knew; at other times at how little they knew. If one was security-minded, one was always on the watch, too much on the watch.

He did not stand up when Hassoun came across. He smiled, but it was not a smile of recognition. No one at another table would have guessed that they already knew each other. Hassoun had brought over a half-filled glass. It contained a yellowish liquid, a scotch and soda probably. He waited till his own martini had arrived, then took his first sip before he spoke.

'That man in the Kasbah,' he said. 'That friend of mine— my Moroccan friend—has been to see him. I want you to find out all you can about that visit. How he came to see him. Have they been friends for a long time. This is most important. I want to know what they talk about. As soon as possible.'

'I see.'

Hassoun finished his drink quickly.

'Is there any need for me to stay?' he asked.

'No, there is no need for you to stay.'

Hassoun rose, bowed, walked away.

Adrian looked at his glass. Only two sips. A whole glassful left. Quarter past eight now. Another half hour. He wasn't going to hurry. He did not often allow himself a second. He was going to linger over his enjoyment. The rehearsal would probably be over. They would go on to the Parade, if they did not stay on at the flat. He would look in at the Parade on his way back. It wasn't worth ringing up; he would stay here and savour the passing hour and the glow that would spread and deepen, minute by minute, sip by sip.

The rehearsal had in fact broken up a little earlier. Beryl and Sarita had been left alone.

'Do you feel like going to the Parade?' asked Beryl.

'Depends on what you have got in the frig.'

'I've some sauerkraut and sausage.'

'Why don't we heat that up?'

'I've enough aquavit left for two and a half glasses each.'

'What could be better?'

They sat facing each other across the table. Beryl raised her glass. 'Skol,' she said.

'Skol,' said Sarita. The schnapps had been kept in the small top compartment. It was very cold. It sent a shiver along Beryl's nerves. She lifted her glass again to Sarita. They looked each other in the eyes as they toasted one another. 'Why did you want me to know?' she asked.

Sarita smiled, a conspiratorial smile. 'Because of the way I felt about you.'

'How did you feel about me?'

'I fell in love.'

'You fell in love?'

'Does that surprise you?'

'Yes, no, yes.'

'You thought it was just one more experiment?'

'When I began to think about it, yes.'

'Because of the way I'd talked about those others?'

'I suppose so, yes.'

'I'm sorry I misled you. From the way I talked, you must have thought of me as being like a man who looks around him at a party, thinking, "Is there anyone that's my type here?" Thinking of it as a piece of casual fun. And it is fun too. I've had my share of that. But with you it was different. I liked you right away, at sight. You were so fresh, so friendly. You were such good company. No *coup de foudre* about it. Simply a liking to be with you. A liking that grew stronger every

182

time we met. You were so nice to look at, and your way of smiling. Every time I saw you I'd find new things to like in you, to admire in you. And it wasn't only that. I was so close to you. I wanted to be more close to you. I wanted to be at one with you, to whisper to you how I felt about you. Which was something I hadn't felt for many years. I'm a lot older than you, remember. And I've lived through a lot; I'm a widow. I'm a Spaniard. I've had to compromise. I'd built up a life of compromise. And then suddenly there was you, and everything was different. I recognised of course that you are what is called a normal woman. Men attract you; you attract them. You've a husband—well, you've told me about him. That's a real relationship. It is something that is built to last—that will last, I pray to Heaven; when I go to Mass, that's one of the things I pray for, that what there is between you and Adrian will survive.

'But at the same time, I couldn't believe that if I felt so strongly about you, there wouldn't be some reciprocity on your side. You know what that French cynic said, "One loves, the other lets herself be loved,"—Maugham quoted that more than once, but I couldn't believe that you couldn't be persuaded to respond a little—*se laisse aimer*. That's how it was with me.'

She paused. She stretched her arm across the table. Beryl slid her hand to meet it. Their fingers intertwined. 'Adrian will be back in half an hour,' Beryl said. 'Next Wednesday he's going to Gibraltar by the ferry. Coming back in the evening.'

'Why don't we lunch on Wednesday then?'

14

As usual, Adrian caught the ferry instead of the plane, and as usual, in spite of the confusion in the customs shed, within less than half an hour he was walking across the asphalt to the gangplank, and looking round to see which other Tangerines of his acquaintance were making the crossing. At a first glance there seemed only one; and that was one whose being there surprised him. Pablo Monterey. 'I didn't expect to find you here,' he said.

'I never expect to find anyone on this barbarous means of transport.'

'But if one is to replenish one's larder, what else can one do?'

'Exactly; what else can one do?'

'I should have thought you, with your Spanish heritage, would have preferred Ceuta.'

'I do prefer Ceuta. But if you have a Moroccan passport, you have a better time with the customs at Tangier than at Ceuta.'

'Ah, I see, that passport.'

'Have a look at the way they'll examine my passport at the gangplank. They'll let you through automatically, but they'll examine every page on mine. You go first, and then look back and watch.'

He did. The inspector turned Pablo's passport over page by page. And there could not be all that many entries in it.

'I see what you mean,' Adrian said when at last Pablo came up the gangplank. 'And what about some breakfast now? Breakfast and tea are the two best English meals. The trouble is that they spoil you for the other two meals—lunch and dinner—which should be better because wine goes with them. This ferry is the one place where I indulge myself in such an orgy. That's less than ten times a year. Let's go and indulge ourselves.'

The restaurant was three-quarters empty. There were not

many first-class passengers, and they, for the most part, preferred to come in later at about eleven—in terms of Gibraltar time—for sandwiches and beer.

Within ten minutes their fried eggs and bacon with toast and marmalade were on the table. In deference to the fact that they were on a British ship, they took tea instead of coffee.

'This really is a good meal, isn't it?' said Adrian.

'It's a real meal, anyhow. You wouldn't get it anywhere except upon a British train or ship. That's what I ask of things, that they should be real.'

'That was a real enough party at your house on Sunday.'

'Was it? I hoped it was. It was real to me.'

'Are there many houses in Morocco where that kind of standard is maintained?'

'On the French side, I suppose there are.'

'Not on the Spanish?'

'Not as far as I know.'

'You are exceptional, you know.'

'Am I? How?'

'Having been brought up to think of yourself as Spanish in the way you have, but without a Spanish father to, I won't say guide you, but explain to you what it was all about; show you what its tradition was, and make you feel that you were a part of it . . . I'm, of course, in an entirely different position. I wasn't brought up as part of a big world—my family, we were simple, professional Englishmen, middle-middle class, minor public school, but it did have a tradition of its own, that I've been quite aware of, and because I never knew my father, I've always felt a little lost, because of that . . . Do you see what I mean? Nothing could be more different than your life and mine, but there is a kinship, in a way.'

Kinship, yes, there was no other word; he did feel a kinship with this man, of his own age, of his own generation, but of a different class, with a different destiny.

Heaven knew what Pablo was doing on this ship. Was it in connection with some subversive operation? Did it bear any relationship with his own presence here; he who was here as a direct consequence of Pablo's activities. He was going in search of information about Pablo. Was Pablo engaged on a similar mission, in terms of his own campaign? It seemed ridiculous, it was ridiculous, and yet it was equally ridiculous that in 1914 and again in 1939 young Englishmen and young Germans, born in the same year, born to the same ideas, should find themselves at each other's throats for no better reason than that they had been born a few miles apart, the other side of this river or that range of hills, divided by a frontier. Had not Wilfred Owen written a poem about that, 'Strange Meeting'? And just as it was pointless for that German and that Englishman to think I've more in common with that enemy than I have with the majority of my compatriots, so was it pointless for him now to be thinking, 'I like this chap. He's got his problems, just as I have mine, I wish him well.' This man was his enemy. He must remember that young Moroccan stretched out in the Place de France; he must think of that bomb tossed at that lunch party at Ceuta. The bomb that might well have been the death of Beryl. They were sitting here now as friends, but they were enemies. He must turn this occasion to his own use.

'You remember,' Adrian said, 'what we were saying the other day about a terrorist trying to blow up this ship. Let's take a stroll round and see how difficult it would be.'

'Why not?'

The ship, as far as the passengers were concerned, was divided into two sections; there was the upper and the centre deck; below, the cars were parked and the stores, the fruit and vegetables, were packed; above that were the first and second class divisions; the second class had their own deck space and benches: the first class had a restaurant and a bar. The bar was provided with a number of armchairs. It was here that the elderly and affluent passed their voyage dozing between gin-and-tonics.

In front of the restaurant was an open stretch of deck to which second class passengers had access. There was no seating accommodation. Extra packages were kept there. Passengers exercised themselves and leant against the taffrail.

Above the bar and restaurant was the upper boat deck, which was reserved for first class passengers. It was uncovered. It was a wide open space, with hard seats round the taffrail and in the centre round a main ventilator shaft, a further row of seats, one on each side. In front of this open space was a superstructure that contained offices and officers' quarters. Two narrow passages led, on either side, to the steps from which you approached the bridge.

Adrian and Pablo went round the middle deck. The restaurant, as always, was half-full, so was the bar. It was a sunny day, and the front and open deck was crowded with passengers. Men bare to the waist were getting suntans.

'Not much scope here for our terrorist,' said Adrian. The seats in the passages on either side of the bar were occupied. 'Let's see how it is on top,' he said.

The open space in the centre was also crowded. But the narrow passages on either side of the superstructure were empty.

'This would be the best place,' said Pablo.

They strolled along the passage to the bridge. 'This is the one, I gather.'

They stood at the foot of the steps with a clear view of the bridge. 'It would be easy to lob a bomb on to it. It could do a great deal of damage. But he'd need an accomplice to warn him that the coast was clear,' said Adrian.

'Yes, he would need an accomplice.'

'Let's rehearse it.'

'How?'

'I'll go down to the end of the passage. You stand at the foot of the steps. How long would it take you to toss the bomb and dodge round on to the other side of the superstructure?'

'Not thirty seconds.'

'Then I'll stand here and wait until there's a certainty that you'll have thirty seconds clear. Then I'll make a sign. You swing your arm, then dodge away. I don't think you'll need anything like thirty seconds.'

'You'll time me?'

'Right.'

Pablo stood by the steps. Adrian stood at the entrance to the passage. There were a number of passengers, but they were busy. One couple was walking back and forth, but they were not coming down the passage. He must not give them an opportunity to change their minds. They were coming closer to him, closer, closer. Only two yards away now, only one yard. They checked; they turned. Adrian made his signal, then he stooped to tie up his shoe. Before he had completed the knot, Pablo was at his side. Adrian looked at his watch. 'Eighteen seconds. And you didn't need the half of that. Within five seconds you were out of sight.'

'Easy, in fact.'

'Provided he's got an accomplice with him.'

'Of course, provided he's got an accomplice.'

'Just stand here beside me, and let's watch and see how often someone does go down that passage.'

They waited; the half-naked passengers deepened their tans. Other couples walked in a circle round the airshaft; others read and dozed on the hard-backed seats. Then, suddenly, a man came up the stairs, and without looking round made straight for the narrow passage. He moved at a fast straight pace. He strode down to the steps, turned round briskly, like a sentry on parade, swung round, walked back again, down the passage, proceeded across the deck to the steps leading to the middle deck, and down the passage to-wards the bridge. Adrian and Pablo looked at one another.

'No chance for our terrorist with that man on the job,' said Adrian.

'And he looks likely to be on the job for half an hour.'

'Our terrorist would have to have an accomplice; there's no doubt of that.'

They began to walk together, just as the solitary sentry type had done but on the other side of the superstructure. Walking side by side is a great inducement to a sense of kinship.

'I suppose,' Pablo said, 'blowing up this ship would be a very useful tactic for a terrorist.'

'If he got the right publicity for it.'

'What do you mean by that?'

'If he did it at the right time, at the right place.'

'What do you mean by the right place?'

'So that everyone could see it—when the ship was quite near to land—when there'd be a lot of people on the beach and on the terrace by the Place de France, just when she was going out or just when she was coming in. It's no good if she was too far out at sea. It's not as though he were going to sink the ship; that's too much to hope for. But there would be an obvious explosion, something that everyone could see.'

'What do you mean by the right time?'

'Doing it when there's someone of importance aboard. The Bishop of Gibraltar, say, or the British Consul General, so that there'd be a reception committee on the docks. That's what is needed. Everyone should talk about it and then the Liberation Committee could claim responsibility. That would be something for Franco to put in his pipe and enjoy the smoking of.'

Adrian watched Pablo closely. The idea had taken root. It would not be Pablo who tossed the bomb, of course. Any more than it had been Pablo who rode down that Moroccan in the Place de France or who had thrown the bomb in Ceuta. Pablo worked through cut-outs, just as he did himself; another source of kinship.

Adrian lost sight of Pablo in the crush of coming off: he would have liked to see who met him. For himself, he had made no plans. He had signalled Groves that he was coming over, but he was not going to suggest that he had come over on a definite assignment. Groves gave him a free hand. There were things he needed to do, people he needed to see in Gibraltar. He telephoned Groves from the Holiday Inn.

'When will you be at a loose end?' he asked.

'I'm always at a loose end when you're around.'

'Then what about right away?'

'Right away'll be fine'.

Groves was as cordial as Adrian had known he would be.

'I presume,' he said, 'that there's enough business attached to this visit for you to charge it as a legitimate expense.'

'That's so.'

'What is the business?'

'A young American who was caught with kif on the Algeciras ferry.'

'How does he affect us?'

Adrian explained how he felt that he might affect British interests.

'I see. I see.' Groves nodded his head slowly, 'You haven't seen him yourself, I suppose.'

'I didn't think it would be a good idea to let the Moroccans know that I was interested.'

'Quite right. Quite right.'

'Hassoun has been round to see him.'

'Hassoun? Hassoun, yes, of course, I remember now. Hassoun. Can you tell me anything about him, more than I know already? How we came to recruit him for example?'

'Do you think Hassoun would like that?'

'I don't see why he shouldn't, unless he has something to conceal.'

'That's just the point. He may have something to conceal. These fellows do. They appreciate their anonymity. They like to feel they've got us in the dark. They bring us information, but they don't want us to know where they get it. They realise that we check their references before we take them on. But those references, once checked, they expect to be trusted. Hassoun would be shocked if he found that you knew something about him that he didn't know you knew. You see that, don't you?'

Yes, he saw it, and the fact that he saw it irritated him. He did not like Groves' being right. He was glad to think he knew something that Groves did not know, and that in point of fact, Groves, as his superior, should know. When he had decided to make this trip, he had asked himself whether he should not take Groves into his confidence. If Groves had been forthcoming now, he would have told him. But as it was—let him find out for himself, he thought. He had his own channels of finding out a little more about Hassoun. He had had his own very secure reasons for making the trip today.

Pablo Monterey had been met at the docks by a small green Volkswagen. Within ten minutes he was siting in the study of one of Gibraltar's more prominent merchants—an Indian called Amin Sirham. Amin's family had left Bombay in the First World War, and he was proprietor of a small chain of clothing stores in former British colonies and protectorates, such as Aden, Cyprus, Baghdad. He had never taken an active part in politics, but it was believed that he could influence events. He was a man in his middle fifties. There were three other men in the room—one of them was quite an old man, the other two were in their middle twenties. They were, all of them, neatly dressed; they had slightly Semitic features; they were dark-skinned. They had a look of breeding. They all with their British background had a vested interest in keeping Gibraltar British. They were seated round a table on which had been set out a tea tray with small cups on it, along with two plates of sugary cakes. Sirham was in a high-backed chair with wide arms; he sat back in his chair his wrists hanging loose.

He greeted Pablo on behalf of the others. 'Welcome, my dear friend, welcome. We are always glad when you can assist us in our deliberations. You allow us to see our problems from another angle. Living here, virtually prisoners on this rock, we often see our problem in the wrong perspective. We are very grateful to you for the information, in particular for the important secret facts you bring us from British sources. You know more about us than we know about ourselves.'

There was a little murmur of agreement round the table. There were smiles of welcome on their faces. They were fond of him. He knew that. But they never, he suspected, regarded him as one of themselves. Had he really got their cause at heart? Was he not a playboy treating as a kind of game what was deadly serious for them? They were, he always fancied, slightly contemptuous of him. It was they who ran the risks, not he. He had kept track on Simms: he knew about Simms' contacts, but it was not he who had ridden down that agent in the Place de France. It was not he who had been entrusted with that mission to Ceuta. 'No, no,' they had said to him. 'We don't want you to get involved with that kind of thing. We want to keep you underground. That's why you are so useful, so invaluable to us. You are someone that nobody suspects. Keep your alibi. You are someone that everybody trusts.' He was useful to them. They valued him. But he was not really one of them.

He chuckled to himself. That was what they thought. Soon they would know better.

'I am very glad to be seeing you today,' he said. 'I have a project of my own. A project that will do our cause a great deal of good. I can carry it out on my own. In only one way do I need your assistance. You would have no difficulty, I presume, in providing me with a bomb.'

'A bomb.' The two words came from Amin. They were uttered with incredulous astonishment. Pablo looked round the table. On every face there was a similar expression of dumbfounded increduilty. Again he chuckled inwardly. He had caught them off their guard all right. He had not led up to his proposition.

'You will wonder why I need a bomb,' he said. 'I will tell you. I am planning to blow up the *Mons Calpe*.'

'The *Mons Calpe*?'

Once again the exclamation came from Amin. He was still too surprised to comment. Pablo smiled. 'Very shortly the British Consul General will be paying a visit to Gibraltar. He will be returning on the afternoon ferry; the one that I shall be returning by tonight. Shortly before the ferry docks, there will be an explosion on the bridge. It will not be too serious a one; by that I mean that though there will be damage, there may not be any deaths. There may be, of course. I hope there won't be. I should be sorry if anything happened to that jovial, bearded captain. I like him, and he has a lively, attractive wife. But you know the old proverb. "You can't make an omelette without cracking eggs." The important thing is that there should be this gesture. Then our committee will issue an announcement. "This is a warning," we will say, "to the Spanish and the British authorities. The

Basque Liberation Committee is not satisfied with the treatment that we are receiving from the Franco Government. Let those in authority beware." It will be a shock to Franco. That is what we need to do: to frighten Franco.' He paused. 'I think it a sound scheme: a very sound one.'

He looked round him. On their faces was an expression that he had not seen before. It warmed his heart.

'When do you expect this to happen?' he was asked.

He shrugged. 'I cannot tell, but I do not think it will be so long. He goes to Rabat next week. When he is over there, the date of the meeting in Gibraltar will be decided. I cannot be sure how soon I shall have an opportunity of finding the exact date. But I shall find it, of that I am quite sure. I expect it within a month, but it may be sooner. I shall be grateful, therefore, if you will get that bomb prepared as soon as possible. Then when I know, I will send you a signal. On the decisive day, I will cross on the morning ferry. I will call in here at noon. I shall leave with the bomb, and then, gentlemen, you can leave the rest to me. Is that satisfactory?'

He looked round him with a smile.

No one spoke. He could not have had a more satisfactory reply.

Beryl and Sarita met at the Minzah swimming pool. They lay out on chairs. They rubbed oil into each other's shoulders. Beryl lay on her face and let Sarita massage her. How strong her fingers were. How firmly they kneaded her. Yet how lightly their tips brushed her back, her sides. 'Why don't we have a sandwich here?' Sarita said.

'Why don't we?'

They drank sangria. Neither wanted to eat, neither wanted to drink. 'Siesta time,' Sarita said.

'Siesta time.'

They went straight up to Sarita's room. They sat beside each other on a chaise lounge. Each knew what was in the other's mind. 'I'm nervous,' Beryl said. 'I'm afraid of being awkward.'

'There's no need to worry about that.' Sarita took Beryl's

face between her hands. 'I promise you you won't,' she said.

The Gibraltar ferry was due in at half past seven. Beryl was back by seven. The water was off, but she had filled her bath that morning. She put her hand in the water. It was tepid after the long day's heat. She put a steel bucket on the stove. She stretched out on the settee. Every nerve in her was tingling. She had never felt so alive, so restless; satiated but insatiable. Hurry, hurry, hurry, she thought. Hurry back. She was wearing a short white bed-jacket, that barely reached her navel. She waited impatiently for the click of Adrian's key. Hurry, hurry, hurry. At last it came. As he entered the room, she stretched her arms sideways above her head.

'You look hot and tired,' she said.

'That's exactly how I am.'

'Then I've just the thing for you. Get out of those clothes quick.'

She took the bucket off the stove. She poured it in the bath. She dabbled her fingers in it. It was almost warm. She poured in some blue essence. She beat it up so that there was a white cloud of foam upon the surface. She flung off her housecoat. 'Hurry!' she called. 'Hurry!' She climbed over the side. She slid along its length. It was deliciously cool. She stretched herself, spreading her legs. 'In quick,' she said, 'your back to me.'

She raised her knees, clasping them around his body, under his arms. She soaped his back, then leaning forward, she soaped his chest, his stomach, letting her hands travel along his thighs. 'Now let's change places, quick,' she said. She clambered over him; his slippery hands kneaded her breasts, moved in a slow caress over her body, lingering between her legs. 'Up,' she said, 'on our feet. Let's wash off all this soap.' Standing facing each other, they splashed themselves with water. 'Now for that big towel.'

They stood on the bathmat, sharing the big, fleecy towel; then letting it fall to the floor; they stood close, close, together, closely clasped; they kissed. She took his hand. 'I can't wait,' she said.

They did not bother to pull back the sheets. It was the wildest ten minutes of their life.

She lifted herself upon her elbow.

'Something long and cool?' she asked.

'Something very long and cool.'

She mixed a campari soda, in a tall glass, with a slice of lime. Its bitterness would quench his thirst. She handed him the glass. She watched him sip it. 'Do you recommend the same for me?' she said.

'What the doctor ordered.'

She climbed up on the bed beside him, propping a pillow underneath her shoulders. 'Tell me about your day,' she said. He told her, but she did not listen. The sight of his body naked at her side excited her. She felt aggressive. This was how she had looked to Sarita, three hours back. 'Did you have a good lunch?' she asked.

'One always has a good lunch at the Rock.'

'Then you aren't hungry yet?' She put down her glass on the bed table. She leant across him. Her fingertips trailed over him, as Sarita's had trailed over her. 'If I were you I should put down that glass,' she said.

Quite a little while later, she said: 'I shouldn't be surprised if you weren't feeling hungry now. Stay there. I'll bring you something.'

She set a tray of open sandwiches between them. He munched in silence. 'Wouldn't you say that beer is what we want with this?'

'That's just what I'd say we want with this.'

The beer was sharp against her palate. It was half past nine. 'This morning we planned to go to the Parade,' she said.

'I know we did.'

'Do you feel like going there?'

'I don't particularly.'

'Then why don't we snuggle up.'

195

She woke, curled up against him, fitted spoonwise. They were naked still. She did not know what time it was. She could not bother to look. There were no sounds from the street. Two or three o'clock, most likely. She was rested and refreshed, but her mind was racing still. The crowded day had left her unappeased. Adrian was breathing quietly. He had no right to sleep so soundly, when she was awake, when she was restless. She began to stroke his chest, gently, gently; she moved slightly aside, easing him on to his back. Once again her fingertips began their slow progression from neck to knees. He stirred. 'He's waking up,' she thought, 'he's in the mood now, though he doesn't know it.' She knelt across him, lowering herself slowly, gently, guiding him. 'Isn't this a nice way to be woken up?' she said.

She had arranged to meet Sarita next morning at Porte's for coffee.

'I don't want our first meeting to be unexpected,' she had said. 'It might be too much of a shock.'

'I don't think it will.'

'All the same, I don't want to risk it.'

To prepare herself, she arrived early. Ten minutes early. She took the second table on the left hand side, beside the window. She wanted to see Sarita first, to watch her walk across the room, so as not to see too soon the actual expression on her face. Let it come upon her slowly, stage by stage.

It did not work out that way, however. A voice from the street called, 'Beryl'. She leant out and there was Sarita on the pavement waving up at her. How silly of her not to have thought of that. There had been no parking place. Sarita had parked further down the street, and it was, just as she had guessed it would be, a shock, that first sight of her. She had expected Sarita to look different, but she didn't.

She watched for the beads across the door to be pressed back. She tried not to gasp; she failed. How exquisite she was at that. As Sarita came up the stairs, she rose. When they met at a party, invariably they kissed; but today they didn't. They looked at each other across the table.

'I feel so happy,' Beryl said.

'Me too.'

They ordered coffee. 'There's something I want to tell you,' Beryl said.

'You tell me.'

'I almost had an affair when I was in America.'

She told Sarita about McCrudden. 'I've always guessed that I should have an affair some day. I couldn't go through a whole marriage without something happening. I wondered if I'd feel differently to Adrian if I did. I supposed I should. I wondered in what way I would. I prayed that it would happen when he wasn't around. In America, last month, I thought, "Now this is how it should be. The Atlantic and half a continent between us. It'll be something that happened in another country, to another person," and I felt cheated over that car accident. I was missing the best chance that I might have. But all the same, when I was on the plane bound for home, I couldn't help wondering how I should be feeling now if I was recovering from a terrific last night. Should I be in any mood for Adrian. I should want thirty-six hours' rest. But as it was, I was looking forward to seeing Adrian. I hadn't been made love to for five weeks. I had missed that. I looked forward to making love again. You see what I mean.'

'I see what you mean.'

'But last night on the contrary, in spite of our time together, I was thrilled to have Adrian back. Doesn't that surprise you?'

'Not all that much'.

There was a mocking, but tender smile on Sarita's lips. 'It's different,' she said, 'between a man and a woman, and between a woman and a woman. With a man and a woman, even in these days of women's lib, there's no real equality; there's the act of possession. The act of being possessed; the man dictates the woman's rhythm; the woman's responses are dependent on the fact on that possession; with a woman and a woman it's altogether different. There's a sharing, being equal partners. You're finding it now; you'll find it more, increasingly.' She paused. There was a twinkle in her eye.

'Why are we discussing this in Porte's across a coffee table. Why don't we go home?'

They lay side by side, their heads raised by pillows, looking up at the ceiling, talking casually; left hand clasped by right hand, fingers intertwined.

'There's another thing that's surprising me about this,' said Beryl. 'As I told you I've always known that I should have an affair one day. I should feel I owed it to myself; that I should need variety; that I should need to renew myself. Now I don't feel that any longer.

'You don't?'

'I feel that I can get all the variety I want with another woman, and that if I did . . . no, this isn't easy to explain. I don't expect you to be faithful to me.'

'I'm glad you don't.'

'And in return I'm not expecting to be faithful to you.'

'I'm not sure that I shall be so contented if you aren't.'

'Won't you . . . I don't think you'd mind. Any more than I would. If you were to say, "You know that Susan Longrigg. I believe I've got a letch on her," I think I'd be able to say, "You have? Good luck to you, tell me all about it." It might even be a link between us. I can picture us, talking it over afterwards with me saying, "Did she do something special that I don't know about. She did, then show me." You can imagine that, can't you?'

'I can.'

'But I can't imagine that with a husband. I remember saying to Adrian, oh, such a long time ago, "I hope you'll be faithful to me, but I know that men are different. If you aren't, though, there's one thing I beg, don't tell me anything about it." But I believe that between you and me it would be an added bond. Another thing to share. If I were to meet another woman who attracted me, I'd think, "what fun it'll be telling Sarita afterwards.".'

'It's heaven, this talking afterwards.'

'And getting excited while we talk.'

'I know, I know.'

15

July was consumed by August. The days grew hotter. The streets were crowded with unfamiliar figures. Charabanc after tourist charabanc blocked the roadways. The Tangier theatre's performance of *A Streetcar Named Desire* was a great success.

On the third Sunday in September, the Archaeological Society held its first picnic of the autumn season. Adrian and Beryl were booked on it. They were to visit some Roman remains beyond Azilah. They packed a thermos of Bloody Marys with their sandwiches. They had also a couple of bottles of iced beer. The rendezvous was at nine-thirty at the Cofficom. There were some thirty members waiting for the President to give them the signal to set out. Most of them were familiar to Adrian, but he was surprised to see Pablo there.

'I didn't know you were a member,' he said.

'I'm not. I've been to Mass. I was on my way to breakfast. I stopped to see what this gathering was about.'

It was a little while since Adrian had seen Pablo. Since the Tangier Players' performance he had not the same check on his activities. It was two weeks since the thread in his diary had been displaced. I wonder, Adrian thought, I wonder.

Beryl was driving, and as the motorcade swung east towards the new road out of town, Adrian looked over his shoulder to see which route Pablo took. He had turned right and was headed up the hill. Tetuan was in the other direction but he might be headed for the Café de Paris. That was the best place for breakfast. Not that he need worry. He'd know soon enough if his suspicions were correct.

He was to know within seven hours. Sarita had been on the picnic, and she suggested on their return that they should look in at the Spanish Consulate for an iced coffee and a swim. He shook his head.

'There are two things I need to do at the flat first. But I won't be long. I'll be right back. I promise you.'

'Can't those things wait?'

'I suppose they could, but they're on my mind. I can't relax until they're settled.'

'You and your mysteries.'

'If you knew how mild they really are.'

'I hope they are. That's all I ask.'

His heart was beating as he hurried up the stairs. He had closed the windows but not the shutters when he left the flat. His study door was open. He sniffed. But he could not detect that particular rich scent that he had come to associate with Pablo. His spirits sank. If Pablo had not come back this morning, then he was either on the wrong tack, or Pablo had become suspicious. If that was the case, he had been banking everything on a horse that had been scratched. If he was wrong, if he had to start again, if he had nothing to show for all these weeks, if he wasn't able to prove to the boys in Whitehall that he was needed, if he lost his job, what would happen to himself and Beryl—what, what, what . . . Had it all been conjecture?

His fingers shook as he turned the key in the lock on his desk. He scarcely dared to take out his diary. Everything in the drawer looked the way it had been. Suppose he had been wrong. Suppose Pablo was not the man. Suppose someone else was at work. He opened the diary. For a moment he dared not look. Suppose the thread were still in place. Suppose . . . Come, don't be a funk, he adjured himself. Be a man. He opened his eyes . . . He sighed. It was all right. All was well. Now he had the proof. It was Pablo. It could not be anybody else. He read the last entry but one: That was the key entry, the one that mattered. 'CG is going to Gibraltar,' he read, 'the week after next. Spending the night. Returning Wednesday's ferry.'

He sighed. This was the test. Now he would know. If the attempt were to be made, it would be made that Wednesday.

'What do I do now?' he asked.

He put back the thread in its right place, stretched it

across the sheet. It had served its purpose. He had baited the hook, and the right fish had nibbled. What did he do now? Should he let Groves know? He should, he supposed, and yet . . . might he not find out more if he held his hand. How much damage would Pablo do? He would toss his bomb on to the bridge. If it was a big enough bomb, and he presumed he would get himself a big one, he would blow the bridge apart. But would there be any loss of life? There might not be, there need not be. The captain would be on the bridge. Adrian would not want any harm to come to him. He was fond of the captain and his attractive wife: no harm must come to him . . . How much danger threatened him? Pablo hadn't had death in mind. He had wanted to issue a warning, to make a gesture. If his man escaped, and why shouldn't he with an accomplice (these IRA men who threw bombs in London always got away with it) if he were left here, undetected and in his own opinion unsuspected, he would be emboldened to try something more ambitious. This conspiracy might be bigger than he could guess. Success would go to Pablo's head. 'I've got away with this,' he'd think, 'I can get away with anything.' If he was allowed to run free a little longer, the whole gang could be roped in. Wasn't it worth risking?

He strode up and down his flat. What a chance. What a chance. He thought again of the captain. He couldn't risk his life. He must give him some warning. He had to think this out. In the meantime . . . There were other angles; what about the assistant. Was it worth risking? Was it?

Pablo was staying the night at the Hotel Lutetia—at the foot of the Rue Velasquez. Time was hanging heavily on his hands. He had not enough to do. His estate occupied only half his day. He could leave it alone for a couple of days and then in half a day he could get the whole thing settled. His engagement with the anti-Franco movement occupied a lot of thought, but not a great deal of action. Then there was Frieda. It had happened so quickly, so excitingly, it had driven most other thoughts out of his mind. But that, too, was very far from being a full-time occupation. He would have liked it to have been, but it simply wasn't. She had very little spare time. She was at the Consul General's beck and call. With his wife in England, his demands on her were incessant.

'You must see how it is,' she said. 'I'm not only his secretary. I'm his hostess too.'

That he could, of course, understand, but he did not see why she should have to be such a universal guest. She was in too much demand. There were not so many unattached young women in what was called the international set. Invitation after invitation. And the infuriating thing was that he himself was not in that set. He was not invited to those parties. He did not see her more than twice a week. And that was not enough: that was not nearly enough. His feelings were hurt, so was his vanity. She was treating him the way some men treated their women, making use of them, calling them up when they were in the mood for them. He was not going to stand for that. He would have to assert himself. These American and European women had to be brought to heel. Moroccans were agreed on that. The women might object at first, but they took a certain pride in their subjection. He had seen more than one woman vaunting her blacked eye in the market. They regarded it as a badge of honour, in the way that old style Prussian officers had flaunted their sabre cuts. He'd never had to resort to that himself. He'd never needed to. But the time had come. Clearly, the time had come. Frieda was a delightful creature, but she had to learn her lesson. In the meantime, there was that enrollment of an accomplice.

That evening in the Parade he noticed Sven Jurgensen by himself. He had not seen him since the last night of the play. Jurgensen, an idea, a very definite idea. He went across.

'I was thinking of you today. Is it possible for you to take a day off from the school sometimes?'

'We seem to have quite a number of public holidays.'

'I have to go over to Gibraltar for the day in a couple of weeks' time, could you come too? As my guest, of course.'

'That would be very nice of you.'

'There's something that I'd like to have you do for me in return. It isn't much. It wouldn't be any trouble.'

'I'd be delighted.'

'It's nothing serious. Just a mild joke I'm playing on the captain of the ship. I'll tell you when the time comes. All I want you to do is keep watch for me when the ship comes up to dock. I want to go up to the bridge without anybody seeing me, OK?'

'OK'

It should be all right. He had hoped at the beginning that he might make more complicated use of him. He had heard about his frustrated Mormon mission, about his anxiety to return to Utah as a hero. He had thought he might enroll him in his own task force. The US was anti-Franco. But the kind of action that he was meditating would not be approved in Salt Lake City. All the same, he felt a genuine kinship with the young American. He too was at outs with his own destiny.

'That'll be fine,' he said, 'a week from Wednesday; I'll get the tickets. Meet me at the customs shed.'

On the following morning, Adrian hesitated over his journal. He did not expect that Pablo would get an opportunity of examining it for a little time. The Fatima did not leave till two o'clock, and in the afternoon he or Beryl was likely to be in. All the same, he would have to make his routine entries, and he would have to slip pieces of false information in between the pieces of actual fact. Not too often though. He had to maintain his own credibility. He must see Frieda this morning and extract some information about 'his nibs' visit to Rabat. There should be something. He ought to be back today. At the end of his entry, he wrote, 'Am curious to learn from CG how much Spain is worrying about Ceuta.'

He usually looked in on Frieda at the time the morning cup of tea went round the office. 'What happened to you yesterday?' he asked.

'I fulfilled my secretarial duties.'

'On a Sunday?'

'Especially on a Sunday.'

There was a half-twinkle in her eye. He remembered how he and Beryl had exchanged glances at Tetuan. He should not be surprised if there was something cooking there. The CG had changed in a number of little ways during the last two months. Perhaps he was consoling himself for his wife's re-solve to be a better mother than a wife. Adrian envied him. Frieda was a tantalising creature. You always felt that she had something in reserve.

He liked her; he felt that she liked him. And he liked her the better for his guessing that they would never really get to know each other any better.

'And what about your extra-secretarial duties?'

'What may those be?'

'The duties that you undertook on my behalf.'

'Ah, those.'

'Well, what about them?'

She shook her head. 'I've done my best. I'm not really much the wiser.'

'You've seen a certain amount of him?'

'I have.'

'And how do you feel?'

'Very much as I did two months ago. I don't feel he's altogether sane.'

'You feel he might do something erratic any moment?'

'That is exactly what I feel.'

'Why do you feel that?'

'Because I don't know what makes him tick. He's young. He doesn't seem without ambition. But he does not really seem to be doing anything.'

'What about that estate of his? It could be a full-time job.'

'It isn't though. It doesn't take up a quarter of his time.'

'And you wonder what takes up the other three-quarters?'

'Yes.'

He was tempted to let her know of Pablo's involvement with the Basque Independence boys, but thought better of it. His sense of security was too ingrained.

Back in his office, he put a call through to his flat. Beryl answered him.

'What about lunch today?'

'I'm sorry. I'm swimming with Sarita at the Minzah.'

'You seem to be seeing her every day.'

'Isn't that in accordance with your instructions?'

'I know. I know.'

'You're still curious about that young Mormon?'

'Of course I am.'

'I'm keeping my eye on him for you.'

'Do that.'

Adrian lunched at the Yacht Club. It would not be staying open on the beach much longer. He wanted to make the most of these last days. As he had expected the captain of the *Mons Calpe* and his wife were there.

'Not many more times here, I'm afraid,'

'I'm not sure that I don't enjoy it on the port as much.'

'It's good to have a change; by the way, I have a kind of warning that I should give you.'

'That sounds alarming.'

'It needn't be. I'm sure it's a false alarm. You know how pranksters ring up theatres to warn the management that there's a bomb planted in the stalls. I've a rumour that there may be some trouble on the journey across on Wednesday week. It might be a good idea to leave the missus behind.'

'I hadn't thought of bringing her.'

'No trouble then. And I should keep my eyes skinned on the bridge, as you're coming into port. Have somebody on guard.'

'I always have.'

'Then that's all right.'

'Does your boss know about this?'

'I'd be choked off if I mentioned it. He thinks I'm an alarmist. I sometimes pray that something will happen sometime, just to prove that I'm not always wrong.'

'Keeping an eye on that Mormon for him.' Beryl was doing

more than that. That afternoon, after their swim, she was
keeping alert Sarita's interest in him.

'You remember saying, oh, at the very start of things, that
if I was interested in him we might agree to share him.'

'I remember.'

'Have you thought about that since?'

'Of course.'

'But how do you mean, share. You really did mean share?'

'Of course.'

'The three of us together?'

'Yes.'

'How would we get that started?'

'Let's think it out.'

They were lying side by side on Sarita's divan. Each wore
a jacket that lay loose and open on their shoulders; left hand
was clasping right hand.

'Suppose that we'd been to the beach, and we'd come
back to shower.' Sarita said. 'You might complain that your
shoulders ached. "I'll massage you," I'd say.'

'And I'd lie on my stomach.'

'That's what you'd do, and I'd stand over you.'

'Why not kneel over me?'

'That would be the second stage.'

'What about Sven?'

'We'd tell him to make himself comfortable.'

'Sitting on a chair?'

'I think so, to begin with; nothing hurried. I'd begin on
your shoulders. I'd do them thoroughly; make a real massage
of it, talking all the time. "Such soft skin," I'd say. "I
shouldn't have thought that skin could be so soft." Then I'd
start stroking lower down; "You're even softer here," I'd say.
Then I'd bring Sven in: "Feel how soft it is," I'd say. He'd
be shy at first. Perhaps he'd be too shy to touch you. I'd
have to take his hand and massage you with it. He'd soon
find himself liking that. Then I'd turn you round. "Even if
it's your shoulders that ache, I mustn't neglect these, I
mustn't make them jealous. Oh, and they are so pretty too."
I'd stroke them smoothly, rolling them in the palms of my

206

hands. It's then I'd change my position and kneel across you. "It's your turn now," I'd say to him. "See how soft, how firm they are." I don't think I'd have to take his hand this time. And then I'd lower my head. "I can't resist," I'd say. I'd kiss one of your breasts. "You take the other one," I'd say.'

'And what a time I should be having.'

'Exactly, what a time you would be having. And then I'd raise my head. "I can't resist it," I'd say. "I've got to kiss her".'

'It would be a real, real kiss. And if that didn't excite him, I don't know what would.

' "It's your turn now," I'd say to him. That would be a real kiss too. It would be up to you to make it a real kiss. "I wonder if he's excited by that as I am?" I would say. Then it would be your turn to play your part. "If he isn't, I ought to be ashamed of myself," you'd say.'

'We could play it as a duet. "But I rather think he is, don't you?" I'd say.'

'By the look of him I'd say he was.'

'Oughtn't we to make sure of that?'

'I think we should.'

'Oh yes, you're right, he is.'

'Ought we to do something about this?'

'It isn't fair to get him into a state like this and leave him high and dry.'

'Most certainly we shouldn't.'

'Which of us first, do you think?'

'Let's toss for it.'

'Why not?'

'The great thing is to keep it light,' Sarita said. 'Never be serious. Keep laughing. If he were to get embarrassed, everything would be spoilt.'

'And the one who lost the toss would take a part?' said Beryl.

'Of course. There would be so many little things that she could do. She could act as a chorus. She could urge him on. "Faster, faster," she could say, or perhaps, "slower, slower".'

'And there are things that she could do?'

'Of course there are.'

'To both of you?'

'Why not?'

'She might whip him, mightn't she?'

'Would you like that? I didn't know that was a line of yours.'

'I didn't know it was myself.'

'What makes you think it might?'

'Being with you puts ideas into my head.'

'We do have fun together, don't we?'

'You remember what Casanova said?'

'He said so many things.'

'He said that it was easier to seduce two girls than one.'

'Why?'

'Because one encourages the other. If the one has taken a certain step, she insists that the other one does too.'

'So that if we're both working together upon that Mormon, we'd find ourselves doing all sorts of things that we'd never even dreamed of doing by ourselves.'

'This conversation is driving me round the bend.'

'Me too, me too.'

Later, a long time later, Beryl said, 'We've got to try this out—and very soon.'

16

Pablo's tension mounted. The days of the week were dragging slowly. Eight days, seven days, six days, five days—the weekend only two days off. The long, long weekend. He ought to go back to Tetuan. He had duties there and responsibilities. Things would get out of hand if he were not watching them. But he could not bear the inaction there. Nothing was happening here in Tangier; it was of prime importance that nothing did happen. But something might happen. And if it did happen, it would be happening here, and he would not hear of it in Tetuan. The right people would not be able to get in touch with him. As long as he was in Tangier and no report had reached him, he would know that all was well. Tangier could give him sureness of security, but the inaction got upon his nerves. He had nothing to do, nothing he wanted to do. He was tempted to go into a bar, but if he took one drink, he would take two drinks. And then no power that he could command would prevent him from taking three drinks. That he could not allow. He must keep his mind alert. He must be able to think swiftly and clearly. Alcohol would relax him, but it was the wrong form of relaxation.

If only the red light district were open still. That would solve his problem. One of those quiet, discreet houses in one of those side streets off the Petit Socco. The front door would be bound in iron across coloured glass. A veiled Moslem would open it; there would be the sound of music; there would be a sweet and heavy scent. He would be shown into a small room with carpet-covered settees: a coloured lamp would be hanging from the ceiling; a plump, elderly woman with a shawl about her shoulders would rise to greet him. She would bow. 'A lady, two ladies?' she would ask. 'Let me see what is here,' he'd say. She would go to the door. She would call out. Four, five small elegant creatures would glide into the room. They would be fully clothed. Their eyelashes

209

would glisten. Their eyes would be darkened. Their lips would be very red. They would smile demurely. 'That one and that one,' he would say. They would take him by the hand, lead him into a very small room that was sumptuously over furnished with cushions, carpets, coloured photographs. They would lead him to a couch. They would pull back the coverlet. They would undress each other, passing their hands over each other's breasts; then they would turn to him, undressing him together, laying him upon the divan, caressing him with their lips and fingertips, ministering to his delight. One by one his anxieties would disappear, brushed away, smoothed by those lips, those fingertips. Such peace of mind, such peace of body; that's how it would have been in the old days when Tangier was an international zone, and that's how it would be today if the old régime was still in force, if Franco had not betrayed the men who had made him the *Caudillo*.

Franco, it was all Franco's fault. It was because of Franco that Morocco had become entitled to 'clean up' Tangier. Clean up, indeed: what did that amount to: rid this part of the world of the opportunities of adult living. Where would Franco be without the Moroccan Spaniards who had won his sceptre for him? What would his grandfather have thought. Could he have forseen what would be the outcome for men of his class and station. *Todo por la patria*. His anger rose at the thought of it. *Todo por la patria*. And he, whose grandfather's blood had been shed 'por la patria', was lost and unemployed—an alien in a Moslem world. His temper rose. He had to take some action. There were no longer any padlocked doors in the Medina. Spanish Moroccans like himself had to rely on supercilious Anglo-Americans who conferred their favours with the condescension of pampered royalty.

'I am rather booked up the next three days, but if you were going to find yourself free, on Wednesday evening . . .' That was what she had said. 'If you were going to find yourself free on Wednesday.'

That's not the way it ought to be. She should be the

suppliant. 'Whenever you happen to be free,' she should have said, 'you've only to let me know. I do have dates, lunch dates, on Monday and on Thursday, but of course, I can alter that.'

That's how it should be, and that's exactly how it wasn't, and here he was kicking his heels, wondering how to put in his time till Wednesday.

He could not stand it. It was more than any man, any real man could. I'm going round. I'm going round right away. I'll get this fixed.

Frieda was dressing for a party. She was surprised at Pablo's calling. Their meetings were arranged carefully in advance. She was also annoyed by it. She was in a hurry.

'I wasn't expecting you,' she said.

'I know you weren't. The idea only occured to me half an hour ago.'

'Why didn't you ring up?'

'I thought I'd bring you a surprise.'

'It's a surprise all right, but I'm afraid I can't ask you in.'

'You can't?'

'I'm going to a party.'

'You are?'

'To one of David's. Patrick's calling for me in twenty minutes.'

'He is, is he?'

She returned to the stool before the mirror and began to pencil in her eyebrows. He stood behind her. Her concentration on her eyebrows maddened him. A party of David's, indeed, and Patrick calling for her. The two most prominent figures in the 'mountain set' from which he was excluded by his birth and station. He who, but for that base Spaniard, would be one of the most respected and venerated of the continentals. She wasn't going to any party of that kind.

She was wearing a dressing jacket and raising his hands, he took it by the collar on both sides, swinging her round to face him. 'You're not going to any party, so don't think you are. You are staying here with me, and you can ring up your smart friends and tell them that you have a headache and can't come.'

'Miss Otis regrets, in fact.'

'Exactly, and there is the telephone.'

She turned on her stool, but it happened so quickly that he could not tell what happened. A pointed heel was stabbed gougingly into his shin. A knee was driven into his crotch, an elbow into his solar plexus. As he fell forward on to his knees, the heel of a hand was struck onto the nape of his neck. He slid sideways on to the floor, breathless, half-unconscious, pain tearing at his shin and groin. She laughed. 'Do you think I'd have let myself get involved with a Moroccan if I hadn't taken lessons in karate?'

She returned her attention to the mirror. He watched her through blurred eyes as she made up her face, tidied her hair, fitted herself into a short-skirted cocktail dress. 'There,' she said, 'I'm ready. In about half an hour you will have recovered. That's how long it took the last gentleman whom I had to deal with. It will have no ill effects. But you should rest for an hour or so. I will help you into that chair. Sit there quietly. I should recommend a strong whisky soda. I expect I shall come back here straight after the party. But I can't be sure. We may go to the Parade or back to Patrick's. At any rate, I don't want to find you here when I get back. I will set my alarm for quarter to nine. You might fall asleep. Probably you will. And when you have recovered, not tomorrow, but the day after, ring me at my office, and remember, I don't bear you the least ill will. Now then, on your trotters, upsi-daisy.'

She held out her hand and helped him to his feet. He did not speak. He was still dazed. The front door bell rang.

'There's Patrick', she said. 'I'll go down and let him in.'

She paused in the doorway and waved her hand. 'Don't worry. You'll be all right. I don't bear you the least ill will.'

He heard the front door close. He heard the sound of voices, then the crunch of wheels on gravel, then silence.

He could not believe that it had happened. Nothing like this had ever happened to him. Had he been told an hour ago that such a thing would happen, he would have pictured himself abject with humiliation. To be beaten up by a young woman! But in point of fact, he felt a curious pride, as though he had been singled out by fate for a unique experience. He did not hate her; he admired her. She was wonderful. He must prove himself worthy of her. She did not bear him the least ill will. On the contrary, this extraordinary episode would forge a new bond between them, would make them extraordinary for one another.

He stood up. Better take a shower, he thought, then have that whisky. He undressed and went into the bathroom annexe. As he lifted his hand to turn the handle on the shower, he noticed that he still had his wristwatch on. He took it off and looked for a place to put it. There was a mantlepiece with a ledge on it. So that his watch should not be spattered by water, he put it behind a small photograph frame. As he moved the frame, he saw that there was a watch there already. He picked it up. It was a man's watch, a gold one with a platinum and silver chain. A surprising object to find in a young woman's bathroom. He turned it over. It was an old-fashioned watch that was wound by a key. The key was attached to the chain. He opened the back lid of the case. There was writing inside. 'Mark Littlejohn from his staff, in homage and affection. Madrid 1962–66.'

It could only mean one thing. Littlejohn had taken a shower here; and there was only one reason for his doing that, there was only one occasion for his doing that. Mark Littlejohn. He replaced the watch behind the photograph. Mark Littlejohn and Frieda: there could be no other explanation. To his surprise, he did not feel jealousy or indignation. On the contrary, he felt a strengthening of his admiration for Frieda. He did not feel 'what a bitch she is,' but 'My word, she is something. She's got away with murder.'

He took his shower, felt rejuvenated and refreshed, went to the wine cupboard, poured himself a two-finger measure, took out a bottle of club soda. He sat back in the arm chair, appreciating on his palate the mingling of strength and the sting of the soda water. He must think this out. A powerful card had been placed into his hand. An astounding piece of luck. What was the most effective use that he could make of it?

As usual next morning Frieda went into the CG's office for instructions. He dictated a couple of letters, handed her a report to file. 'Is that all?' she asked.

'That's all.'

She stood up. 'Then I am afraid that I've something rather serious to report.'

'You have?'

'I'm afraid so, sir, a serious breach of security.'

'Indeed.'

'Yes, sir, one of the senior members of your staff has been taking showers in the bathroom of a lady to whom he is not married. He left behind the proof of his presence there.'

She handed him an envelope. He opened it. 'I see,' he said.

'A very serious breach of security, don't you think?'

She was standing close beside him. He stretched out an arm; he took her hand in his. His fingers stroked her wrist. She had expected him to make a joke about it. But he didn't. His face assumed a serious expression.

'I don't know,' he said, 'what I should do without you.'

It was the last thing that she had expected to hear him say.

'Every day you mean more to me,' he said. 'I didn't think it was going to be like this. I didn't mean it to be like this. I thought . . . I don't know what I thought. I was lonely. You are very attractive. Why not, I thought. At my age a last fling, why not? an opportunity like this might never come again. If I thought it out at all, that's what I did think. And then it became altogether different from anything I had dared to dream; it wasn't because you were more attractive, because you were younger. It was that, but it was much more than that. It was unlike anything I'd known. It was a different order of things. I don't know what I'm going to do without you.'

'I know,' she said, 'I know.'

And to his astonishment, to his relief, he felt that she did know: that she understood what she meant to him. Even

214

though he knew that he did not, that he could not mean to her anything approaching what she meant to him. But the fact that she did understand gave him a sense of peace, of fulfilment greater than he had ever known. He had the feeling for the first time in his life, and at this late day, of being where he belonged.

Beryl looked at the calendar. Four days late and for the second time. She, who was never late. She added back the days. That first time she and Sarita had bathed together at the Minzah. The day that she had welcomed Adrian on his return from Gibraltar. It was the most dramatic occasion, series of occasions, of her life; if this should be the result of that, well, good luck to it. It was appropriate. I'll give it three more days, she thought.

On the third day she decided to take action. She was almost sure, but she needed official confirmation. 'I've an idea,' she said to Adrian, 'that I need to go over to Gibraltar.'

'Yes?'

'To see a doctor, one of those female things.'

'What's wrong with our doctors here?'

'Nothing, but if you go to a doctor here, the whole town thinks you're pregnant.'

He laughed at that. It was as well to tell the truth, as far as possible. If she went to ask a local doctor on this issue, it would be all round the town by cocktail hour.

'When did you think of going?' Adrian asked.

'Wednesday.'

'By the plane?'

'Yes.'

'I'll drive you to the airport.'

Was there a tone of relief in his voice? She fancied that there was. She remembered how anxious he had been that she should go to Ceuta on a certain day. Was there the same anxiety in his voice today? There couldn't be, and yet, Wednesday, and by the plane, and he would drive her out and meet her. She hesitated, deliberated, and then shrugged. She had to go to Gibraltar anyhow.

Pablo sat listening to the morning news. It was the usual kind of news. This time the kidnapping was in Rio de Janeiro. This time the kidnappers were demanding the release of seventeen members of their organisation, in addition to a ransom and safe transportation to a neutral base. The release of prisoners; that gave him an idea. He had not known what he could demand from the British Consul General in partial liquidation of his blackmail account. Here was a clue. Why not the release of that hippie with the kif. It was a first step anyway.

He put a call through to the Consul General's residence. He spoke in French, giving his French a Spanish accent.

He had a certain difficulty in getting through, but he was insistent. 'You will not know who I am. It is not necessary for you to know. You have never heard of me. I am one of the Basque Liberation group. I have proof that you have been conducting an amorous intrigue with your secretary. The British Government will regard that as a very serious offence. Unless you do exactly what I say, this evidence will be sent to the appropriate authorities. You must do what I tell you. You must secure the release from prison of the young American who was caught trying to smuggle kif into Algeciras. You must get him released and put on the next Yugoslavian liner that sails to Genoa. You may be doubtful of my powers. I will give you a proof of my powers. If that prisoner is not released, and with your powers you can get him released, a very unfortunate incident will take place on the *Mons Calpe* on its Wednesday sailing from Gibraltar. I am told that you will be on that sailing yourself. You will realise that I am not indulging in idle threats. You will not be in any danger yourself, provided that you do not interfere. But it will be a lesson to you. You have been warned.'

There was the click of a replaced receiver. Littlejohn sat forward at his desk; his elbows rested on it, his chin supported by his fists. So it had happened again. Once more the danger of a scandal; and this time he would not be forgiven, not with his present seniority. He had had his warning—all those years ago. 'This once we can overlook it,' they had said, 'and with your wife backing you up. But not a second time; no, not a second time.'

There would be no alternative to resignation; on a diminished pension. Vera was well off. He had investments of his own. He would not be in an impossible position. Far from it; but retirement in England, under those conditions, with people whispering behind his back; with no real authority in his own home; with his old friends scattered. How many dreary accounts had he not read about retired officials, sitting in the Sports Club talking about India and Malaya: a typical Maugham character, and in his own case there would not be the dignity of an honourable retirement. He could imagine people whispering behind their hands when he left the room. 'Old Littlejohn, you heard about him, didn't you. Trouble in Tangier. I never got the facts, the exact facts, but it wasn't a pretty story. Rotten luck on his wife. She's been very good about it.'

He shivered. No, no, no. Not that. He thought back over what the man had said. Who could he be; what did he know. What precisely was he threatening. What had made him think that he, Littlejohn, would be on Wednesday's ferry. There had never been any suggestion of his going to Gibraltar. From what the blackmailer had said, this whole plot had been determined by the fact of his being on that sailing. Some wires had got crossed somewhere. What wires: where and how. 'I'd better be on that ferry,' he thought. 'I'd better find out what it's all about.'

Next morning he asked Frieda to book him a day return on Wednesday's sailing. 'I don't want anyone to know about this trip of mine,' he told her. 'Book it in your name, and until the ship has sailed, I don't want anyone here to know I've gone. I shall be lunching at the Rock. If anything crops up, you can get me there.

'Is anything likely to crop up?'

'A hundred to one against.'

'Is there anything about this that you'd like to have me know?'

217

'No, or well, yes.' He hesitated. He did not want to let her know that their secret had been discovered. It would seem as though he were accusing her of an indiscretion, and if she had not been indiscreet, how could anyone have known. He had not talked himself. He was sure of that. But she—that was another matter. There was nearly always one person that one had to tell—the one person that one swore to secrecy. For most women that was one of the chief attractions of a love affair, talking it over with another woman. A man could tell a woman what he thought about her, about how wonderful he thought her, the things about her that made him think her wonderful, but a woman could not tell a man that: she had to keep him guessing. That was an essential part of her *métier de femme*. But she had to talk to someone —usually another woman, or perhaps to an earlier lover; sometimes perhaps to a pansy. Frieda must have talked to someone. But he did not want her to know that he guessed she had. At the same time, in case of an emergency she ought to have some idea of what was happening. 'I'm not certain of what it's all about myself,' he said. 'You know, of course that there's an American tourist in prison in the Kasbah; a chap who was trying to smuggle kif to Algeciras.'

'I've heard about it, but I've got no details.'

'Apparently the Basque nationalists are interested in him. They want me to get him out of gaol. Of course I couldn't do it, but they don't know that. They still think the British are all powerful. At any rate, the Basque representative over here is threatening me with reprisals unless I get him out. Something, he says, is going to happen on that ferry that will convince me that he means business. He has somehow got the idea that I am travelling on the ferry. I don't know how he got that idea, but he has.'

'Do you know who is the Basque's representative in Tangier?'

'I don't.'

'It might be worth asking Adrian Simms.'

'I'd thought of that, but I don't want to ask him. We're under different managements. I don't think there can be anything in it, but I feel I should go on board and see for myself.'

'You'll take care of yourself, won't you?'

'I'm going armed.'

17

Wednesday was a bright and sunny day. Beryl cooked breakfast for them both. The flat looked very fresh; autumn scents drifted in from the garden.

'Don't you wish you were staying here?' he asked.

'It'll seem all the nicer when I get back. What shall I bring you.'

'One of those gadgets that shoot lemon juice.'

'I won't forget.'

He drove her to the airport. The colours were beginning to change; soon there would be rain and the fields green again. The sidewalk in front of the airport was crowded with passengers. Two charabancs were unloading their groups of tourists. 'It's a relief to have no luggage. See you tonight,' she said.

'I'll be here. Don't be tempted to come back by the ferry.'

'Why should I be?'

'I don't know, but don't be.'

He's very insistent about my coming back by plane, she thought.

Adrian reached the Consulate shortly after nine. He went straight to Frieda's room.

'Can I see his Nibs?' he asked.

'I'm afraid you can't.'

'Why not?'

'He isn't here.'

'Where is he?'

'Halfway to Gibraltar in the ferry.'

'And when's he coming back?'

'Tonight.'

'You could knock me down with a feather.'

'In that case you'd better take that chair.'

'You're very right; I had.'

He sat in it and stared at her. 'When did he decide this?'

'Yesterday morning.'

'Had he any special reason?'

'Yes.'

'Can you tell me what it is?'

'If you're so curious, hadn't you better tell me first why you're so curious.'

'I'm curious because I've reason to believe that a bomb is going to explode on that ship this evening.'

'How long have you known that?'

'I've only known it for certain thirty seconds ago.' He explained why he had only this very moment known for certain. 'I knew that the Basques had an idea of planting a bomb on that ship. I knew that they were planning to plant it when a VIP was on board.'

'But the CG only decided to sail yesterday.'

'I let them think that he would be travelling today.'

'Did you give the ship any warning?'

'I told the captain, but I had no real reason for believing that anything was likely to happen today. It's too long a story to tell you now. And anyway it doesn't matter. I've made a mistake. The thing is for us to decide what we should do now. Can you reach the CG in Gibraltar?'

'He's lunching at the Rock. He'll arrange it so that if a message does come through, he'll get it.'

'Then if we tell him exactly what is going to happen, he'll be on his guard.'

'Do we know exactly what is going to happen?'

'Yes.' He told her that the bomb would be tossed on to the bridge when the ferry was within sight and sound of land. 'So that if we warn the CG,' Adrian said, 'he can take the necessary action. He can warn the Governor: he can warn the police. It's out of our hands. He has all the information that we have. There's only one question: who's to warn him, me or you.'

'If you don't mind, I'd prefer to do it.'

'I'd prefer that too.'

'And I think I'd find it easier to get a line through to the Rock; also if anything goes wrong with the call, I'm in the right place to take action.'

'It should be all right. I think I've told you everything.'

One thing, though, he had not told her: that the Basque representative in Tangier was Pablo Monterey. It did not seem essential. He was certain that Pablo would operate through a cut-out.

Littlejohn always did himself well when he lunched at the Rock. He ordered à la carte, and he did not consider the cost. The Rock had a special supply of Beluga caviar, which it got from Russian ships. He started off with that. Then he had an Angus steak which was flown straight from Scotland. He had two vodkas with the caviar and a half bottle of the best red Burgundy that was in stock. There was always a good one. He had just finished his first glass of vodka when a page boy called him to hear Frieda's story. 'Yes,' he said, 'yes, I see.' He listened, thinking as he listened. 'And you've no idea who this liberator is?' he asked.

'I'm afraid not.'

'Adrian might have an idea.'

'I could probably find him if you really want to know.'

'No, no, it doesn't matter. It wouldn't be anyone I know, and I'm very grateful to Adrian, very. Please tell him that. Though of course, I shall be seeing him tomorrow. When, of course, I'll be seeing you. Perhaps—if you weren't busy—no, I'll tell you what. I'll make straight from the ship to Porte's. I might be needing a martini—in fact I'm sure I shall. So let's meet there and play it by ear—and I'm very grateful, more grateful than I can say to him, to you . . . It'll be all right. I know it'll be all right. Thank you. Bless you.'

To Frieda listening in the Consulate, it seemed as though he were talking to convince himself. I ought to be there, she thought. I should be there.

Back in the dining room, Littlejohn picked up his vodka, lifted it, swallowed the half of it in one quick gulp. He spread his toast thinly with butter, then more thinly still with caviar. He squeezed his slice of lemon over it, lifted it to his mouth. How good it was, the condemned man's last breakfast. He chuckled. Was it? It well might be.

He knew exactly what he should do, what his duty was. He

should call the Governor. The Governor would alert the police. The ship would be patrolled. The potential blackmailer would be arrested. There would be no explosion, no harm would be done to anyone. That was what he should do. And that was exactly what he was not going to do. If he did his duty, his obvious duty, his own personal scandal would be general knowledge. The blackmailer would have his day in court, and his own personal life would be in tatters.

He had a readier solution. He had his revolver in his pocket. He would not tell the Governor or the police. He would be there alone when the blackmailer went down the passage. He would be there alone, and he would shoot to kill, and his secret would die with the blackmailer. It might not work out that way. The blackmailer might have accomplices, desperate and dangerous men. This well might be his last meal: but if that were to be so, he would be out of the picture with his record clean. No one would know; no one would listen to what the blackmailer might have to say. He, her Majesty's Consul General, had done what he had considered to be his duty, and he was dead. Nothing would be amiss.

If, on the other hand, his bullet ended the career of a man who had a bomb upon him, that surely would be accounted as a gallant act. He had a clear cut issue.

The waiter cleared away his place. A trolley was wheeled up. A blue flame was flickering beneath a silver dish. The wine waiter was pouring the first sip of Burgundy into his glass. He raised it to his nose. Ah, the authentic bouquet. If these were the last glasses of wine that he was destined to savour, they should be worthy of that honour. The head-waiter sliced the steak: just how a steak should be, burnt on the outside, almost black, then a deep red, then a line of pink. And afterwards a slice of cheddar cheese. They always had good cheese at the Rock—firm, sharp cheese; and with it a glass of Harvey's Hunting port—no coffee; then an hour's nap. Whatever happened later, he was going to enjoy the next two hours.

In the doctor's hospital up the hill, the white-coated doctor rose to his feet.

223

'I don't think there's any doubt at all,' he said, 'though we can't be quite certain until we have had the test.'

'When will you have that?'

'On Friday morning.'

'Will you write me the result?'

'I'll telegraph.'

'No, don't do that. My husband might see the cable. Just send a note "Congratulations" if that is the answer.'

'I am sure it will be, and I shall be expecting to see you over at the end of the month.'

'Four weeks from today.'

The room had been cool. The heat of the afternoon sun dazed her. She stood on the door step, blinking at its reflection off the yellow stone. So that was that. It was the last thing she had foreseen. She thought she had been careful with the Pill. But you could never be sure. It had fooled her once. But that had been her carelessness. She had been careful since—or at least she thought she had. She had not wanted a child. There was plenty of time for that. She did not want to complicate her life. Nor had Adrian. They had gone on from week to week, from year to year, thinking of it as one of those problems that you thought you had solved, when you had only shelved it. One of those things that they would make up their mind about some day. There was plenty of time, they had thought, and now suddenly there wasn't. They would have to replan their life.

She walked slowly down the hill; as she turned into Main Street a voice called, 'Beryl!' She turned and there was her young Mormon.

'Sven, what on earth are you doing here? In term time, on a weekday.'

'I'm playing hookey.'

'Why?'

'An idea of Pablo's. He wants to play a practical joke upon the skipper.'

'You came on the *Mons Calpe*?'

'Yes.'

'What kind of a practical joke?'

'He wouldn't tell me. He said it might spoil everything if I knew. I have to keep cave on the upper deck, so that he can slip by on to the bridge.'

'And when is this to happen?'

'Just before we dock.'

'And he brought you over here, all expenses paid, simply to do that?'

'That's what he said.'

'It seems a very expensive kind of joke.'

'That's what I thought.'

'Well, good luck to it.'

'Shall I be seeing you on board?'

'No, I'll be . . .'

She checked. There was something fishy about this. Why should Pablo want to play a practical joke on the skipper of the *Mons Calpe*? Why should he put himself to all this trouble and expense. Pablo was a curious creature. Nobody knew very much about him. He wasn't a Spaniard; he wasn't a Moroccan. He did not belong anywhere. No one had seen anything of him till he joined the Tangier Theatre Club. She remembered suddenly how anxious Adrian had been that she should come back by plane instead of by the ferry. Had he known that something was going to happen on the ferry? If something was going to happen on the ferry, she should be on it.

'Yes,' she said. 'I shall be on the ferry. We'll have a drink together.'

The evening plane from Gibraltar was due to ground at Tangier at half past six. It was never ahead of time. Adrian reached the airport at twenty-five past. He watched it circling in the air, the sunlight glinting on its silver wings. It was good to see it: good to know that she was on it, that whatever might be happening at sea, she was safe, up there.

The aircraft grounded, taxied slowly down the runway, slid past an Iberian machine that was waiting to take off for Madrid. The ground crew hurried forward with their trolleys and their gang-ways. The door swung open; the airline hostess stood at the head of the steps, bowing to the passengers as they came off one by one; they were laden with parcels.

Beryl never hurried to come out. She disliked standing in queues. She always waited till the last passenger was through the door.

One by one they came: they were thinning out now. A very fat man, festooned with packages was limping his way on to the top rung. Now it would be Beryl. Her straw hat with the yellow ribbon and her yellow and black blouse would be filling the gap over the hostess' shoulder.

It wasn't though. The gap beyond the hostess was still dark. She couldn't have waited all this time. There was only one explanation; she wasn't on the plane. She'd missed it or . . .

He hurried from the gallery to the information desk. He had a diplomatic pass that allowed him certain information. The man at the desk knew him. He drew out his list of passengers. Mrs Adrian Simms, no, he said, no; she had been on this flight, but her name was taken off.

Cancelled her flight. That could only mean one thing. She would not be staying in Gibraltar. She had no friends there. She had no luggage with her. She must be on the ferry. What had happened in Gibraltar to make her change her plans?

There was a telephone box near the bank. He put a call through to the British Consulate. Could he speak to Miss Fitzgerald, please.

'Frieda, this is Adrian. Beryl isn't on the plane. She must have changed on to the ferry. Have you heard anything?'

'No.'

'You got through to the CG all right?'

'Yes.'

'How did he take it?'

'As you'd expect. You know what he is.'

'I don't as a matter of fact.'

'He never flaps. He takes everything as a matter of course. He wouldn't let it interfere with his lunch.'

'He gave you no instructions?'

226

'No.'

'You'll be going down to the docks to meet him?'

'Of course.'

'I see.'

He paused. 'I'm glad that you are the kind of person that you are,' he said.

The ferry was due to dock at half past seven. It was very often late. It was liable to be held up by rough weather and also by late arrivals. The ferry waited for its passengers on Wednesdays. It was always heavily booked because of the day excursion rate. Today there was little wind. The sea looked calm. The actual crossing would be smooth. Adrian paced the terrace by the Place de France. He had left his car outside the flat. He would have plenty of time after the ship docked to walk back to his car and drive down to the docks. There was always a long delay at immigration. Each passport would be cautiously examined.

He sat on one of the stone seats looking over the straits. Three shoe-shine boys importuned him. He knew them all. 'We'll toss for it,' he said. 'You two first, and then the winner takes on the last one.'

'But that's unfair; the third one only has one chance of losing.'

'Next time he'll be the first.'

They laughed. They fought it out between themselves. They enjoyed themselves. He would now have a good shine, and he would be left in peace.

On the horizon—to the right—he could distinguish the prow of the *Mons Calpe*. In quarter of an hour, he should be able with his field glasses to distinguish passengers on board: not well enough to recognise them, but to distinguish their actions, to gather what they were about. 'What wouldn't I give to be able to see Beryl now,' he thought.

At that moment Beryl was sitting beside Sven Jurgensen in one of the deep armchairs in the bar. They had been sitting there for half an hour. They had just begun their second gin and tonic. Beryl had organised her voyage carefully. She had made a reconnaissance. She had noted which Tangerines were on board. She had remarked—and been surprised to remark—the Consul General. She was surprised that Adrian had not mentioned that he would be crossing. She had seen Pablo and Sven. She had strolled on the boat deck as the ship sailed out. There were a number of tourists. There were at least two package tours. It looked by and large a very customary kind of crossing. Nothing particular to notice either way. Perhaps she was on the wrong tack altogether. She might well be. Married to a man in the Secret Service, it was easy to start fancying things. Well, and if she was, there was nothing lost. She would have worried Adrian by coming back on a route that he had not expected, but that was something that could be overlooked. Anyhow, it was for her now to behave as though nothing untoward were to happen. It had been planned that her young Mormon should assist in the playing of a practical joke upon the captain. It was for her to prevent that joke being played. She suspected that the joke was not as innocent as young Sven thought. What it was she did not know; there was no means of her knowing. But she would prevent, or at least hinder, Sven's participation.

She started to look for him when the ship was in mid-channel. She found him pacing the boat deck and fell into step beside him.

'Isn't it time for that drink we promised ourselves?' she asked. She led him down into the lounge section of the bar.

'I'm for a gin and tonic. Are you for the same?' she asked. 'Why not?'

She handed him an English one-pound note.

'As you probably know, dirhams are no use on this ship. Give the boy a fifteen pence tip.'

She settled back cosily in her chair. 'It's weeks since we've had a real talk just ourselves,' she said. 'We've always been meeting in groups or with Sarita, and that isn't the same thing, not quite; these other people, after all, they're English, or they're Europeans; we are different, we are Americans, more or less of the same generation too. We see things in the same way basically—when we had that first talk together, at that cocktail party, I thought we were going to become real friends, but that's not the way it's gone, friendly though we've become, friendly though we are. That first talk was the only real talk we've had. That's why I'm so happy for this opportunity—being ourselves together, without being interrupted. I want to know how this place is striking you, how you are feeling about it all, how you are feeling about yourself.'

She had her campaign worked out; she wanted to get him talking about himself, so that when Pablo eventually came up, she would find it easy to get rid of Pablo. 'Don't bother about that', she would say to Sven, 'that's not important. Let's have our talk now.' It shouldn't be difficult; Sven could have so few chances of talking about himself.

'I've been wondering so many things about you. In particular, what you've been doing about girls.'

'Not very much.'

'You've been thinking about them, though.'

'Naturally.'

'And what have you been thinking. No, don't tell me. Let me guess. I'll tell you what I think's been on your mind, you tell me if I'm wrong. Is that fair?'

'That's fair.'

'Now before we start, how old are you?'

'I'm twenty-two.'

'So you went on your mission when you were twenty.'

'That's right.'

'And you knew from the start that you *were* going on one.'

'If I was called to go.'

'You were fairly sure you would be called.'

'I supposed so, yes.'

'That meant that you had to be careful during your last year in college. You could go out on dates, but if you had a serious affair that would have gone against you.'

'I suppose so, yes.'

'Not that you considered it very seriously?'

'I can't say I did.'

'You had decided, hadn't you, to leave all that kind of

229

thing alone till you came back from your mission. I've had quite a few Mormon friends. I've known girls who were Mormons. They've told me how excited they all get about the young men who come back from missions. Those young men have glamour. I heard one girl say, "They go out boys. They come back men." The dream of every young girl at BYU is to find a man when he's back from a mission—ready to fall in love, after two years of being on his best behaviour. And Mormon girls aren't puritans: they are strict, but they are not prudish; they believe, how shall I put it, that young people should have fun in bed. Isn't that the way it is?'

'That's the way it is.'

'And I suppose it's the same, the other way round, I mean.'

'I'd say so.'

'When you go off on a mission, you have a very firm resolve, to follow the rules, but all the time you're looking forward to the time when it'll all be over and you're thinking about the girl you'll find, that you'll fall in love with, that you'll marry; and then all your self-denial will be rewarded.'

He nodded.

Beyond his head, she could see Pablo in the doorway, watching them. Was he trying to make a sign to Sven to warn him that his time was nearly up? Sven mustn't notice him. I'm talking now, but soon I'll get him talking, and when he's once got talking, he won't stop.

'People make fun nowadays,' she said, 'of the young man keeping himself pure for the one woman: that old Victorian idea, the modern young woman wouldn't say thank you for the man who has had no experience. And it's true that that Victorian ignorance was at the root of a great many unhappy marriages, but that doesn't mean that the ideal—as an ideal —was not a fine one. The ideal is surely for a young man and a young woman to fall in love with one another, for the first time and the last time. That's what you thought then, and it's what you are still thinking, isn't it; at heart?'

Again he nodded. Another minute, she thought, and I'll have him talking; once he's got started, he won't stop. She still had her eye on Pablo. He was fidgeting. He was getting nervous. Another minute, and he would be coming over, but within that minute Sven would have begun to talk.

'I've been so wondering what you have been thinking of Tangier: or rather how you have been thinking of yourself here in Tangier. It's a funny place; there's no high code of morals. It must have been a surprise to you. It must have been a shock to you. Six months ago you pictured yourself as a missionary for another year; now you are in a world where anything within reason is permissible . . . Tell me about Sarita.'

He started. This was the best approach: a direct attack, his defences swept away.

'I'm very close to Sarita, you know that,' she said. 'She tells me most things. She's very attracted to you, but nothing has happened, has it, yet?'

He shook his head.

'Why not?'

He hesitated, then in a great overflow of confidence, it came pouring forth. 'I'm attracted to her, of course I am attracted to her. But am I in love with her? I don't know. I've never been in love. I've thought about being in love. I've wondered what it's like. I've thought of how exciting it might be to be in love with somebody I couldn't marry. Because I couldn't marry Sarita, or at least she wouldn't want to marry me. She's older. She's a Spaniard. I haven't any money, but more than that, she is a Catholic. I may not be a devout Mormon, but I couldn't marry someone who was not a Mormon, or at least couldn't become a Mormon . . .' He gabbled on; nothing could stop him now.

She interrupted him. 'Why bother about marriage? She wouldn't want to marry you.'

'I know; that's what makes it all so difficult. I don't say that you should only make love after you've been married, but I do think it's wrong to make love to someone whom you know that you can never marry; there's a difference, isn't there?'

'Of course, there's a difference, a big difference.'

'And in this case, you see . . .'

Once started, there was no stopping him. Pablo left the doorway and came across. She raised her hand, waving it in denial before her face. 'No, no,' she said. 'This is very important. Go on, Sven. Come back later, Pablo.'

She turned back to Sven. 'Go on, go on.'

Pablo hesitated. His nerves were on edge. He had reached a high point of tension, the point he had been approaching for two weeks. In ten minutes time it would be all over. He could see through the porthole the lighthouse on Cap Spartel. In twenty minutes they would have docked. He could not wait any longer. Was the accomplice so important? He had thought, he was. But was he? He leant forward, stretched out a hand to touch Sven's shoulder. But Beryl intervened. She struck his hand away. 'No, no, please go away.'

Sven did not seem aware of Pablo's presence. 'With a woman like that . . .' he was assuring her.

Pablo turned away. He could not argue it out. He must avoid a scene. He must not attract attention. The success of his getaway depended upon that. The police would be busy with their cross-examinations. 'Did you notice anything peculiar?' they would be asking. He must be anonymous. He walked along the crowded passageway to the steps leading to the boat deck. The sun was lowering in the sky. It cast a reddish glow on the Kasbah. There were still some bathers at the Yacht Club. There were not many passengers on the boat deck. They were clustering in the hall way with their luggage, preparing for a quick getaway. He was wearing a light rain coat. He held the bomb in his right hand in his pocket. The passage leading to the steps was empty. No one would notice him. Ten quick steps, the bomb tossed high on to the bridge; before it landed he would be on the other side of the superstructure out of range. Another thirty seconds and he would be on the lower deck mingling with the crowd.

He stepped towards the bridge. Only five seconds more. His hand took the bomb out of his pocket.

'Stop! Hands above your head!' The voice rang out like a

sergeant major's. He swung round on his heels. A man holding a revolver stood behind him. The British Consul General. They stared at one another. Both lost their heads, simultaneously. The Consul General fired; Pablo threw the bomb.

The noise of the explosion did not carry across the water, to the terrace by the Café de Paris, but Adrian saw its consequences, saw the flash, saw the crack and crash of the superstructure; flames leapt from it, splinters of boarding were scattered across the boat deck. Through his field glasses he could see passengers and crew scurrying back and forth, but he could not discern what was happening. The ferry was continuing its course. Beryl could not be in any danger. There was no sign of fighting. The bomb was not the signal for an outbreak. It was an isolated incident. Presumably, it had achieved its purpose. Why had it happened though? Surely with the CG's warning, the police could have intervened. What had happened? There was nothing that he could do. His car was fifteen minutes walk away. He could be at the docks within half an hour. There would be a long delay before all the passengers were off.

He had a special pass to let him on to the docks, but the police guard shook his head when he presented it. 'No, no,' he said and gave no reason. There was a large crowd gathering on the pavement of the Boulevard d'Espagne. The police were keeping the roadway clear. He drove back along the waterfront, found a parking place beyond the Yacht Club, and walked back to the barrier. Official cars were driving to and from the docks. He did not see anyone he knew. He asked what had happened, what was happening. Shoulders were shrugged. A Moroccan had been shot. There had been a murder. Something had exploded. Rumour upon rumour. An ambulance drove up, then an ambulance drove out. A car flying a French Flag drove up. It was no good, his waiting here. Beryl would never find him. When she came off the ship, she would find a taxi: or someone would give her a lift. Perhaps the CG would . . . If he was alive, that was to say. There was nothing for him to do. Better drive back and wait.

As he stood on the terrace of his flat looking along the road, he was reminded of the day when he had stood there after Beryl's trip to Ceuta. The same kind of incident. The same kind of anxiety. Then he had not known what had happened. This time he did. But this time he did not know how it had happened. What had gone wrong? How much was he to blame? He had tried to be so clever; that had been his mistake. Trying to hoist the cloak and dagger boys with their own petard.

He had not long to wait. A taxi drew up outside. Beryl got out first. She was followed by a young man who seemed familiar. Why, yes, of course. Sven Jurgensen. What was he doing here? They came up the stairs, just as Beryl and Sarita had, with a sense of drama, but without the exuberance that Sarita and Beryl had had that day, so close in time, so distant in events that was linked so inextricably with this. These two were deadly serious.

He said to them as he had said to Beryl and Sarita. 'What would you like to drink?'

'We've been drinking gin and tonics.'

'Could you use a dry martini then?'

'We could use something hard and strong.'

He kept his gin in the upper compartment of the frigidaire. His 'drys' were not the equivalent of Madame Porte's, but they had their cachet even so. He served them in silver goblets which he kept also in the freeze compartment.

'That's what I wanted,' Beryl said.

'Can you tell me now what happened?'

'Unless you can tell me more than I know.'

'A bomb exploded on the ferry. That's all I know.'

'How do you know that?'

'I saw it from the Place de France.'

'You were watching for it?'

'I knew that something like that might happen.'

'And did you know who was going to throw it?'

'No.'

234

'It was Pablo Monterey.'

'Oh.'

'Are you surprised?'

'Yes, but not altogether. I knew that a bomb might be thrown. I didn't know that Pablo was the one to throw it.'

'Did you know that the Consul General would be there when it was thrown?'

'It was the last thing I expected. What happened to him?'

'He was very badly injured.'

'How badly?'

'I don't know. They say that he'll recover.'

'What about Pablo?'

'The CG shot him.'

'What?'

There was a pause. There was a hard look in Beryl's eyes.

'What was our young Mormon doing there?' he asked.

'So you don't know that?'

'Why should I?'

'I thought that you knew everything; it's because of him that I was on that ferry.'

'How so?'

'I met him in the street. I asked what he was doing in Gibraltar. He said that Pablo had brought him over because he wanted to play a practical joke upon the captain. Sven was going to keep 'cave' while Pablo played his joke. That's how it was put. Pablo playing his joke. When he told me that, I remembered how anxious you had been that I should take the plane and not the ferry. I felt that there was something fishy there, knowing you.'

'Knowing you.' Is this the end of my marriage, Adrian wondered.

'So I decided,' Beryl was continuing, 'that I'd go on the ferry instead of the plane and find out what was cooking, and if I sensed that it was dangerous, I'd throw in the monkey wrench.'

The telephone rang. It was Frieda.

'Are you alone?' she asked.

235

'No, but they can't hear what I'm saying.'

'You've heard what happened.'

'I just have, but only half the details. How is he?'

'How's who?'

'The CG'

'Oh, he's all right. It's bad, but he'll recover.'

'I didn't know that Pablo was in this.'

'I know you didn't.'

'Was it the explosion?'

'That's what they are going to say it was. There's no point in going into details.'

'You wouldn't like to come round here.'

'No, I don't think so, no.'

'Is there anything I can do?'

'No, I'm afraid not, no. They're flying him to Gibraltar. I'm going across tomorrow.'

'That was Frieda Fitzgerald . . .' he told Beryl.

'What had she to say?'

'Nothing immediate. He's bad, but he's all right.'

'Did she sound worried.'

'Of course. I asked if she'd like to come round here, but she said no.'

'Licking her wounds alone, I suppose.'

There was a curious tone in her voice, but he made no comment. He had never felt further from her.

'What about some food,' he said, 'you must be hungry.'

'Yes, we could use some food, Sven and I.'

'Shall we go out?'

'No, I'll fix something here.'

It was eight o'clock. 'Time for the news.' He switched on the radio. The headline announcements came through from London. A bus strike threatened in the midlands. A summit conference proposed in Zurich. A French diplomat kidnapped in the Argentine. The England team picked for the tour in India. Another decline on Wall Street. What a number of other things had happened that afternoon.

Sven left them early. They sat on opposite sides of the Moroccan room.

'I still don't know how much you knew of all this in advance,' she said.

'I didn't know anything for certain till I got back to my office after seeing you off.'

'But you knew that something might be happening.'

'I would have said it was a hundred to one against, at least.'

'Don't you think that you should have warned me?'

'I should have if I had known you were going on the ferry.'

'Do you want to tell me what you learnt at the office to convince you that there was going to be this attack?'

'It's not important, but I'll tell you if you like. I learnt that the CG had been warned that something would happen on the ferry this afternoon.'

'Why should that affect the CG so much?'

'He was being blackmailed. The attack on the ferry was intended to convince the CG that the blackmailers were in earnest.'

'I don't see how the two fit in.'

'I didn't then; I don't altogether now.'

'What did you know?'

'I knew that the Basque Independence group—about whom I have talked to you—were planning, now shall we call it, a gesture.'

'Did you know that Pablo was involved in this?'

'I knew that he was connected with the group.'

'Did you know that he himself would be carrying out this bomb attack?'

'No, that I didn't know. I thought one of his underlings would be doing it.'

'What about Sven; you promised that he would not get involved in this.'

'I didn't know he was involved in it.'

'Is that the truth?'

He hesitated. He hadn't known, but at the same time, would he be telling the truth, the complete truth, if he denied foreknowledge?

'I didn't know he would be involved,' he said, 'but I knew that somebody would fill his role.'

'I suppose I see the way it was,' she said. 'You made a promise. I thought for a moment that you'd broken it, but I see you didn't. Pablo was involved in this, *that* you knew, but you didn't know he would be the one to throw the bomb, and you knew there would be an accomplice, but you didn't know it would be the Mormon. That's what I think's so terrible about this job of yours; you don't know who's involved. You don't know who you may be involving; you don't know whose life you may be ruining. There's Pablo dead; there's the CG maimed, and by the skin of his teeth, by the skin of my teeth, the Mormon's got off scot free, and who's the better off for any of it. That's what maddens me— who's any better off?'

18

For two days Littlejohn was under sedation. He had received the full impact of the explosion on his right side. If he had received it on his left side, near his heart, it would have killed him. He had compound fractures of his leg and shoulder. His head and face were cut. He would limp for the rest of his life. He would be unable to lift his arm. On the Friday evening he had put through a telephone call to Vera. 'I have played my last game of golf. You're not to worry,' he had told her. There was nothing to be done. It was something that could not be hurried. There was no point in her coming out. He would not be in his office for six weeks. He could have no official duties. She would have nothing to do. Far better for her to stay in England and keep an eye on Julia. He would be taking sick leave as soon as he was well enough. Let them wait till then.

To Frieda he had said, 'I didn't want her here. She would get on my nerves. I couldn't stand it. It's because of her really that I'm in this mess. I can't explain, but all this is really on account of her.'

If Vera had come out in July, he would not have got involved with Frieda. He would not have laid himself open to that blackmailer. None of this would have happened. He had risked his life, rather than face the ruin of his career.

For him lying back now among the pillows, in the hospital, his problems had resolved themselves into a simple series of equations. This had led to that, and that had led to this. He should not have got into this mess with Frieda, and having got into it, he should not have taken the insane solution as her Majesty's representative, of shooting his way out of a predicament. It was unforgiveable. It was, in fact, an attempted suicide. He had been desperate, and he had taken that alternative. He did not know what attitude Whitehall would adopt. His injury would no doubt be regarded as a mitigating circumstance. But if he offered his resignation, he did not imagine that any great efforts of persuasion would be made to keep him at his post. He was near the age of retirement. He could be registered as disabled in the call of duty. His pension would be adapted to his situation. He had breasted the tape.

But it was not only his career that had ended on the boat deck of the *Mons Calpe*; his marriage had as well. He could not go back to Vera after this, with this between them. Even if she did not know, even if she was never to know the full implications of his folly.

And that was what he was saying now to Frieda. 'I don't want to force any ultimatum on you. I don't want you to make any answer to what I'm going to say. I want you to know what's on my mind. I'm going to retire; my mind's made up on that. And I'm going to end my marriage. That was the other casualty on that boat deck. My marriage and career were linked in this; they've gone together. You remember what I said to you a few days ago, about this having come to mean so much more than I expected.'

'I remember.'

'That was true; so much more than true. I'm not going to say that I can't picture the rest of my life without you. I could make something of my life alone, of course I could. I wouldn't drink myself into a stupor, and I'm older than you, half a generation older, but I do think we could make something of a life together, and I wouldn't be asking you to nurse an invalid. I could be a companion . . . and I have plans for moving into a new line of work. I've got a second string to my bow. I want you to consider it.'

'I'll consider it.'

She smiled. It was a smile that held a promise. He had the sense that he had had with her before, that he could trust her utterly, that she would keep her promises.

He changed the subject. 'What about young Simms?'

'I wouldn't know.'

'I expect he's worrying. I don't want him to worry. He's a decent chap and he's no fool. I've something to suggest to him. I'd like him to come out here on Monday morning.'

240

Beryl slept late on the Monday morning. Adrian had already left when she awoke. The mail brought her a typewritten envelope from Gibraltar. It contained a single word: 'Congratulations.' Well, and that settles that, she thought.

Her course was clear cut now; straight back to Oklahoma. She wouldn't find it difficult to argue Adrian into that. She had to have an opportunity to think things out. She didn't know, she could explain, if she would be able to go on with this kind of life. He would be ready enough, presumably, to let her go. Then later on . . . the child would be born over there. It would have American citizenship. That was the main thing. She would play the thing by ear. McCrudden. That was another issue. That could wait. The great thing was to get away. She could not go on with things the way they were.

That morning she had a date with Sarita, at Porte's at half past ten. They arrived there simultaneously. 'Let's make pigs of ourselves,' Sarita said. They chose their cakes with care. They took three each.

'And I'm going to have chocolate not coffee,' Sarita said, 'American coffee is the best there is. But chocolate must be French or Swiss.'

'What have you heard about it?' Beryl asked.

'Heard about what?'

'About the bomb.'

'What everyone has heard, the Basque Liberation boys again.'

'What have you heard about Adrian's being involved in it?'

'That he knew more than he should; that he acted rather cleverly to have known so much, but that the CG behaved rather stupidly.'

'Is that what your father-in-law said?'

'He went across on Saturday.'

'Then that's the official story, that's, well . . . it's fine for Adrian: his career's all right, but for me, no, it's too much. The same thing again, Ceuta and now this. He hasn't been really open with me; I don't see how he could be in that kind of job. I'm sitting on a volcano all the time. He promised me after Ceuta that he'd tell me everything, but you see, he didn't . . . I can't go on with this—I'm American, not British. I didn't know what I was taking on. I've told you how we got married . . . It wasn't love's young dream. It was . . . I won't say it was making the best of a bad job, but that's what it really was. It's been a compromise . . . How did it strike you looking at it from outside?'

'It didn't seem that you'd been dealt too good a hand.'

'That's what I've felt, and I'm only twenty-four. Why should I settle for a second-best so early?'

'Exactly.'

'And for Adrian too; he would be better off with someone else, with one of those typical career wives . . . this can't go on . . . the same thing over and over again. How would you feel if you were me?'

'If you're going to get out of it, now's the time.'

'That's what I feel. By the way, do you know how our Mormon got involved in this?'

'I wanted to ask you that.'

She explained to Sarita.

'He's so unspoilt'; she said, 'when he was telling me about his dream of going back after his mission and finding the girl who had been waiting for somebody just like him—it all sounds very sophomoric—two young things keeping themselves pure for one another, but it's rather lovely too. It is the *ideal*. Perhaps he should be allowed his shot at it.'

'Perhaps.'

'He'd have had fun with us.'

'We'd have had fun with him.'

'But we might have spoilt something for him.'

'We might; we'll never know.'

They had finished their three cakes and their jug of chocolate. They looked at one another, self-questioningly. Beryl would like to have told Sarita about the baby. But she did not want that story to get round Tangier, yet. The news of the separation was another matter. She'd be glad to have that bruted round. A pink bill lay on a plate between them.

'I couldn't tackle another cake,' said Beryl.

'And it's too early for martinis.'

'I know what I'd like to do.'

'It's what I'd like too.'

'But I don't think we should.'

'No, I don't think we should.'

'Something might get spoilt.'

'Something might very well get spoilt.'

'Last-time occasions can go wrong.'

'It's better not to know when it is the last time.'

'Like Monday was.'

'Exactly, like Monday was.'

'How little one thought at the time, how often one would relive that time.'

'It's been good, hasn't it.'

'It's been very good.'

They divided the pink bill between them. 'Let's give her a good tip,' said Beryl. They rose to their feet. There was a mist before Beryl's eyes. She raised her right hand to her face: half kissed her forefinger, laid it against Sarita's mouth. And that is that, she thought.

Across the channel Littlejohn was looking better than Adrian had expected. The arm held up on a splint, the leg suspended by a pulley were disconcerting, but he did not look in any pain. It was difficult to realise that four days earlier he had been so near to death. His manner was warm and cheerful; in the way that it had been these last few weeks, in contrast to what it had been when Adrian had been posted there.

'You're looking better than I expected, sir.'

'Thank you. Yes, I'm all right, or at least I shall be. As it is with these modern wonder drugs, I don't feel any pain; just a little discomfort. That's about all, and that's not much. We don't know what pain is in this modern world, or perhaps we are more sensitive to the little that we have.—Do you know what Nelson's chief worry was when his arm was being amputated?—that the steel of the surgeon's knife was cold. After that he had a glass of boiling water kept in the surgery to heat the knives. No, I'm not worrying physically, and I hope you're not mentally. Frieda gave you my messages?'

'Yes, sir.'

'You're not to worry. I'm thoroughly satisfied. And I'm the one that counts—in this instance; though I'm not your direct boss. I'm not sure about Groves. I fancy that he's not too pleased.'

'I was afraid he mightn't be.'

'He thinks that you've been acting behind his back, and you did, didn't you?'

'Yes sir.'

'And that by his standards was very wrong. He wants to run his own show himself, and take all the credit. Ambitious fellow, can't say I'm crazy about that type, myself. The sooner you get away from him, the better.'

'That's how I was feeling, sir.'

'Are you thinking of resigning?'

'It isn't really any life for Beryl. She never knows what may be going to happen next. She isn't English. If she were in an American organisation, she'd feel differently. She'd feel it was for her own country.'

'Yes, I see that. What do you propose to do?'

'Go to America and get a job there, a teaching job—with my M.A. and with my languages and with an American wife, I don't think it would be difficult.'

'You've discussed it with Beryl?'

'Yes, she thinks it might work out. She could go back to college, get her master's, do some teaching too. American wives do that kind of thing.'

'So I've heard. Don't think too much of the idea myself, but if you do that, would you mean to emigrate?'

'I could become a resident alien. I shouldn't lose my nationality.'

'You've thought it out rather thoroughly.'

'One has to, hasn't one?'

'Of course, of course . . . and you wouldn't mind saying goodbye to England?'

'I feel I've lost touch with England, sir. My old friends are scattered. I haven't any roots there now. My mother is bound up in her grandchildren and her nephews and nieces' children. I don't belong there any longer. I felt that very much my last time over. I haven't any life there into which Beryl could be fitted. She'd never feel at home there.'

'She means a great deal to you.'

'She means everything. She's my entire life.'

'And you think with her you could make a real life for yourself in the United States?'

'Yes, sir, I think so, yes.'

'That's what I hoped you'd say.'

There was an ironic twinkle in Littlejohn's smile. 'Your plans fall in with mine,' he said. 'That bomb was as climatic for me as it was for you. We all, if we're wise, have two strings to our bow. And I have for the last year been working out a plan with your own top men to form a new special branch in the USA, that will work in very closely with the US authorities. I may be second in command of that section, and what we are looking for is English residents in the US who are accepted by Americans as being one of them, who have bona fide employment and who could be trusted to impart and hand on information. I thought you might be one of the Englishmen I could enroll.'

'I'd be doing the same kind of work that I was doing here?'

'Up to a point, but you wouldn't be—how should I put it—you wouldn't be cloak and dagger there.'

'I wouldn't want to be working against the USA.'

'You wouldn't be; far from it. You'd be working against the enemies of the USA, and if there's one thing in the world now that matters more than anything, it is that Britain and the USA should work hand in hand. This is all only tentative as yet. What I suggest is this: that you apply for a year's leave of absence. There is no need for you to resign, yet. You are entitled to that leave. You have put in a solid spell of work, and a very good report will go in on you. You will go to the

245

USA with Beryl, and you will make enquiries about getting a teaching job; when you have the firm offer of such a job, you can come back to England and arrange to enter the USA as a resident alien; it is essential that the drill of it all should be carried out correctly, that your record should show you as having entered the USA with the definite intention of making your home and working there. Once that is done, you can enroll with us; we can, as you may guess, arrange for funds to be paid to your credit in a bank in Zurich. There should be no problems. I look forward to the outcome of all this, with the greatest confidence.'

'And I can leave Tangier right away?'

'The sooner, the better. I don't imagine that your final interview with Groves will be—oh, well, he's a reasonable man. Between you and me, I suspect that he will be not sorry to place somebody of his own selection at your desk. Birds of a feather, if you follow me.'

Adrian was back soon after six. Beryl braced herself, as her ears caught the click of his key in the lock. 'It shouldn't be too difficult,' she thought.

They would each know how to behave, as though nothing were at stake. Neither wanted a showdown.

'How did it go?' she asked.

'Not quite the way I expected.'

'No?'

'If you had told me when I woke up this morning that I should end the day planning to go to the United States?'

'As what?'

'As a prospective professor of Eng. Lit.'

His eyes were twinkling. He was in the highest spirits.

'Hadn't you better begin right at the beginning?'

'I don't know that it has a beginning.'

'Then start at the end, I'm told that that's how detective story writers set about their novels. They start at the end, and then work backwards.'

'But I don't know the end.'

'What do you know?'

'That's what I'm wondering myself.'

'Have you been drinking with the Consul?'

'As a matter of fact, that's the one thing he overlooked.'

'Then that I can put straight. Scotch or campari?'

'Scotch.'

But he did not sip it; he put it on the long, low table facing the long, low Danish sofa and swung his leg over the low Danish chair.

'It's been the most extraordinary forty minutes of my life,' he said. 'I went up there expecting—I don't know what I was expecting. Frieda told me not to worry, but I had put up a black. I had gone outside my instructions. I'd run risks that I had no right to run. I'd double-crossed my boss—at least not perhaps double-crossed, but kept him in the dark, and as a result there's the CG in a shambles and Pablo dead. I couldn't have done worse. What's saved me really is the fact that they don't know what I've done, and Pablo, the one man who does know, dead men tell no tales. That secret's buried. They know what I discovered, but they don't know how I discovered it, and because they never will, I'm the white-haired boy . . . and the wide gates are opening.'

She stared at him, astounded. She had never seen him in this mood before; nothing could be less like the scene she had expected.

'But I'm talking in riddles. I'll come to the point,' he said. 'We're going to the USA as soon as I can get a visa, and that shouldn't be long. You remember how we talked that time about my getting a teaching job out there. You told me that I'd have no difficulty in that, with my degree and with my languages—and my having an American wife. Then, as soon as I have got it, I'll come back to England and apply for an alien immigration permit, which I can get with the definite promise of a job, and then—now this is the key point—there's a new branch of Anglo-American security being formed, and the CG is in on it, they need men with some experience in this game who could get a bona-fide job in the US. There are not so many men around with those qualifications.'

'Had the CG been thinking of you in this connection before all this?'

'I'm not certain. I think not. He was pleased with me, perhaps because he did not know the whole story, and I'm not meaning to let him know it. He was ready to recommend me for something good somewhere else—but then when I told him that I was through with this kind of work . . .'

'You told me that. How did you tell him that?'

'I said much what you said the other night. About the worst of this job being the not knowing who might be involved, whose life might be ruined, there's Pablo dead and the CG maimed, and the Mormon saved by the skin of his teeth, and who's any the better off for it, you said.'

'And that's what you said to him?'

'More or less. I told him that it wasn't a life for you.'

'You told him *that*?'

'I said that you weren't English after all, if you were involved with an American organisation you might feel differently.'

'You turned the whole issue upon me.'

'Of course, that was the whole point of it, and he saw my point. He asked me what I proposed to do. I told him about our idea of my coming out to Oklahoma for a teaching job.'

'Our idea?'

'We'd discussed it, hadn't we?'

'Not very seriously.'

'Maybe you hadn't, but I had.'

She was still dumbfounded. She had never taken seriously that idea of hers. She had thought of it as just one of those things that a husband and wife used as small talk.

'And what did he say when you told him that?'

'He was delighted. Nothing, he said, could suit his plans better. He told me about his new racket. I was exactly the kind of man he needed, so he said. It would mean my leaving England. I was prepared for that, I told him. I had no real roots there any longer. I had no life over there into which you could fit. You'd never feel at home there, because I couldn't feel at home myself. He saw my point. He was very

248

nice about it. "She means a great deal to you, doesn't she," he said. "Of course," I said, "She means everything. She's my entire life." '

'You told him that?'

'What else?'

'But . . .' It was the biggest surprise she had ever had. 'That's really true?' she asked.

'Of course.'

'Why didn't you tell me then? Why did you tell him, not me?'

'I thought you knew.'

'How could I know if you didn't tell me?'

'Isn't that the kind of thing that husbands and wives assume about each other?'

And that, she thought, was how husbands lost their wives. She remembered her telling Sarita on the way to Ceuta that she had found herself marrying a man who had never told her that he loved her. Was that how the English were. How did their women and men communicate? In some kind of short-hand. To have to learn secondhand, through the intervention of a Consul General, that you were your husband's entire life. Thank heaven, she had learnt in time. She could settle for this all right.

His entire life. Was that really what she was. And to have him tell her so casually; as something assumed. What more might she not find out about him. She saw him as a new person: with new eyes. She was his entire life. He was going to build a new life round her; their life. And she was going to be the mother of his child, and in that recognition she felt the first stirring of a maternal instinct, not towards the future child, but towards him who had become hers in a way that she had never guessed. If she was his entire world, then he had become her responsibility. During the next eight months she would be subjected to a whole series of new feelings and emotions. But now the first focus of them was he himself. She felt protective.

Now, she could tell him about the child; he was still chattering away about their immediate plans. What a surprise for him, she thought. But just as she was about to interrupt him, she was checked by the first expression of that protectiveness. 'No,' she thought, 'no, he's had as much as he can take in one day.'